Birth Offering

By
Anthony Hains

Damnation Books, LLC.
P.O. Box 3931
Santa Rosa, CA 95402-9998
www.damnationbooks.com

Birth Offering
by Anthony Hains

Digital ISBN: 978-1-62929-035-5
Print ISBN: 978-1-62929-036-2

Cover art by: Ash Arceneaux
Edited by: Sally Odgers

Printed in the United States of America
Worldwide Electronic & Digital Rights
Worldwide English Language Print Rights

For Ann

I would like to acknowledge the kind people at Damnation Books for all of their assistance in helping a new author learn the ropes of fiction publishing.

In addition, and more importantly, I would like to thank my family for all of their support; from the late nights working on the computer to reading various drafts. Ann and Anastasia, thank you.

Prologue

The house was larger than it looked on the outside, where it appeared to be nothing more than a shack on wooden pilings. Once inside, rooms begot rooms that extended in a seemingly haphazard fashion, suggesting little forethought on the part of the builder. Yet, the pilings under the house were spaced with precision in an effort to protect the dwelling from occasional high surf and the unforgiving tidal surges of tropical storms.

In one of the rooms, a small white woman of about twenty lay on a single bed in the final stages of labor. Perspiration soaked her fine reddish-blond hair, dramatically darkening its color and pasting it to her head. Her cries of anguish filled the room. Two additional women, one black and one white and about the same age, worked in tandem in preparation for the delivery. The black woman, who had nursing and midwife training, periodically reached for a small cross that hung on a gold chain around her neck.

The white woman had none of her training, but was present because her moral code demanded it. As a person of privilege she needed to give back in some capacity. For the first time in all of her years of service, however, the white woman's expression was set with fear.

Standing in the hallway outside the room, a young black woman silently watched the unfolding drama. She was approaching the six month of her own pregnancy, and she trembled with unease.

"Eugenia," the white woman said, "I can see the head."

"The dragon stood before the woman..." Eugenia murmured, and again clasped the cross around her neck.

"Please, we can't be distracted," the white woman whispered in reply, although she too was uneasy. "I refuse to believe..." she whispered to herself, trying to hold on to some sense of normalcy.

"Please, oh please God, don't let it eat my baby," the girl wailed, her eyes begging the other women.

"There now, you don't know what you're saying. Your baby will be fine. We'll take care of it," the white woman said and then gazed intently at Eugenia.

With a final cry the exhausted girl bore down and the infant was in the white woman's arms. Her eyes flared in shock and disbelief.

"Carolyn?" Eugenia began, and then stopped. She saw there was no umbilical cord.

The new mother's eyes glazed over and she whimpered. Her complexion paled to a pallid gray within moments. Eugenia exhaled slowly, trying to prepare for the all too certain nightmare to come.

"My Lord in Heaven," Carolyn gasped. The head of a second baby appeared. The young woman was delivering twins.

In the hallway, the mother-to-be backed away from the door with such force that it appeared she was shoved.

"Oh, my God...Momma!"

Eugenia didn't answer, although she now knew her daughter was observing from the hallway. She stared with amazement as the second child was born. The cry of the first turned into an unholy shrieking. It squirmed in Carolyn's arms. She placed the firstborn on the bed besides its brother to keep from dropping it.

"No, Carolyn..." Eugenia cried.

The first twin swiped at its brother, and blood sprayed.

"Dear God..."

The firstborn swiped again, missing this time. Both infants wailed.

"Carolyn, take the second child to another room," Eugenia said.

Carolyn reached for a spare baby blanket from a nearby pile and wrapped the second twin. She gathered him to her chest, away from the flailing arms of the firstborn. Neither infant had been cleaned and blood and mucus were everywhere. Carolyn could not believe the sight.

The first twin continued to howl. Eugenia raised her voice above the cacophony to call her daughter in the hallway.

"Child! Help Mrs. Tryon, she must save the baby."

The young woman in the hall did not acknowledge her mother. She was riveted at the scene unfolding in front of her. The new mother was lifeless on the bed, all color drained. Her firstborn was hungry, and it had started to eat.

"Eugenia?" Carolyn was also paralyzed.

"Sweet Jesus!" Eugenia searched frantically for something among a pile of instruments. She picked up a pair of scissors. "This can't go on."

Carolyn's entire frame shook when she noticed the scissors. "Eugenia...can you?"

Eugenia peered at Carolyn, her eyes a chasm of dread.

A shrill squeal came from the bed, and both women turned to see the firstborn glaring at them while poised above the young woman's body. Blood smeared its lips.

Then, it smiled.

"Yes, dear God," Eugenia answered. She set her face and deliberately strode to the bed. She spread the scissors, exposing the cutting edge. The blade slashed swiftly, just once, and blood sprayed the far wall. The scissors slipped from Eugenia's hand and fell to the crimson bed sheets. Carolyn shuddered but reached determinedly for the scissors and did the same. All the while, she hugged the second infant to her breast with her other arm.

The room, blessedly, fell silent.

"My God," the young woman planted in the doorway whispered.

"Let's move, Cassie," Carolyn said to her, "this baby might be hurt."

* * * *

A young man startled awake after dozing for a few minutes at most. Vague images, terrifying in nature, remained from an impossibly short nightmare. The visuals, really not much more than fragments, threaded into his consciousness. Ink black eyes tinged with red...teeth like blades fresh from the whetstone, ripping and tearing...a cavern of death... He knew the images well, as they've been a part of his existence for the last eight of his twenty-one years.

"Jeremy? What's the matter?"

Jeremy realized he had propped himself up on his elbow in bed. His girlfriend, in bed with him, looked up at him with a concerned but still amused expression.

"Oh, man. I'm sorry." He eased himself back down and caressed her. They were in his dorm room and his roommate promised not to return for a few hours. The passion of their lovemaking still lingered. Jeremy was aware that their relationship was moving into welcomed, but uncharted, territory. He needed to come to terms with the contents of his dreams, and that meant telling her about his past.

"I just dozed off, and, I don't know, it caught me by surprise." Now didn't seem the time.

"Hmm, am I that boring?"

"What do you think? Do I look bored?" He resumed kissing her.

Much later, Jeremy was on the phone with his father giving him updates about classes and how he felt he was getting serious with his girlfriend.

"I've got to tell you something else, though. I started having the dreams again." After a few moments of silence, Jeremy continued. "I think it's happened again."

His father sighed. "I'm sorry son. You know I'd give anything to make this go away. You seem to be attuned to these events. God knows why."

"I know, but just in case I need to—"

"You know you can count on me."

"Thanks, Dad."

"You know who you can talk to, don't you?"

"Yeah. I was thinking that too."

"Not to throw a monkey wrench into this thing, but...this girl, the one you're getting attached to...have you told her?"

"No. I'm still trying to figure out how."

"Are you sleeping with her?"

Jeremy blushed, embarrassed even though no one else was in the room. "Yes, Dad, I am." He had always been honest with his father, no reason to change now.

"Then you need to talk to her. Whatever you say will be the right thing." Silence followed for a few moments. Jeremy sensed a lightening of the atmosphere. "By the way, your mother wants to know, when can we meet her?"

* * * *

"Is the child safe?"

Eugenia sipped a cup of tea and returned it to the saucer on the coffee table before answering.

"Yes, he is." She sat in the living room of a small house outside of Charleston, visiting Aunt Tessa. Her close-cropped hair, rapidly turning white, graced her dark face. Aunt Tessa wasn't really an aunt, at least not in the familial sense. They were more likely second cousins twice removed. Emotionally she was Eugenia's aunt, her mentor...the woman who taught her and supported her.

"The body of the other...the demon child?" Aunt Tessa asked.

"Gone. As far as we know."

"Let's pray it is gone. We don't want it back."

Eugenia nodded, and breathed a sigh of relief. She was feeling more in control.

Aunt Tessa stared earnestly at her. "You did the right thing."

Chapter One

Ryan felt really hot inside the car even though the air conditioning was going full blast. Regardless of time of day or direction of travel, the sun always shone on his side, and the midafternoon glare added to the misery. The barely tinted windows and a pair of sunglasses provided only minimal relief.

"I think this'll be good for us. You'll make all kinds of new friends." His mother glanced at him briefly before returning her attention to driving. They were traveling on I-26 south of Columbia and headed toward the coast, the move to South Carolina almost complete.

What's the matter with the ones I am leaving behind? he thought. He knew better than to blurt this out and risk another argument.

Scanning radio stations was fruitless as Ryan couldn't find anything he liked. He risked another rebuke by inserting the earbuds for his iPod. His mother thought listening to music this way was antisocial because it inhibited conversation, and typically made her feelings known immediately. Fortunately, she overlooked this particular transgression, at least for now.

Ryan and his mother had been snapping at each other all day. She criticized him for every little thing, while from his perspective everything she said was just plain stupid. The heat and the glare added to the atmosphere in the car.

Part of the problem was that the past few weeks she had adopted this fake sense of enthusiasm. The lilt to her voice was ineffective in relieving his sullenness, and it did little to brighten her facial expression or mood. Her brow was furrowed most of the time as if she tried to concentrate on basic things like breathing and walking. Her eyes were sunken and red, and missing that essential spark that suggested brain activity was present inside her head. She had not resumed her work, either, and that would be the true indicator that she was more or less back to normal. When she took on jobs to illustrate more children's books, then he might feel more relaxed about her.

If it came right down to it, Ryan would admit he was acting like a jerk a lot of the time. She missed his dad too, and neither could make sense of his unexpected death.

He remembered the day his father died as though it was yesterday. The accompanying grief still simmered inside him, ready to boil over at the slightest provocation. He wondered if he would ever be able to shake this reaction. He supposed he would eventually, but right now images arrived unbidden, bringing him back to that day.

Ryan was in history class when a call came for him to go to the principal's office.

"They said to bring your backpack too," the teacher reported. The rest of the class 'oohed' and 'aahed' on cue.

"Dude, what'd you do?"

"You're screwed, man."

"Pharmaceuticals in his locker." The class hooted with this remark.

"Shut up." Ryan smirked. He zipped up his backpack and hoisted it over his shoulder while the teacher tried to regain some control.

"All right, you clowns, calm down." The teacher tried half-heartedly for order.

Ryan sauntered down the aisle trying to look cool, but inside he was worried. *Why are they calling me?*

"Mister Perry, they'd like to see you sometime today, I think."

The hallway outside of the classroom seemed almost alien and hostile, but he worked on keeping his mind blank as he made the trek to the office. The secretary practically whisked him into the principal's office as if he was some kind of VIP.

"You can go right in, Ryan."

Only the principal and his mother were in the office, and her back was to him when he entered. He was confused, trying to recall what he might have done to get into trouble.

The principal stood. "Ryan, why don't you sit down?" He motioned to a chair next to his mother. He placed his backpack on the floor and slid into the seat. Only then did his mother turn to look at him. Her eyes were puffy and red. She looked as if she had been knocked senseless.

Ryan knew what happened before she said a single word. He clasped his hands and squeezed them into his stomach. *No, Mom, don't say it. You can't say it. Please no, please don't say it.*

"Honey," she said, and then stopped. Seconds went by and she looked around the room. She looked everywhere but at him. Tears poured out of her eyes like flood waters over a dam. Ryan didn't think it was possible to shed tears at that rate.

"Ryan," she resumed, "your dad collapsed at his office today. He had a serious heart attack." She clutched wads of damp tissues in her hands and tore them slowly in anguish. "He died at the hospital."

Ryan's world ended.

His father had not been the type of guy who lived through Ryan's accomplishments. Oh, he was always around and available. They shared a passion for baseball, for instance. He went to Ryan's games, but he always clapped and cheered for all the kids. He wasn't like some other dads who yelled instructions or advice, or worse yet, embarrassed the kid publicly after he did something wrong. When the game was over, they talked about what happened as long as the momentum was there. Once it was gone, well, they would move on to something else. For them, baseball was huge...baseball was exciting...but it wasn't the be all and end all. There were so many other things to do. Everything was natural when it came to his dad, nothing felt obligatory—which is what Ryan thought other parents were doing, as if they were mentally keeping track of a parenting to-do list.

What Ryan really missed, though, was the ballast his father provided. When shit happened, his father was like the Navy SEALS arriving, offering to help Ryan think through the problem. Oh, he'd get pissed at Ryan for doing stupid things, what father didn't? However, they would size up the problem and look at it from multiple angles. Weighing the pros and cons for courses of action often made things seem so manageable.

Who would have thought this guy would drop dead at his desk for no reason?

Now, his mom tried to play his father's role along with hers, and she couldn't make it work. It wasn't her fault. She was more into being perky and sharing feelings.

A couple of months ago, his mom came up with this new idea. She thought it would be a good idea to make a fresh start. She wanted to move back to South Carolina where she grew up. Ryan wanted no part of it, even though he was supposed to be "part of the discussion". In the end, he really had no say, and that was that. They were moving to South Carolina.

One concession from Mom was they would move after Ryan completed the eighth grade. So, they stayed in Wisconsin for six months after his dad died. He was able to attend a few parties, play baseball in the spring, and he even had the chance to make out with Abby Fitzgerald. Then it was time to prepare for the move. That's when his mom started with the, "oh, we're starting on a whole new adventure" crap. Why this bothered him he had no idea. Things went more or less downhill from there.

One of the hardest things about leaving was not saying goodbye to people, and God knows that was hard enough, but watching her get rid of their belongings. She sold furniture they wouldn't need by placing advertisements in the newspaper. She held a huge garage sale. Ryan watched items go that had always been a part of his life, carried off by strangers on the cheapest terms as if suddenly insignificant. He felt sad in a way he couldn't explain.

"Look," his mom offered, "only twenty more miles." A sign indicated the distance to their exit.

"Thank God." Ryan sat up straight and adjusted the seat belt so he was more comfortable.

* * * *

"Whoa. Check this out." Todd turned to Melissa, his expression truly excited like a little boy. A few yards from the beach they walked onto a hard-packed path in the middle of a wooded area of huge live oaks, pine trees, and palms. Upper branches from the oaks on either side of the path joined above them, creating a tunnel-like effect. Moss hung like green streamers over their heads. The entire space was like a chapel, quiet and serene–although with the many imprints of sandals and bare feet, the setting was clearly well visited. Other than a little kid on a bike some way down the path, they had the place to themselves.

Todd's reaction to their find was an example of one of his endearing traits. He was often wowed by the simplest things. Here was a guy who grew up in the mountains of South Carolina and who loved to be outside. When Melissa visited him over spring break last year, he took her for day hikes into the mountains. He pointed out certain spring flowers and various rock formations. He was well versed in geology and the impact of weather on his section of the Appalachians. He explained all this natural beauty with awe and reverence. When he started talking about the negative impact of acid rain, she swore she saw moisture in his eyes.

"We used to walk home from church when the weather permitted," his mom told her one evening during her visit. "Once Todd was able to walk on his own, that short walk turned into a cross country trek. We had to stop and look at every bug and every rock. His sisters got to the point where they dreaded the whole Sunday routine. His father and I had to take turns hanging out with him while the other one walked home with the girls."

While Todd and his family were oriented towards hiking and camping in the mountains, Melissa's family members were beach people. She was astounded to hear he had never been to the coast. They made a plan. After graduation and before graduate school, they would take a beach trip together. Todd wanted to camp at the beach, though, and she wanted a condo or a small beach house. They compromised. The first leg of their vacation was camping while the second half involved staying in a resort on Kiawah Island. Melissa couldn't wait for the clean sheets and the showers.

Todd continued to stroll ahead, shifting his perspective from the ground to the canopy above. He also slowly rotated so that he could share his wonder with her.

"You should watch where you're going, you know."

"Yeah...Is this cool or what?"

"I thought you'd be impressed."

"I really need to read up on the plants and vegetation. I suppose we can go hiking in there." He pointed towards the forest area. "There are paths I do believe. Let me look." He bounded on his bare feet into the greenery. She continued on slowly as Todd disappeared into the brush. She heard him talking at a distance. Leave it to Todd to meet and carry on conversations with strangers. They were probably into ecology or local wildlife by now.

"Yeah, there're paths," he called back to her. "I want to come back with some shoes. Although, the ground is pretty soft." He paused, and then continued, "Hey, we can have sex in here."

"Would you be quiet! Shhh. God," she hissed back at him.

She heard him talking again, but couldn't make it out. *I'm going to kill him.* Someone could have just walked by and heard that whole thing. It dawned on her that whoever he was talking to was probably standing right by him all long. She grew even more furious at him. *Probably it's another guy, and they're just yukking it up out there about screwing in the woods.* She heard a laugh. *Yep, that's what's going on.* She decided to wait right here on the path, and glare at him as he approached.

Melissa expected him to reappear any second, but the wooded area was quiet. Within seconds, more laughter was followed by the sound of someone swinging a golf club. A driver, to be exact. *Now they're talking about golf? God.*

"Todd?"

There was no reply. She heard some rustling, most likely a bird or small animal. She approached the edge of the path, looking in the general direction where Todd went exploring. He should have been easy to see in his bright yellow T-shirt and multi-colored swimming trunks—enough color to make him stand out in a semi-tropical jungle.

"Todd? What's going on?" She followed his path into the abundant green landscape. "Is this some ploy to get me deep into the forest so you can have your way with me? It won't work, you know." Still, he didn't answer.

Melissa felt a sense of unease deep in the pit of her stomach. "Todd, are you okay?"

Then she saw a small patch of his yellow T-shirt. He sat on the ground with his back leaning against a tree. The sleeve of his left arm was the only part visible.

"Todd, are you hurt?" No reply. She ran towards him. "Todd!"

As she reached the tree, Melissa's feet slid from under her as she tried to stop. She landed hard on her hip. She reached for Todd, but he didn't react to her. In fact, Todd was not focusing on anything at all. He was immobile, and his body was not aligned correctly in what should have been the area of his physical space. The surrounding area was wet, and Melissa saw the liquid was sticky and red. She wanted to scream but couldn't. Her throat felt clenched shut. She stood up to run away, but only managed one step before she was dead.

* * * *

After his father's funeral, Ryan's grandmother stayed with them for over a month before returning to South Carolina. She helped with the cooking and the laundry, but she mostly was instrumental in keeping everyone on schedule. She woke Ryan each morning, kept after him to eat his breakfast and dinner, pushed him to shower, comb his hair and brush his teeth. Homework was fair game too. She went online to look at the school's homework website to examine whether Ryan was on target with his assignments. The whole Velcro-grandmother thing got really annoying pretty fast. Ryan found it easier to keep one step ahead of her and do everything on his own to avoid her over-the-shoulder-nagging, which he had to admit was probably her intention in the first place.

The talk about "moving back home" didn't start until right before his grandmother left. Ryan overheard the two of them weighing the pros and cons of South Carolina. He exploded, running into the room screaming that *he* wasn't leaving.

"How could you do this to me? No fucking way am I moving to South Carolina!"

His mother and grandmother sat in their living room, looking up at him and nodding, as if they understood completely. His shouts echoed in his head. He never said "fuck" to his mother before, and he expected her to pounce all over him. Instead, she just sat there as if he asked her how cold it was outside.

"Ryan, I know this is hard, but right now we are just talking about it."

"Bullshit! You've already decided. I bet you have."

"Honey, really, no. Please sit and let's talk about it."

"No! You never listen to my side! I don't want to leave. Everybody I know is here. You can't make me leave."

"Sweetheart, please sit," his grandmother said quietly. "We can tell you what we've been thinking."

"No, Grandma." Ryan realized he was crying and he couldn't control it anymore. His voice got higher. "You don't care about me. I want to stay here!" His chest exploded with an enormous sob, and the crying was like a raging beast that had escaped from its cage and could no longer be contained. Coherent sentences became single words, many of them swear words, and his face streamed with tears and snot. Despite his upheaval, even Ryan couldn't understand where this came from. In the end, his outburst didn't sway his mother or grandmother. Quite the opposite, they remained maddeningly composed throughout his tirade. The eventual outcome of his meltdown was obvious to everyone from the start when he stormed to his room sobbing.

The cause of his despair was not the loss of friends, he soon realized. Of course, that prospect scared him, along with the fear of what would happen if he didn't make friends at his new school. Strangely enough, it was how his friends changed toward him that helped him understand leaving would not be too devastating. They acted as if he had some strange disease or was too fragile to handle basic things. With onset of baseball season, his social life went more or less back to normal. Practice and games provided the fodder for much discussion, as did renewed debates about girls in their class. No, the real reason was that he felt he was deserting his father.

"I don't want to leave Dad, it's as if we're leaving him behind," he said carefully, willing his voice not to break. He had finally stopped sobbing, and his mother sat at the edge of his bed, brushing his hair from his forehead. "I'm afraid I'll forget him."

"I know," she answered him. "I have thought the same thing. Then I think, no matter where I am, I won't be leaving him behind. He's still with me in my heart. I think that helps."

Ryan thought for a moment and then said with a slight smile, "You sound like a greeting card."

"I know, I can't help it." She leaned over and kissed his forehead.

Chapter Two

Sunlight peeked from around the window shades of Ryan's new bedroom. The digital alarm clock said 11:14, and he had slept soundly for almost thirteen hours. Yesterday was a day of unpacking, sorting, moving, and rearranging things. He'd dreaded the activity, but the whole process turned out to be rather fun. He was the go-to guy for anything requiring muscle, and his grandmother kept plying him with all kinds of snacks.

Ryan stretched and then sat up in bed. He loved his room. It had plenty of space for his desk, clothes, and belongings. His grandmother bundled her internet, phone, and cable service, so they had great TV options and wireless services. She even bought a new smart phone for him.

He heard his mother and grandmother busy downstairs in the kitchen. Much of their dishware and kitchen supplies made the move with them. Both women were in the process of reorganizing the cabinet space to incorporate the additions. Figuring he ought to get moving, Ryan sprang out of bed to head to the shower.

The house was quite awesome. It had two wrap-around porches that extended two sides of the house. The top one served three of the bedrooms on the second floor. The porches had round, white columns connected by stately arches, along with decorative railings. The house was a blazing white with evergreen colored shutters.

Inside, the house was all wood. Hardwood floors finished in mahogany were covered with ornate throw-rugs in the living, dining, and "smoking" rooms (now called "the den", his mother informed him), and matching runners in the hallways. Wainscoting the same shade as the floors ran everywhere. Many of the rooms had pocket doors, which Ryan loved to play with during visits when he was younger. He thought it was magic that you could push a sliding door and make it disappear into an adjacent wall.

The main stairway was lit with stained-glass windows of

dazzling color. The stairs contained no rugs or carpeting, but were just the finished wood. As a result, it was quite noisy, and Ryan could always hear people clomping up and down the stairs, even when that was not their intention. No surprises by serial killers in this house.

Shower finished, Ryan dried himself off and placed the towel around his waist. He opened the bathroom door slightly in an attempt to lower the humidity. Looking in the mirror he saw the same kid staring back that he always saw. Not for the first time, Ryan wondered how he looked to girls. Did they think he was too skinny? He was slender, true, but he considered himself athletic. There was baseball and he rode his bike a lot. There were always touch football and pick-up basketball games. He had taken up jogging to build up stamina for baseball season, although lately he had seen why grown-ups would do it to relieve stress. In the months after his father died, he found himself enjoying the solitude and the self-imposed regimen. The outcome of all this was that his body had gotten quite well toned.

He thought his hair was his best asset. He liked the color, which was a golden blond like melted butter. His mother always said some women would pay top dollar to achieve the color that came to him naturally. During the summer, sections bleached to an even lighter shade as he spent time outside. Therefore, he tended to keep it on the long side. Ryan remembered Abby Fitzgerald commenting on how awesome it looked before they started making out behind the school last spring. So, yeah, the hair was a real plus.

His scar was a different issue. Ryan turned slightly to his left so he could see his right side in the mirror. The scar, eight to ten inches long now, extended from below his right shoulder blade towards his ribcage then curved downwards in almost a straight line to his hip.

"How did you get that?" was one of the most frequently asked questions growing up, and often by complete strangers when he was at the pool or the beach or in the locker room.

"The doctor had to repair something when I was born," he would offer, or sometimes he just shrugged. He didn't know anything else, because that was all his mother told him. At this point, it was such a regular part of him he rarely gave it a second thought.

* * * *

He had some new clothes, and chose to wear a pair of blue and white plaid shorts and a blue shirt. He thundered down the stairs and the slap of his bare feet on the wood pounded throughout the house. For some reason, this struck him as funny and he amplified the effect as he went down.

"Good heavens, a herd of elephants." His grandmother beamed at him when he entered the kitchen.

"What's for breakfast?"

"Breakfast? Sweetheart," his mother answered, lifting a stack of bowls into a cabinet, "it's almost noon."

"Okay, lunch then."

"If he wants breakfast, he can have it." His grandmother positioned herself behind him when he sat at the table. She swooped down, threw her arms around him and kissed the top of his head.

"Hmmm. Smells like boy."

"Hey, what's that supposed to mean?"

"Nothing...it's sweet."

"I think she means sweat."

"I just took a shower."

"How much longer beyond the thirty second mark were you in there?"

"Mom," Ryan warned.

"Okay, you can have breakfast or lunch, your highness."

Ryan surveyed the kitchen. The place was a wreck as the two women tried to re-arrange the space so his mother's stuff could fit in too. He was starving, and thought about fixing versions of both meals, but reconsidered when he anticipated his mother's reaction.

"I think I'll go with lunch."

"Bread's over on the counter. Meat, cheese, lettuce and everything else is in the refrigerator. You can do it yourself, my big boy."

"After you eat," his grandmother said, shifting topics, "are you going outside to play?"

This was the type of question if asked by his mother would warrant a snotty reply. She knew it too, because she shot him a look that suggested "watch your tone". From his grandmother, though, it was kind of amusing.

"Grandma, I'm fourteen. I don't 'go outside to play' anymore."

She feigned shock. "To think the child doesn't play anymore–how terrible."

Ryan snorted and shook his head, then asked, "Grandma, can I bring my sandwich upstairs and sit on the porch?"

* * * *

The second level porch was accessible from his grandmother's bedroom. She had French doors that opened to the porch overlooking the front yard. From that vantage point, Ryan could walk to where the porch curved elegantly to overlook a side garden and an expansive brick terrace. Interspersed within the terrace were brick edged planters which contained geraniums and roses, along with other plants Ryan couldn't begin to name. In the midst of all this, he spotted an outdoor glass table surrounded by chairs. He supposed you could eat meals outside, but could not imagine trying now. The weather was ungodly hot and humid, and the mosquitoes within the shade of the garden were killers. He was drinking a can of cola, and the condensation ran off the can like a faucet. The climate was a far cry from Wisconsin.

The house was located in the historical and fashionable section of town. Palm trees grew in the yards and beside the street, along with huge oaks covered with moss hanging from the branches like delicate scarves. The neighborhood was actually a square, with old homes—many of them antebellum—surrounding a small park. Additional oak and palm trees graced the park, which served as an attraction for people to stroll at a leisurely pace to beat the heat while enjoying the locale. Horse-drawn carriages containing tour groups were present, with the guide's comments about the area drifting leisurely up to Ryan on the porch. The tourists snapped pictures of the park and surrounding homes with their digital cameras and cell phones, and Ryan was confident he was in some of the shots. His grandmother said their town could never be confused with Charleston as a tourist destination, but they were starting to receive their fair share of visitors—nearly as many as Beaufort and Georgetown. Ryan found it amusing just the same to be considered a tourist attraction.

Beyond their neighborhood, other residential streets fanned out containing additional historic homes. One of the streets to the south turned into the downtown district. Most of the buildings were renovated, and the main street was dotted with cafes, coffee shops, antique shops, and arts and craft stores. Not a single fast food restaurant chain or coffee franchise could be seen in the immediate area.

Surrounding the residential area were saltwater marshes, and wooded areas filled with pines, massive low country live oaks draped in Spanish moss, and Cyprus trees. Some of the narrow unpaved roads that led away from the square and toward the coast remained undeveloped. The woods in these areas were so robust that the oaks and pines towered over hiking paths and narrow roads. They created a cathedral-like appearance, often blocking sunlight except for an occasional flash breaking though the canopy with golden radiance. Ryan's grandmother told him this was an idyllic place to find trails for hiking and running. He was intrigued with her description, and curious about checking these out.

Further on were beach houses and then the ocean was maybe a mile or so away. Ryan sensed the salt in the air with the breeze that was blowing inland.

He sat in a wicker chair to eat his lunch. With his last mouthful, Ryan shifted his lunch plate from his lap to a glass-topped wicker table adjacent to his chair. He stood up, ambled to one of the white porch columns and leaned against it. The sky was too hazy for him to get a clear view of the marshes or the ocean. Instead, he followed the black wrought iron fence that surrounded the perimeter of his grandmother's property. The fence was about five feet tall, and the ornate bars comprising the vertical portions ended in threatening looking spikes. The main entrance of the fence at the front of the house had two gates that swung inward. Ryan thought it looked cool.

While he inspected the property, Ryan noticed a kid sailing by on a skateboard. Directly in front of the house, the kid looked up in Ryan's direction. His expression suggested recognition, and he waved to confirm it. Ryan was puzzled because he had never seen the kid before. The kid rode out of view behind some trees. Ryan walked along the porch a few feet and leaned over the railing to try and catch sight of him again.

"Ryan!"

He was startled by his mother's yell. "What?"

"Be careful, you're going to fall." She looked up to him from the brick terrace in the garden.

"Geez, Mom. I'm not going to fall. God." He was exasperated. "You practically scared me into falling." Ryan still leaned over the railing. He noticed two air conditioning units directly below him, surrounded by the same wrought iron fencing that ran along the perimeter of the property. There was even a small gate as part of the enclosure to allow access to the units in case of service. He wondered what possessed his grandfather to think about putting the fence around the air conditioning in the first place. Surrounding these units, in turn, were wax myrtle and gem magnolia trees to block the view of the unsightly hardware.

"Wow...imagine falling onto these things," he mocked his mother.

"Or worse, the sharp spikes of the iron fence..." she replied seriously. "Your grandmother told me she has some dry rot in that area of the wood you were leaning against. It could easily break off and you'd come crashing down."

Ryan couldn't believe it. Of all the stupid things..."How can there be dry rot? It's so humid here."

"Okay, maybe it's wet rot, Ryan. I don't know. Just do me a favor and don't lean on it."

* * * *

Miranda watched the upstairs porch long enough to make sure her son was safely away from the railing. Of course he wasn't going to fall. He was just an active boy exploring new surroundings. Yet, she couldn't help seeing danger at every turn. There were situations in which he could fall or cut himself or trip or drown or pick up germs or...or God knows what, but there was always a catastrophe lurking behind every corner. She hated herself for thinking this way, but there it was. She knew she was driving Ryan crazy with her hovering. Granted some of his moodiness, probably a lot of it actually, was hormonal. You don't get through puberty unscathed, and she was talking about the parental perspective. As a kid, well, the teenage years were always exploding in turmoil of one sort or another. Miranda was forty-three and didn't have a firm memory of her own adolescence (maybe that was the mind's gift to adults—amnesia related to your teen years), but she had recollections of fun and exciting times and dreadful memories of unmanageable self-doubt. Lord only knows what it would be like to go through that decade again today, and being a male at that.

What angered her to the point of despair was the fact that she had to make this journey with a teenage boy all alone. *Damn it, Phil, you weren't supposed to leave me this way. How the hell am I supposed to do this?* She'd had this one-sided argument with him quite often over the last six months or so. Every now and again she could imagine how he would respond if he was present. *What, you think I planned it this way?* She smiled at these comments she made up for him. *No, Phil, I know you didn't, and I know you would have loved to see him grow up.* This didn't change the stark reality that everything regarding Ryan rode on her shoulders. The only frame of reference for raising a boy was growing up with Charlie, the brother who was two years her junior. Sadly, he provided a distorted perspective at best. A sullen and directionless young man who wanted to portray himself as edgy or uncompromising, Charlie just found himself in and out of rehab until their father said it was time to get a job and leave home. He was in his mid-twenties by then, and left to find work in California, of all places. He somehow managed to make a living, although Miranda thought it was done illegally involving drugs and God only knows what else.

Ryan didn't seem to be anything like her brother. Miranda had to admit the kid was pretty low maintenance, and extremely independent and self-reliant. As a toddler, Ryan was always saying, "Ry-Ry do it". He had to do everything, put on socks, shoes, coat, take turns raking leaves with Phil, you name it. The downside to all of this was that tasks took forever. The upside was that they found themselves skating through childhood with minimal hassle. Miranda recalled an occasion when Ryan was five. She woke up around four thirty or five in the morning to the smell of food cooking. Both she and Phil raced to the kitchen and found Ryan cooking pancakes. He woke up hungry and figured he could do it. Oil, eggs, pancake mix, milk...the ingredients were spread out all over the kitchen. The thing was he did a pretty decent job. He knew from watching them prepare numerous breakfasts, and lately helping with breakfasts, that he had to be careful with the burners and not let the pancakes burn. They found him standing on a chair, spatula in hand, keeping due diligence. Phil, of course, thought it was hilarious. Miranda didn't know what to make of it.

Sitting with other mothers at baseball or soccer games

would often be an eye-opener. Litanies of incomplete homework, holes punched in walls, drinking, brooding silence for days on end, fighting, back talk, swearing–many of these on a daily basis. Ryan had his moments, by God, he could argue with the best of them, not to mention his reaction to Phil's death and the plans to move back to South Carolina. On the other hand, he was also so even keel at the same time. He was able to make personal adjustments and then go on with the next task. He got this from Phil, she knew that. Phil's main strength was being pragmatic. He was a realist who always demonstrated how not to make a mountain out of a molehill. You've got a problem? Well, let's deal with it. Ryan was drawn to that style like a bee to honey.

The other women at the games noticed this, with admitted envy. Miranda had to acknowledge she enjoyed their comments. The irony was that she couldn't claim genetics, since Ryan was adopted. This was just a good example of nurture playing a bigger role than nature, and a father's strong impact on his son. With Phil gone now, however, Miranda worried about Ryan's ability to handle his life's pressures on his own. He certainly showed independence, but she frequently found herself wishing for some dependence on his part. A boy still needed his mother. Or, let's be honest, she needed him to need her.

Within minutes of their spat, Ryan joined Miranda and her mother in the kitchen, volunteering his services. "All right, I suppose you want me to do something."

Miranda saw her mother's face beam with joy. Ryan's mere presence seemed to draw this out of her.

"There's my sweet grandson. I knew we could count on you to help."

* * * *

Ryan placed his foot on the seat of the wooden kitchen chair to tie his left athletic shoe. He helped out with some chores, and earned free time for himself by doing the work without complaining. He took two steps towards the back door, and then remembered to take some water. He reached back to the refrigerator, opened the door, grabbed a plastic bottle, then closed it with his foot. At that moment, his mother came in.

"Good, I was just coming to remind you."

Ryan waved the bottle at eye level to indicate he was one step ahead of her.

"Honey, please be careful. Drink a lot, and stop to walk if the heat gets to you."

"Yeah, Mom, I know. You must think I'm so stupid."

"No, it's not that..."

'Gotta go," Ryan interrupted. His Mom-radar started sensing another overprotective worry speech coming on, and he wanted to get the heck out of there before he was trapped. "Love you." He bounded out the door. He felt a little guilty doing it, but this tendency of his mother to foresee danger was getting old. In his heart he understood where it came from, but she had to understand he was growing up, and he was going to want to live his own life and do more things. He could only imagine what kind of wreck she'd be when he started driving in two years. She'd probably dole out his driving privileges like a miserly banker. Then there were girls. What happened when he got a girlfriend? Would she be scrutinizing everything? Would she force him to sit down to have heartfelt chats about relationships and sex and shit? He could only imagine the embarrassment. God, the mine fields that awaited him!

Ryan crossed the street and jogged on the paths in the park. He dodged tourists as he made his way to the Old Bay Road which cut through the woods. Two of the tourists were incredibly beautiful girls about his age or a little older. The both wore tank tops cut pretty low, giving him a great view of their breasts. They smiled at him as he went by. He smiled at them in return, but as he felt the first stirrings of arousal he focused his concentration on the route he planned to take for his run.

After fifteen or twenty minutes, he exited the residential area, and entered an alien world. The tunnel effect of the oak and pine trees lived up to its reputation. The upper boughs shielded him from the sunlight while Spanish moss draped branches at various lengths. The spiky fronds of small palmetto trees clustered with other bushes on the ground. The clamor of town life quickly subsided. The humidity almost had a life of its own, pressing down on Ryan as he ran. He was glad for the water, and reluctantly acknowledged that maybe his mother was right for a change.

Within five minutes, the air was very close, almost smothering. The breeze, sounds of birds, and flight patterns of various insects disappeared. The sudden stillness was a little unnerving.

Ryan was now very conscious of being isolated.

You really are alone. There is no one around to...help you.

He was starting to spook himself, and felt stupid for it. The pat-pat-pat of his footfalls was distinct against the stark silence. Sweat ran freely down his face.

You're so alone.

A figure blocked his path about fifty yards ahead.

He used the hem of his T-shirt to wipe sweat falling into his eyes. They started stinging, so it took him a second to refocus.

The figure was gone.

He's hiding in the woods. He's going to get you, Ryan.

Stop it.

Ryan was positive there had been someone further ahead. The figure was silhouetted against the sunlight at the end of the wooded tunnel. It was a guy, a kid maybe–a boy, but now he couldn't see him.

The live oak canopy, quite charming only moments before, was now sinister. Someone was nearby and *watching*.

He was reminded of last fall when he and his friend Daniel were in the mall and some guy approached them in the food court area.

"Hello boys. How about I give you each fifty dollars if you let me take your picture."

"What?" Ryan couldn't believe he just heard this. He started to walk away but Daniel said, "Fifty dollars for our pictures? Sure."

Ryan was speechless but grabbed his friend by the upper arm and shoved him away from the creep with surprising ferocity.

Daniel was incensed. "Dude, what the *fuck*? That's an easy *fifty bucks*."

"You stupid shit," he hissed. "The guy's a child molester or a serial killer. I'm trying to save your ass." Ryan kept pushing his friend away from the vicinity of the man.

"Really?" The implications were dawning on Daniel. When they turned back, the guy was nowhere to be seen. When they reported him to a security guard, Daniel made it sound like he, and not Ryan, had been on top of the situation. Ryan just stared in disbelief. By the time they got back to school, the story had blossomed into a narrative of dramatic escape that involved dodging automatic weapons fire during a near abduction from a network of human traffickers. Although he never said it aloud, Ryan thought if he hadn't been forceful, there would be pictures of Daniel, naked and terrified, all over the internet and Daniel's body would be somewhere at the bottom of Lake Michigan.

Ryan's gut told him to get the hell away from that guy wanting to take their picture. He got the same kind of warning here. Something was terribly wrong.

Ryan stopped jogging. The stillness was complete.

A short burst of menacing laughter sounded.

You're gonna get hurt. Badly.

The bushes and shrubs to his left rustled. The shaking of palmettos, smaller pine trees, and other bushes suggested something advancing on him. Something was low to the ground, and driving forward at a surprisingly rapid pace despite the thickness of the brush.

Similar movements started off the right side of the narrow road. Vegetation trembled, actually *moved*, as the mass charged towards Ryan.

On the left, the forward advance paused. Ryan caught a brief glimpse of a head, bare chest, and hair flowing back into a mane as the figure dashed to the ground to resume forward movement.

That was a boy. Right? Had to be. But how...

How could it be? The figure was bent, near the ground, moving too quickly. It didn't seem...human.

A second glimpse through palmettos...an impossible angle, haunches driving, thigh muscles straining. Then a cry, high pitched, excited, and malevolent.

You're dead if you don't move NOW.

Ryan's nervous system finally kicked in. He nearly fell on the first twisting step, but somehow he righted himself and started pumping his arms and legs.

The humid air felt as if it was smothering him and he gasped. His brain focused on escape, and he feared he wouldn't make it. *Oh God, what's happening?* He couldn't feel his feet on the path. He was getting light-headed and shaky. His hands and fingers tingled. Pounding footfalls behind him sounded closer and closer. The two figures charging through the forest on either side of him had burst through, but just out of his peripheral vision. Low to the ground, at times they seemed to run on four legs. Dogs? No. Wolves? No. Now on two legs. Kids? No, something dangerous, something with claws...

Something would grab him or trip him any second now. There would be claws and teeth as these things fought over his flesh. They would tear him apart while he screamed his last breath.

Sunlight ahead, maybe twenty yards, the oak canopy was thinning, something swiped at him, just barely missing. If he could just make it out of the tunnel...Another swipe caught his collar, ripping his T-shirt to shreds down the middle of his back. Somehow he kept going, pulled, churned his legs, staying on his feet, screamed his way forward, to get...to... the...sunlight. He broke away, practically flying, and then sprawling along the ground, skinning his palms and knees. He scrambled to his feet ready to fight the approaching...

There was nothing there.

The Old Bay Road looked as inviting as it had when he first entered about thirty minutes before. In fact there were two bicyclists riding on the path further down the tunnel.

He collapsed onto the ground, laboring for each breath.

What the hell?

He felt his T-shirt. It was intact.

"What the hell?" he said aloud between breaths. He noticed a street with some traffic, and houses dotting the landscape. The busier section of the town was about a mile away. He noticed a car parked on the road. A man jogged up to him.

"Son? Are you all right? I saw you come running out of the woods and falling. I stopped when I could." He was probably about his mom's age, with straw colored hair very thin on top. He wore glasses. Ryan was glad to see a human.

Ryan shook his head, saying, "Yeah, I'm okay."

"Well, you look...well...you should drink your water, at least."

Ryan was amazed to find the plastic water bottle on the ground just a few feet away. He picked it up and felt unsteady. He shrugged off this sensation, unscrewed the cap, and drank half of it in one gulp. It was warm, but tasted great.

"Careful, now, don't get sick." The man still looked at him intently. "Can I give you a ride somewhere? I can take you home."

Ryan considered this for a second then said, "No, really, I'm okay. I think I could use the walk."

The man's expression suggested walking was the last thing that he needed. "Do I know you? You don't look familiar."

"No, I just moved here."

"Ah. I thought so. My name is Arthur Beaumont. I thought I knew everyone in this town, so I figured you had to be someone new."

Ryan didn't know if he was supposed to add something to the conversation. He'd rather just go home, but he supposed this was southern hospitality, so he should be polite. "Yes, sir."

"I'm a science teacher at the high school, biological sciences, mostly. You'll be attending?"

"Freshman, in the fall. My name is Ryan." He stood up and held out his hand.

"A pleasure, Ryan." The teacher shook it. "I will certainly be seeing more of you. Are you sure I can't help you? I'd love to take you home, and meet your folks."

"That's okay, really, I'm just fine."

"Well then, I guess I should head off." He turned away and walked for a few feet, and then looked back. "You're sure now? It'd be no bother, and I hate to leave you with that walk back to your grandmother's."

"No problem. Thanks anyway."

* * * *

They had pizza and salad for dinner, normally something Ryan loved to eat. That night though, his mind kept returning to the Incident in the Tunnel, as he now considered it, capital letters and all.

"You're awfully quiet tonight," his mom announced midway through the meal.

Ryan thought he did a pretty good job keeping up the conversation, but obviously he wasn't fooling anybody.

"Just tired. The run took a lot out of me. I think you were right about exercising in this heat." Ryan hoped admitting he was wrong and she was right would throw her off balance. It worked, sort of...

"From now on, if you go running, do it earlier in the day. That'll mean getting up earlier."

"Um-hmm." He was non-committal.

After dinner they had plans to watch a DVD–"something the whole family could enjoy", which meant something Ryan would not enjoy like a chick flick or a G-Rated goofy family comedy with talking pets or something. It turned out to be the latter. Ryan was bored to tears, but watched with them in an effort to be a good sport and to throw off the scent that something troubling had happened to him today.

Around ten he announced he was going to bed, claiming he was too tired to keep his eyes open any longer. He kissed his mother and grandmother goodnight and went upstairs to brush his teeth and go to the bathroom.

When he returned to his room, he undressed, flicked off the light and literally fell into bed. Clasping his fingers, Ryan placed his hands behind his head and stared at the ceiling, waiting for his vision to adjust to the darkness.

What did happen out there? Why was he so scared of two kids? They looked smaller. He was positive he could've kicked their asses.

After the school teacher left, he walked home. By the time he got there, he felt as though he was going to puke. Luckily he could avoid his mother and grandmother, who were back at it in the kitchen, by shouting a quick, "I'm back" and moving as quick as he could upstairs to the bathroom. He sat on the floor until the symptoms passed, and then took a shower.

It must have been the heat. Wasn't that what people always said? Heat stroke or dehydration? There were no strange kids chasing him through the woods. Likewise, nobody was behind him, although he would swear on a stack of bibles that he glimpsed that one kid.

He wasn't even aware of falling asleep until he turned over to look at the clock. It said 4:25. Ryan didn't recall closing his eyes. He propped himself up on his elbows, startled into alertness. Had he heard something? He remained motionless for two minutes, and then made himself stay that way for another minute. There was nothing, although he heard the ocean breeze combing through leaves outside. He was thirsty, however, that was clear. Maybe he had been severely dehydrated.

Ryan went out to the hallway. Everything was quiet, and he could see nothing was moving because the hallway was dimly lit with nightlights. He tiptoed downstairs to the kitchen for some ice water. He grabbed a plastic cup and filled it with ice, careful not to rattle the cubes when removing them from the freezer.

Ryan walked into the dining room, sipping his water. He stood before the French doors and saw his full body reflection. Since he was wearing only his boxer shorts, he considered moving away from the window so he wasn't seen from the street.

A head appeared outside a few feet from the glass, just over the reflection of his right shoulder. Someone was on the porch looking in.

Ryan gasped and dropped the plastic cup of water. It hit with a dead sound and water splashed on his ankles and shins. He involuntarily stepped back. The head now had an upper body and moved forward. Ryan saw he looked at himself, or his double. Yet it wasn't his double, really. This other Ryan-thing looked diseased. The skin was a mottled lifeless green, and the eyes nearly black except for a hint of red like the underside of hot charcoal. The lips pulled back into a semblance of a smile to display teeth that seemed to be chiseled into uneven jagged shapes. As the figure reached the window, it lifted and placed its hands palms up on the glass and leaned towards Ryan. The fingers looked vaguely like talons. The nail of the left index finger tapped softly on the glass as if in greeting. The hair on Ryan's neck stood on end.

From behind him, a hand brushed the skin of Ryan's back between the shoulder blades.

Child. Barely a whisper...

Ryan screamed, and turned to see a dark face with eyes that looked directly into his with concern. After this brief silent communication, the eyes shifted to over his shoulder and looked out the window.

"Go!" the dark face commanded the figure sternly...before fading away.

Ryan sensed the sound of feet hurrying down the stairs. Somebody called his name, but he couldn't tell who or why because he was falling. His face slapped the back of a wooden dining room chair...then his entire body slammed onto the floor.

Chapter Three

"Almost done. Just a few more." Above him, the doctor suturing the cut above his right eyebrow was in view. Ryan's face and head throbbed. "You'll end up with five stitches above your eyebrow and four below the eye on your cheekbone. You're lucky you didn't do any damage to your eye, but you'll have quite a shiner. You're also fortunate you don't have a concussion or any broken bones. There..." She snipped the surgical thread as she finished. "Let's have you sit up."

The emergency room lights illuminated everything in a harsh manner. Ryan blinked, and noticed the dried blood on both hands, and streams of it soaked into his T-shirt. His hair felt matted and gritty, suggesting that blood dripped in that direction too. He felt like shit, and must have looked really pathetic because as the examination table shifted into a sitting position, the doctor gently took the right side of his face in her hand and gave him a pat. Her eyes showed compassion, and she looked as if she felt sad for him. Ryan thought she must be a mother.

The name embroidered on her white coat said, "Cassandra Pullman-Batista MD". The color of her eyes and skin were the same dark brown. In addition, her skin was moist and creaseless which made it difficult to tell how old she was.

"Are you using drugs or alcohol?"

Ryan wasn't expecting this. "What? No. I swear..."

She stared at him. He was glad he asked his mother to wait in the waiting room.

"Okay, once, no, twice. Both times it was beer, and just one can. I didn't even finish the can the second time. I was at a friend's house, and it was last year. His dad has cases of beer in the basement."

"What about the hallucinations? Ever have them before?"

"Hey, look, I saw the kid. He looked in the window. I'm not making it up." He hadn't told anyone about the Incident in the Tunnel. God, what would they think if they knew about that?

"The old black women behind you in the dining room?

Who told the kid to get lost?"

Ryan sighed. He lowered his head into his hands, "Crap. I don't know."

For the second time in a few minutes, Doctor Pullman-Batista placed her hand ever so gently below his chin and raised his head so he looked directly at her.

"You may have been out of the sun too long today, and you may have been dehydrated. Maybe you northern boys just don't have the stamina." She smiled at him as he started to protest.

"Ryan, I'm joking. I'm sure you're tough enough to handle it. I am not joking about this, though...you have been through a lot this past year. Your father died, and you're still grieving–even if you don't know it. You moved to a whole new part of the country away from your friends and all of your support."

Ryan was caught off guard with the ease in which she moved into personal territory. Maybe it was her gentle manner or her way of saying things.

"You're under a lot of stress. You're confused. Most adults have trouble coping under similar circumstances. So, it is really possible that your mind is playing tricks on you."

Ryan nodded to show he understood. All of a sudden he felt incredibly drained, and everything hurt.

"You've been here less than a week, right? So, you don't know any kids yet. I saw your mother enrolled you in school. You'll soon meet some kids there, and things will start falling into place for you. My daughter's your age, by the way, and she'll be going to the same high school."

He smiled weakly at her.

"I am going to write a script for pain medication. I'll give it to your mother. I'll send the nurse in to put on the dressings and explain to you and your mother how to change them. In the meantime, you are to obey my orders. Rest today, take a nap, and eat well. Read a book. No running around. Agreed?"

"Agreed."

* * * *

Following orders wasn't difficult. His grandmother and mother took turns hovering. They made sure he was well fed. He took a nap willingly. He went on Facebook to catch up with kids in Wisconsin. He took a nap unwillingly by dozing off while reading. By late in the afternoon, he felt somewhat better, although he was starting to go stir crazy. He wanted to go outside, but that was off-limits as far as the two women were concerned.

On one of the shelves in the downstairs den he found all of the children's books his mother illustrated. Ryan's personal favorite was about a boy angel who had the opportunity to play little league baseball. The cool thing was that eight-year-old Ryan served as his mother's model for the main character. Ryan still had his own personal autographed copy from his mom ("to my special angel") and the author in his room. He still felt a rush looking at it six years later, and could picture himself showing the book to his own kids in the future ("that's me, do you believe it?").

Next to his mother's books was the collection of family photo albums. He grabbed two of them and then sprawled on the couch. He flipped through, checking out the gradual changes in people year after year. Many of the pictures had similar poses, around the table at Thanksgiving, opening presents at Christmas, couples dressed up in formal attire for another night of celebration related to this or that event in South Carolina society.

There were pictures of kids, of course. His mom started out as a baby and grew into a teenager, sometimes singing in school musicals, sometimes soaking wet with a towel wrapped around her after she finished an event at a swim meet, sometimes mugging during her birthday parties, or posing for prom pictures. She was always smiling, at ease with the camera. It was different for Uncle Charlie. He often scowled or partially turned from the camera. There was no consistency or theme to his photos, he often just stood in the background and tolerated whatever event was captured on film. The few photos of normal childhood activities often had a desperate feel to them, as if someone tried to capture a glimpse of what could have been, but wasn't meant to be, an occasional athletic venture that ended shortly thereafter or some short-lived extracurricular club activity.

Ryan didn't see Uncle Charlie that often. He was in the "entertainment business" on the "coast", but not affiliated with any entertainment Ryan was aware of. When he was around, Uncle Charlie was nothing but a bundle of frenetic energy, with non-stop, pointless, and self-absorbed talking. He was annoying. During his father's funeral service, his cell phone kept ringing. One time he actually took a call. Somebody must have said something to him later, because at the house afterwards, he came up to Ryan and said, "Hey dude, sorry for the phone. I just have so many things in the fire right now."

Ryan didn't know how to respond politely to something like this, so he spoke from the heart, "Uncle Charlie, you're a complete asshole." Those were the last words they exchanged.

Ryan's grandfather, Franklin Tryon, was a wiry guy who was also energetic. The difference was his energy had purpose. Ryan remembered him vividly, even though he had been dead for five years. He was always looking for something to repair or build or improve. Installing a wrought iron fence around air conditioning units was a good example, followed by planting trees and shrubs around the fence. Professionally he was a lawyer, but was a huge advocate of community service. Ryan knew this was how he met his grandmother. She too was involved with community service, although her interests focused on helping the less fortunate. No one could accuse her of doing service work for recognition. She did it out of principle or obligation.

Midway through the second album, his father appeared. "Miranda and Philip's Wedding" was a huge feature. His father had a bemused look in many of the pictures, even as the years went by. He appeared to get along with his in-laws because there was no sense of impatience in any of the shots. Like magic, Ryan showed up a few pages later. Since he was adopted, there were no pictures of his mom pregnant. He just appeared, ready for action. Ryan sucking on his toes, Ryan trying to stand up for the first time, Ryan on a tricycle, Ryan learning to ride a two-wheeler, Ryan playing in the Wisconsin snow, Ryan snowboarding.

"Well, young man, you look like you're in a nostalgic mood."

Ryan looked up from the album and noticed his grandmother standing over him. She had a bouquet of flowers in her hand.

"Yeah," he replied. "It's kind of fun looking at the pictures. Everyone looks so different on the one hand, but the same on the other. Do you know what I mean?"

"I do." She sat down at the edge of the sofa, and he moved his feet by bringing his knees up so she could fit comfortably.

"I look at old pictures and it seems the event just happened yesterday, but then I look in the mirror and I see this old woman and I think 'how can this be'?"

"Nah, you're not that old."

She smiled warmly in reply. "Thank you for that compliment."

Ryan found himself inspecting a picture of his father. He was sitting on the downstairs porch drinking a can of beer, wearing a pair of khakis rolled up practically to his knees. He was barefoot, and his legs were propped up on the railing. He had a wry smile, and was obviously enjoying himself.

"Dad was pretty happy, wasn't he?"

"Pretty happy? Oh my heavens, Ryan. He was very happy. He and your mother were very happy together. He found enjoyment in just about everything."

"You liked him, didn't you?"

"Very much. He was friendly, polite, and easy going. I was so thrilled that my daughter married a man who cared so much for her and was so decent to her. We couldn't wait for their visits, and then when you came along, the visits became even more special."

"I miss him, you know?" Ryan said. "It still hurts inside."

"I know, sweetheart, and it probably will continue for a long time. But you know what, all the good qualities he had? He had plenty of time to pass them along to you. You remind me of him in many ways."

"Really?" Ryan felt himself grinning like a little kid. He couldn't help it. He liked the comparison.

"Yes, really."

Ryan was satisfied. "What's up with the flowers?" He nodded to the bouquet in his grandmother's hand.

"Well, speaking of nostalgia, I was thinking of walking to the cemetery to check out your grandfather's grave. It's been awhile, and I imagine it's a mess."

Ryan recalled accompanying her in the past to help spruce up the grave site. Going again sounded appealing. "Can I come?"

"Of course you can. Let's tell your mother so she doesn't worry that you've escaped against medical advice."

The walk to the cemetery was only about six blocks. The late afternoon sun was blocked frequently by palm trees and live oaks, but the heat was still oppressive. Their walk was more of a leisurely stroll, but Ryan still felt a thin sheen of perspiration developing on his skin. His grandmother, amazingly, did not seem to be troubled at all by the warmth.

"Do you remember me teaching you how a gentleman escorts a lady while walking?" she asked as soon as they left her property and set foot on the sidewalk.

"Um...not really." He looked at her sheepishly. He had no clue what she was talking about.

"Oh dear, it's time for more lessons. You never know when you're going to need it."

Ryan groaned inwardly, but he didn't know any of the kids in the area, so he wouldn't be too embarrassed if he was spotted taking part in an impromptu charm-school exercise.

"First, my dear boy, a gentleman always walks on the outside closest to the street. The lady walks protected on the inside."

"Why? Protected from what, I mean?"

"All kinds of things...so she won't step in road apples, for instance."

"Road apples?"

"Manure, dear. Horse droppings in the street or near the curb from the horse drawn carriages."

Ryan couldn't help smiling. "Horseshit you mean." Then he laughed.

"If you must. Although, gentlemen wouldn't use such language."

She was trying to act stern, but Ryan could see she enjoyed his playfulness. "Okay, road apples it is."

"That's better. Now, the gentleman offers his arm to the lady. So, hold out your arm." Ryan did. "Bend it slightly so she actually takes the crook of your arm. See, a lady now has support." By this time, his grandmother had now taken his arm and they were strolling together.

"Okay, besides manure, what else does this protect a girl from?"

"Oh, splashing puddles, runaway horses..."

"Runaway horses! God. How dumb."

"It's convention, Ryan."

"Yeah, but, the guy takes all the risk and does all the work."

"Yes, indeed, he does." She kept smiling at him.

"That's weird."

They continued to walk arm-in-arm for a block before his

grandmother asked, "Do you remember to use your "ma'ams" and "sirs"?"

"Yes..." Ryan purposely stretched out his pause, "...ma'am. At least around you for sure." Ryan was trying to suppress a grin, but he knew he wasn't being successful.

"Humph. We'll have to see about that too."

As they reached the cemetery, Ryan's entire frame trembled slightly. He managed to recover quickly with little more than a slight hitch in his pace, so his grandmother didn't seem to notice his reaction. The setting for the cemetery was beautiful, just as Old Bay Road was beautiful – before the ground fell out from under him. The area was only about half a block and was adjacent to an Episcopal Church. The setting probably dated back a century or two, with huge oak trees draped with Spanish moss. Palmettos dotted the paths among the gravestones and headstones. Ryan still felt nervous, but his reaction came not from walking among graves. That really didn't bother him. Rather, the similarity of the cemetery to the tunnel of Old Bay Road was a little too close. He couldn't help imagine strange kids watching him from behind the markers.

Ryan's grandfather was buried midway towards the southern end of the cemetery. His grandparents had burial plots because their families had lived in this town forever. Ryan remembered a number of summers ago when his mother and Uncle Charlie were joking with their parents about how they couldn't be buried with them in the family cemetery. There was literally no more room. His grandfather had all of the adults laughing when he replied that "the view stinks from there anyway". Within a year, he was to take up residence in this very location.

Franklin Tryon's burial site had a pretty decent view. It was off the main path, so the foot traffic was not extensive, and when Ryan and his grandmother visited in the past, they pretty much had the place to themselves. The grounds were well maintained, and tourists were frequent, but they tended to stay to the main trails. The headstone had an arched top and was rather plain with the name "Tryon" boldly presented front and center. Towards the lower left was "Franklin" accompanied by his dates of birth and death. On the lower right was "Carolyn", with his grandmother's birthday listed.

Ryan dropped to his knees in front of the headstone. "Does

it feel creepy seeing your name written here, Grandma?"

She chuckled. "Heavens, no, Ryan. We all go sometime." Her first act was to remove some old dying flowers from a vase in front of the stone, and insert the next bouquet. Ryan's job would be to dispose of the dead flowers and get some water for the new ones from a faucet near the church.

Ryan wasn't so sure if he felt as cavalier as his grandmother did. If he saw his name written like this with the only thing missing being the date of his death, he'd certainly feel creepy. He ran his hand along the edge to the top of the arch. Below this point was an image of a live oak tree. Other markers had other images like crosses, flowers, and anchors. Some markers had statues of Jesus or angels. There were even huge mausoleums, which seemed ridiculous to Ryan. They were kind of crass.

"Why do you have a live oak tree engraved in the stone? Does the oak have any meaning?" he asked.

"Yes. An oak on a headstone means strength. Does that sound like your grandfather?"

"Definitely." Ryan knew this symbolism really appealed to his grandmother when she thought about her husband. Still sitting on his haunches, Ryan traced his index finger over the oak tree. The lawn felt comfortable under his knees and shins. He sensed that his grandmother was looking at him so he turned. Sure enough, she was gazing at him with a warm smile that communicated both affection and sympathy. She reached out to him and he felt her hand caress the back of his head before sliding down to the side of his face where she patted his check gently.

"I think an oak would have been appropriate for Dad, too." His father was cremated, which was okay, but if he had been buried then "strength" would be a perfect symbol for his father.

"I agree. We've been very fortunate to have such men in our lives, you know."

At the instant, Ryan realized his grandmother probably still felt pain for her loss. Here he was still feeling moody over his father. He never even considered that old adults grieved for a long time, too.

His grandmother gave him a final tap and returned to pruning and cleaning. The site looked great, but he saw she attended to the removal of the smallest twigs or fallen leaves.

"How badly do you miss Grandpa?"

She brushed away a few stray acorns from the grass in front of the headstone. Ryan had to get off his knees so they could be sure she located them all.

"After all these years," she said, "the intense pain has lifted. You know how that pain feels. You don't wake up one day and it's gone. It's very gradual. I still miss him. Whenever something new happens, I still say to myself 'I've got to tell Franklin that', and then I realize I can't."

"I know. I do the same thing. I'll go, 'I can't wait to tell Dad...whatever' but then it hits me that I can never do that again."

"I'll let you in on a little secret. I do still tell things to your grandfather. Only, I'll do it in my mind so people don't think I've had a nervous breakdown." His grandmother pointed at her head with her finger.

Ryan smiled at her remark. He hadn't thought of trying this.

"You know something my dear boy? I think we're just about done here. Ready to help the old lady with the running around chores?"

"Sure." He bent to pick up the discarded flowers and retrieved the vase with the new ones. "Back in a second."

Ryan ran to the church, disposed of the old bouquet and filled up the vase from a faucet. As he returned to the grave site, he noticed his grandmother standing silently before the headstone. She was framed among the varying shades of green from the oaks and the palms, and her presence seemed so natural. He knew she was talking to his grandfather, so he slowed to give her the privacy. For some reason, the sight produced a catch in his throat, bringing tears to his eyes. He wiped them away quickly before approaching her.

"Ready?" She turned to face him as he drew near.

"Yep, all done." Ryan placed the vase in front of the headstone.

"Let's go home then."

Ryan stood up straight and offered his arm to his grandmother.

"Think now. Which way are we walking home, and where will you and I be relative to the street?"

Ryan thought. "Oh, yeah." He moved to her opposite side and lifted the other arm. She took it.

"Nicely done," she said and smiled at him.

* * * *

Ryan was startled into wakefulness, but disoriented as to where he was. He sat up and swung his legs over the edge of the bed. Okay, he was in his room...South Carolina. His clock read 4:17.

Wait, wasn't this like last night? Am I dreaming?

His head still ached, and other parts of his body were stiff and sore. He rubbed his arms and then his legs. He stood up, his muscles complaining.

Somebody ran up the stairs, pounding heavily on each wooden step as if running in hiking boots. Ryan froze, terrified. The footsteps reached the top and charged towards his room and stopped bare inches before his door. The silence that followed was so complete Ryan wondered whether he had somehow been mistaken. Why anybody else hadn't woken was baffling.

Something with the force of a battering ram crashed into his bedroom door.

Ryan jumped. *Holy shit!*

Another slam and Ryan thought he heard wood crack. He turned on a desk lamp.

He looked for something to protect himself.

What?

His baseball bat.

Another crash and Ryan sensed the door rattle.

He ran for his closet and opened the door. He was throwing clothes, fumbling in the dark for the *damn bat*. The next crash was so intense Ryan practically felt the impact on his chest from six feet away. Where was his mother, why wasn't she yelling for him?

Call the police.

He checked his night table for his cell phone. Not there. In his pockets? He found the shorts he had taken off before going to bed. Not in the left side pocket, but, yes, in the right pocket. Turned it on: pressed 9—

Another explosion and the door seemed to bow inward. Ryan expected it to shatter. He dropped both the phone and the bat.

The battering stopped.

Ryan held out his arms in anticipation of the next attack.

It didn't come. Instead, the door knob turned soundlessly.

Ryan shuddered. Somehow this was more alarming than the pounding noise.

The door swung open ever so slowly, but there was nothing standing in the doorway. Lights were on downstairs, but no noise, no movement, no *breathing*. Nothing.

Ryan cautiously stepped towards the door. Something had to be there, around the corner, there had to be. Just like in the movies, the guy with the axe, wearing a hockey mask.

Ryan knew he couldn't just stand there waiting for this thing to attack his mother or grandmother. He retraced his steps and picked up the baseball bat. Without giving it any second thought, he sprinted out his room to avoid the monster hiding around the corner. He ran to the staircase and then spun around, bat held high above his head in an exaggerated batting stance. The hallway was empty.

He lowered the bat from over his shoulder. As he did so, he realized his right side was wet. Looking down, he saw blood. A lot of it. Every time he rubbed his upper arm against his side he smeared blood. Blood flowed freely down his side into his boxers, which were now soaked, and then the blood continued to run in rivulets down his right leg. It pooled at his foot. He raised his right arm to find the source and saw his scar had been split open the entire length, from below his shoulder blade to the opposite end which sat just above the waistband of his underwear.

There was a cry from the doorway of his room. He turned to see his double, the same kid standing outside the dining room window just twenty-four hours before, charge him at a full sprint. Ryan barely had enough time to register that its eyes, glowing red on a black background, were filled with rage.

Then the Ryan-thing was on him—and went right through him before disappearing. A scream echoed in the hallway. Ryan realized he was the one screaming, and that he had lost his balance. He fell down the wooden staircase.

* * * *

He babbled like an idiot, trying to explain himself. "The same kid had gotten in."

"He was banging down my door."

"Didn't you hear it?"

"How could you sleep through that?"

"He cut me! Look at all the blood coming from the scar."

"Don't you see the freaking blood?"

Somebody got him some water, as if that would make a difference. They took turns trying to calm him down, sooth him. Telling him, "easy, take it easy...don't get up too fast". They found him sprawled on the stairs, crumpled and agitated. They helped him into a sitting position. He wasn't bleeding from his side. He was bleeding from his head, the left side this time, so another trip to the ER was in order. The wetness he felt wasn't blood but urine. He had wet himself. Ryan was humiliated. The stink of pee had settled in the hallway. His underwear was drenched and a good sized pool was at the top of the stairs. His left arm was killing him. He cursed with pain.

"Mom." Ryan reached for his mother's hand, beyond devastated. "What's wrong with me?"

* * * *

Doctor Pullman-Batista had trauma duty again.

"This was not what I had in mind when I told you to obey my orders."

Five more stitches on his left hairline, three more on his left eyebrow, and a simple fracture of the left wrist. The x-ray procedure was just a blur to him. Ryan dozed during much of the suturing with the help of the pain medication. This time, his mother stayed with him in the examining room. He caught portions of the conversation between his mother and the doctor.

"Mrs. Perry, what is going on?"

"...he keeps saying he's seeing his double..."

"...psychiatric history?"

"...adopted...don't know..."

"...uncharacteristic...level-headed...no problem..."

"...other trauma..."

"...scar?" Ryan sensed someone lifting his shirt to examine his side.

There was silence, followed by additional whispering, then...

"May I?"

"Oh, sure, Mom. Come in. Doctor, this is my mother, Carolyn Tryon."

"Hello Cassie," his grandmother said.

Ryan caught that, and he sensed a change in the room. He lifted his head and focused his vision. His grandmother noticed him looking, so she smiled and patted his knee.

"Mrs. Tryon. It has been a long time."

"You know each other." It was a statement from his mother. Ryan almost said the same words, but as a question.

"We go back a few years, dear," his grandmother replied. "I used to work with Cassie's mother. Oh, I'm sorry, I am forgetting my manners. You're Doctor Pullman-Batista now." There was a sense of admiration in his grandmother's voice.

"It's quite all right Mrs. Tryon. I feel bad that I didn't make this connection." She motioned her hand towards Ryan. "I think I just put two and two together in the last thirty seconds...Am I right?"

"Yes, my dear, you are correct."

Ryan was confused. At first he thought it might be the drugs, but then he learned that his mother was feeling the same when she said, "This is sounding very mysterious. Exactly what are you two talking about?"

His grandmother calmly replied, "The last time Doctor Pullman-Batista and I saw each other was the night of Ryan's birth."

* * * *

As far as Miranda was concerned, this was just one more in a series of tremors to disrupt her daily living. Her mother's bombshell certainly took Ryan and her by surprise. Even though he was still disoriented from his trauma and pain medications, Ryan started pumping them for information. His questions were unfocused, which agitated him even further. He kept trying to sit up, and Miranda decided the adults needed to sort this out before subjecting Ryan to any more turmoil.

"The three of us need to talk. Outside."

"Wait, Mom...what? Hold it...no..."

"Ryan, honey, no. Lie back. I'll talk to you, but I want to get this straight."

"Oh, but Mom!"

Miranda looked at him sternly and he complied, although he mumbled under his breath and looked wounded.

She stepped back and made an after-you motion with her arm. The doctor and her mother left the exam room in front of her. As she exited, Miranda closed a sliding glass door to separate themselves from inquisitive eyes and ears of her son. She kept her back to him, but she imagined him peering through the glass trying to make sense of the discussion. Around them were other physicians, nurses and family members in consultation. No one paid them the slightest bit of attention.

Her mother initiated the conversation. "Miranda, this might not be the best place."

"Mother, you're kidding. You mention something like that in front of the boy and then expect me to drop it under the pretense of social etiquette?"

"No, darling." Her voice lowered slightly. "It's just that this whole thing is really involved."

"What has Ryan's birth got to do with his current health problems?"

Neither woman spoke for what felt like an eternity. Finally, Carolyn replied, "I'm afraid it might have quite a bit."

* * * *

Special Agent Jeremy Lund from the Behavioral Analysis Unit knelt among the small palmetto trees within the woods of Old Bay Road. He was centered within a large sweeping area surrounded by yellow crime scene tape, examining a series of tracks discovered by local police. The tracks were predominantly footprints but there were a few handprints. Narrow indentation marks were visible in front of the feet and hands where the toes and fingers would be. The tracks were small, suggesting they were made by a child or children—there were two different sets scattered across the scene—who were probably male and around eight to twelve years of age. In addition, the tracks were made with more force than would be expected by kids that young.

More importantly, they were made in the vicinity of a gruesome murder scene.

Lund scanned the immediate vicinity from his vantage point, trying to get a handle on the perspective of the kid who made the tracks. There was a lot of green for sure, and the vegetation had provided ample cover–if the kid had a reason for seeking cover. Which, Lund feared, he did.

The live oaks provided shade, but the air still had an oppressive tropical feel. Lund had discarded his blazer earlier in the morning in deference to the coastal South Carolina summer temperatures. He actually enjoyed the hot, muggy weather, and typically preferred this over anything remotely on the cold side. Spending the first twelve years of his life in Alabama and the next ten only a few miles from here likely produced his affinity for a climate many found intolerable. Living the last twelve years in various locations in Virginia essentially sealed the deal. He would never be able to acclimate to a northern climate. As it was now, enduring the relatively mild winters of northern Virginia, as many of his colleagues considered them, was the closest thing to misery in his recent experience.

Lund sighed and stood up. Because of a knack for public speaking, he frequently gave workshops on research updates and best practices for investigations into serial homicides. His masters' degree in mental health counseling also permitted him to speak with authority on psychopathy issues. In a recent training with local and state law enforcement offices in North and South Carolina, discussion arose about how local authorities might recognize when they had a serial killer on their hands. The topics included number of victims, duration of time between events, risk level of victims, commonality of victims...the number of factors was surprisingly complex. As part of the commentary, Lund provided an illustration about a series of suspicious deaths over a five year period. The occurrences were not frequent, but all involved deaths due to savage attack. Injuries appeared to be the result of a slashing motion of claws, but DNA evidence was inconclusive. What little came back suggested some biological class of birds had been present during or shortly after the murder. One technician, off the record of course, suggested the markings reminded him of archosaurs, a term for animals whose representatives include modern birds and reptiles. These anecdotes received a chuckle from the audience, and Lund played into it with a theatrical shrug. At the same time, other forensic evidence like footprints made by an athletic shoe and auto carpet fibers were present. Lund suspected a serial homicide event was occurring, but he didn't have enough evidence to qualify for the definition. This was an open case for him, so he still doggedly pursued it when he had the opportunity.

Actually, Lund was fairly confident his running hypothesis of what had caused these deaths was on target. He could even explain the strange DNA evidence. At this stage of the game, however, any disclosure of his ideas would invite scorn, and that was putting it mildly. To his surprise, six months hadn't gone by when he received a call last night from the chief of police describing the deaths of two college kids. The chief noted the similarities of her case to Lund's presentation and called him. Within an hour, Lund was on a plane from DC to Charleston.

The victims were a young couple, Melissa Tompkins and Todd Jester. They had recently graduated from college and taken a vacation before starting graduate school. They had a romantic relationship, and everyone expected them to become engaged. An eleven-year-old Boy Scout collecting litter in the woods with his buddies as part of community service project discovered the bodies. Todd and Melissa had been dismembered and beheaded and piled within a small clearing within a few yards from where Lund stood. The Boy Scout was drawn by the odor, thinking it was spoiling garbage. The kid might never be the same.

Lund found the locals had done a decent job with the crime scene and generating potential witnesses. When the news broke about the disappearance of the couple, and the later discovery of the grisly remains, another young couple bicycling on Old Bay Road came forward and reported seeing a teenager running away from their location the previous day. House to house interviews with neighbors found a woman who reported seeing her old biology teacher talking with, and seemingly trying to assist, a teenage boy around the same time. It didn't take long to identify Arthur Beaumont, who willingly provided what he knew to the police. Lund had gone to Beaumont's house this morning before he arrived to examine the crime scene.

"I don't know if I can tell you anything more than I already told the police," Beaumont told him. Lund noticed he was in his forties with thinning wispy hair that was not very cooperative at staying in place. He was outside watering his flower beds when Lund pulled up in front of his house.

"I understand, and I realize this is a shot in the dark, but I wanted to hear for myself what you saw."

Beaumont nodded. "Well, I just happened to be driving by when I saw this kid sprinting along the Old Bay Road. He had just come out of the canopy area, and right in front of me he stumbles and goes flying. The landing had to hurt."

"Was he hurt in any way?"

"No. At least he didn't appear to be. He might have had a scrape or two on his knees. I would be surprised if he didn't, but otherwise, no."

Lund considered his next question. "What was his emotional state like?"

Beaumont gave this careful thought. He brought a hand up to his face and rubbed his lips. "My initial impression was he was frightened. His eyes were wild. I could say terrified, but I don't want to sound overly dramatic. He had been running hard and he was very winded from his effort." Beaumont paused again. "So, his emotions and physiological reactions had been hard to differentiate at first glance."

"Did he mention what had upset him?"

"He didn't say he was upset at all. He shrugged off my help and assured me he was all right. I saw him glance down the road as if he was expecting something, but I may have been over-interpreting his intention. Overall, I came away from the interaction thinking this was a very polite young man."

"Did you see anything?"

"Not a thing, other than those two folks riding bikes down the road."

Lund wasn't learning anything new that wasn't in the police report. Beaumont was right in that regard.

"How big is the kid? Did he appear strong?" Lund saw this question was something novel for Beaumont.

"Hmm. We chatted briefly, and I found out he will be a freshman this fall in my high school. Well, not my high school, but where I teach. So, I know he is fourteen or thereabouts. He is probably a little taller than average. He seemed in good shape, and the way he was running I would guess he is a very good athlete. So, in that regard, I guess he is strong."

Lund was at a loss for a follow-up question, and was going to thank Beaumont for his time when he noticed Beaumont's eyes spring open wide in alarm.

"Good Lord, Agent, you don't think the boy committed these crimes do you? Is that why you are asking about his size and strength?"

"I'm just following all leads at this point, Mister Beaumont. I don't have ideas at all."

"Well, I can't imagine such a thing. This kid was very polite and social given the circumstances. Also—now you would know more about this than me—his clothes were clean, other than perspiration and dirt from his fall. Wouldn't someone who committed these murders be covered in blood? Well, there was nothing like that at all, I assure you."

Now, standing at the crime scene, Lund knew Ryan Perry was not involved with the murders. In fact, he never really considered the kid as a suspect. The timing didn't fit, for one thing. It was highly likely the murders occurred even before the Perrys arrived at their new home. For another, the footprints were too small for a slightly above average fourteen year old. Even though young Mister Perry appeared to be a strong athlete, he was not the kid who produced the forceful tracks on the ground. There were multiple eyewitness accounts of Ryan Perry running upright like a typical kid.

No, whoever made those tracks ran while hunched over, and therefore using hands occasionally, and the pace was fairly powerful. And the narrow indentation marks in front of the foot and handprints were made by talons.

Ryan Perry was not a suspect, but he may have seen something. It was time to talk to him.

Chapter Four

Miranda always feared someone would come out of the blue and take away her son. The birth mother who changes her mind or the biological father who reappears to assert his parental rights–these were her nightmares. However, after all these years, the likelihood of this seemed remote.

This account of Ryan's birth, though...she could not get her head around it. There were legal ramifications. Then there was her mother. What was she thinking?

"Mrs. Perry," Doctor Pullman-Batista said, "Believe me, I am only realizing the extent of this issue as we speak. I am not even sure what to make of it."

The story was long but eventually Miranda had it straight. A young girl came to Eugenia Pullman, the doctor's mother, in labor. Someone had told her Eugenia would be able to help. Carolyn Tyron happened to be present since she often assisted Eugenia with health related services to the African-American community. The girl was deeply distressed, and appeared mentally ill. She rambled on about a curse, and feared for her baby's life.

"My mother became convinced the girl was possessed." The doctor mouthed the last word, and looked around to make sure she was not overheard by her colleagues. "My mother is a trained medical professional, Mrs. Perry, yet she has always held onto the folklore practices and healing skills of our family ancestors, specifically a favorite aunt."

Carolyn Tryon continued the story. "Miranda, at first, I didn't believe it for a second. After that...quite frankly, it was chilling."

"Let's cut to the chase," Doctor Pullman-Batista said. "Twins were born, and the mother died horribly giving birth. One twin also died, but the other survived, though he was injured in the process. The scar on Ryan's back is that injury. I was pregnant with my daughter at the time, newly married, and home for a visit before starting medical school. I saw the whole thing."

Miranda waited, expecting more.

"I needed to save the life of that baby. I knew you wanted badly to have a child, Miranda. I gave him to you," Carolyn said, barely above a whisper.

Miranda leaned against the glass door of Ryan's exam room in the ER. Competing responses flooded her mind. Why wasn't she told about this? Were they saying that somehow these past events were impacting Ryan now? Mostly, *"What the hell were you people thinking?"* wanted to jump from her lips. She suppressed the urge though, knowing that challenging their course of action would put everyone on the defensive and not address the immediate concern. With a sense of irony, she realized this was how Phil would be thinking if he were here.

Miranda pushed herself off the glass and took a step or two away from her mother and the physician before turning to face them. "I'm too overwhelmed to think clearly at the moment. I don't...I don't know what to make about all this...let alone know what I should communicate to Ryan." She turned to Doctor Pullman-Batista. "His problems...the falls...the visions...could there be something wrong...I mean, an illness..." She couldn't put her fears into words.

The doctor exhaled slowly before she responded. "Yes, it could. There's always drug abuse, neurological or psychological concerns...Look, when was his last physical exam?"

"Last summer."

"I think we can ease some of your worries. He's going to need a check-up for school, I think. Let's start there. I'm not a pediatrician, but I know a few who have a skill for working with teenagers. Do you need a referral?"

"God yes, please." Miranda felt some initial relief. At least this was a step in the right direction.

"Hold on a second." Doctor Pullman-Batista excused herself and walked off while digging a cell phone out of her white-coat pocket. She left Miranda and her mother alone. They were silent for a few minutes.

"I'm sorry Miranda. I should have said something."

Miranda looked at her mother, and realized that she wasn't angry with her. After all, who could have anticipated something bizarre like this? If she had known any of these facts would it have changed the course of their history?

Miranda recalled the afternoon she received the phone

call from her mother. She was home working on her second book illustration. It was late winter and snowing heavily, and she remembered standing and leaning her butt against her desk and looking outside when she answered. For the longest time, she couldn't understand what her mother was proposing. She kept repeating, "Mom, wait, what are you saying?" Then, it hit her like a thunderclap, and she nearly fell to her knees.

A baby? We can adopt a baby?

There were some minor hysterics. She called Phil at the office. He was intrigued.

He left the office early, but it still took him forever to make it home because of the snow. They discussed the opportunity. The entire idea was novel to them because they never considered adoption. Then there were the issues like no crib, no clothes, when would they ever find the time...

Of course Phil started asking the nuts-and-bolts questions. Is the adoption legal? What were the birth parents like? Have the birth parents consented? Always practical, that was Phil, but with each question, he was clearly growing excited too.

The birth parents would not be a problem. They'd abandoned the baby.

The situation was unusual for sure, but this solution would be best for all...

Not really adequate responses by any stretch of the imagination, but they could overlook them...

A boy. A baby boy.

Milwaukee's airport was shut down until the next day due to the snowfall. Waiting to catch the flight to Charleston seemed like an eternity. When they finally arrived, they had generated a number of to-do lists for what was needed, so they felt somewhat in control of what was going to happen next. That sense of control didn't last long once they had Ryan home and the day to day realities set in. At the time, though, the sense of control was important to them.

Miranda burst into tears when she took Ryan in her arms after walking into her parents' house. Even Phil shed a few. Her mother was ecstatic, and her father had the biggest grin on his face she had ever seen.

On top of everything, Ryan was absolutely beautiful.

No, thinking back, if she had known the facts it wouldn't

have mattered. She wouldn't change anything.

"No, Mom. I'm not sure you should have told us. Maybe your decision not to was the best thing. You had no way of knowing."

Carolyn nodded, trying to blink away tears.

"We'll just take this a step at a time, and consider all the options for sorting this out." *Just what Phil would say*, she thought again.

Ten minutes later, the doctor returned. "Sorry for the delay. Doctor Renee Barrington." She handed Miranda a computer generated appointment slip. "I went to Med School with her. She is a great colleague. It just so happened she had a cancellation at noon tomorrow, and I took the liberty of making an appointment for Ryan."

Miranda was impressed. She wondered whether Doctor Barrington really scheduled patients for noon or if Doctor Pullman-Batista pulled a few strings. "Thank you very much for doing this. I don't know what to say."

"You're welcome. It's the least I can do. You have your hands full. Renee is my daughter's pediatrician, so she comes highly recommended. She'll be a good fit for Ryan."

* * * *

He had seen the doctor leave and then come back and hand his mother a piece of paper. When his mother returned to the room, he immediately started his questions.

"So, what was that all about? What did Grandma mean? What were you talking about?"

"Ryan, easy, calm down."

"Wait..."

"Ryan, honey." She rubbed his good forearm. "Shhh. My mind is going in a million different directions, and I need to process everything. I can't talk about it right now. I will though, I promise. Give me a little time."

Then she dropped the bombshell. "I have an appointment for you to see the doctor tomorrow. For a physical. Her name is Doctor Barrington. The ER doctor highly recommends her."

"What? Oh crap." He groaned loudly. "Why do I need to see another doctor? What more are they going to check?"

"Ryan, I'm sorry. I know this is the last thing you want to do, but you need a physical and we need to rule out certain things. We don't know what is causing you to have these dreams."

"They're not dreams," he replied through gritted teeth. "I am not imagining it. I saw that kid." He closed his mouth tightly and pressed his lips together. He was determined not to speak to her until he felt good and ready.

He maintained his silence while he was released and his mother signed all kinds of papers. When they entered the car, he resumed his interrogation.

"C'mon, Mom, what'd they say?"

His grandmother left the hospital before they did so she could prepare something for all of them to eat. He was astonished to find himself starving as usual.

"Ryan, let's give it a rest for now. Please don't ask me again."

"Mom, it's my life, don't you think I ought to know?" How much time did she need to process things?

"Ryan..." Her tone took on an edge. "If you don't want to spend the rest of your life in your room without your laptop, cell phone, or any other electronic devices, you better stop right now."

"This sucks,' he said under his breath. Ryan knew when to quit, and this was it. Still, he slumped in the seat and sulked. *What did she mean when she said she was there when I was born?* He saw the doctor and his grandmother working hard to convince his mother of something. Their facial expressions said urgency. He heard his mother say, "Absolutely not!" at least two or three times. What next step or course of action was she "absolutely not" going to allow?

Lunch was quiet by their standards. The two women made small talk about chores or shopping, but it was all surface stuff. Ryan sensed the reluctance to talk, and counted his blessings. The awkwardness kept the pressure off him for the time being. There were no probing questions about how he felt and what he was thinking. While he resented their badgering, he knew something really odd was happening to him. Two nights in a row of seeing and experiencing strange visions, falling and getting really hurt...

The pounding on the door last night...how could he imagine that? The blood running from his scar... which had burst open. He saw it... and felt it. Yet...yet...it was just gone...seconds later there was no blood...it was gone. He couldn't just make that up. He couldn't have been dreaming it.

No...no, dammit...I was awake...that was no dream, man... that...that thing...that shitty thing did something to me...

He recalled the doctor asking about psychiatric history... was he crazy...would he be hospitalized...was he a danger to himself? What would it be like talking to a shrink? How would people react if they found out? God, he would never have any friends.

"Sweetheart, you look tired. Do you want to clean up and take a rest?"

"Yeah," he replied truthfully. "I do feel grimy."

* * * *

Miranda sat on the edge of her bed listening to the shower run. She kept having images of Ryan slipping in the tub and hurting himself again. The past forty-eight hours contained non-stop excitement of the worst kind, with most of it involving streams of blood flowing from her son's head. As they were eating lunch she caught whiffs of sweat and urine, and she knew he needed a shower. They couldn't get the stitches wet for twenty-four hours, so she considered alternative means of cleaning his hair and face.

"I've got an idea," she told him as they walked up the stairs together. A stained-glass window situated on the staircase landing provided a swath of color to his face which seconds before had looked pale and gaunt. "I can wash your hair in the sink...I think the faucet is high enough for you to get your head under. I'll have you hold a hand towel over your face to protect the stitches, especially the new ones over here." She pointed to the left side of his face. "The dressings will help protect them too."

The plan worked well. She helped him take off his shirt, careful not to catch anything on the stitches. She widened the arm-hole as much as she could to get the shirt over his cast which started on his forearm and ended midway up his palm. He leaned over the sink, and she was very careful not to send water cascading over the towel. She massaged his hair with shampoo as best she could without hurting him, and watched the rust colored water flow down the drain.

When Ryan stood up, he arched his back slightly to

compensate for leaning over the sink for so long. She knew it must have hurt, but he didn't say a word. She helped him pat his hair dry, and then took a fresh washcloth, wet it and applied a small amount of soap. She very carefully washed his face. He stood silently, and Miranda observed he now stood a little taller than her. His eyes, a light brown in color, did not leave her face. They appeared as big as silver dollars, and Miranda realized with tremendous guilt that the boy was deeply afraid. She would need to sit down and talk to him.

"That feels so much better, Mom. Thanks."

"Remember, you can't get you head wet when you go in the shower, and you can't get your cast wet either."

"Okay."

"One second, I've got another idea." She opened a narrow closet adjacent to the shower and searched. Within moments, she pulled out a plastic bag from the grocery store.

"We can place this over your arm, and keep it attached with this." She opened a drawer in the vanity and found a black elastic hair band. "Put this on the upper part of the cast, not on your arm. Otherwise you might cut off the circulation...make sense?"

"Yeah."

"Still, try and keep it out the water anyway." She paused, and then asked, "Would you want me to stay in here to help you?"

"No, that's okay. Can you get me some clean clothes though?"

"Of course." She went to his room and found a few items. As she was about to leave, she stopped and returned the T-shirt she picked out. In its place, she pulled a button down short sleeved shirt which might be easier to get on over the cast. Ryan approved of her choices, so she left the bathroom. She stood outside the door just in case – of what, she wasn't sure. After a few moments and against her better judgment she called through the door, "Is everything okay? Need any help?" She prepared herself for a snotty adolescent response. Instead she heard...

"I think I'll be all right, Mom. Honest. I'll call you if I need anything."

She moved to her bedroom and waited for him to finish. Ryan actually took about ten minutes, which was long for him. She sensed activity from behind the door, and also heard him swear quietly to himself. She resisted the urge to move to the door.

"Mom?"

"Yes, honey?" She forced herself to move at a deliberate pace. "Everything okay?'

"Yeah, but could you help me for a second?"

She knocked quietly, and then entered. He had managed to get his underwear and shorts on, but he obviously had been struggling. He sat on the closed toilet lid, and she helped him work on the shirt, with her doing the buttons.

Ryan looked up at her and whispered, "Thanks." His face crumpled, and tears spilled down his cheeks. Then he was in her arms, head bent down into the crook of her neck. "Mom, I'm so scared."

"I know." The intensity of his emotional reaction surprised her. Then, he had been pretty distressed at the hospital and during the ride home, and his behavior was so unlike him. His pouting in the car was quite a throwback to when he was five, a nearly perfect imitation of bygone days. She held him silently, and gave him all the time he needed.

He composed himself rather quickly. "I'm sorry for being a pain in the butt, Mom." He sniffed.

"Sweetheart, you're not. You're having a rough time. I'm sorry I have been grouchy with you," Miranda finally said as Ryan pulled away. "Your dressings are a little wet. Why don't we change them, and I will tell you what I know."

* * * *

Agent Lund sat on a bench in the park outside the Tryon house. A horse-driven carriage loaded with tourists had just left his field of vision, so the tour guide's commentary and clip-clop sounds of the horse were fading.

This was the second time today waiting outside the house. He came earlier after leaving the crime scene and sat on this same bench trying to get a feel for the neighborhood before knocking on the door. Just as he was ready to stand, a car pulled in the Tryon driveway. He was shocked to see a battered Ryan Perry gingerly step out of the car. Lund had been surprised a few times over the years while working on cases, but this image really pulled the rug out from under him. The boy looked as if he had been worked over by a gorilla. Before he talked with the kid, Lund would need to find out what the hell happened to him.

"I'm not hearing a convincing argument why I should disclose privileged patient information, Agent Lund." Doctor Pullman-Batista stood with her hands on her hips. They were adjacent to the physician and nurse bullpen in the emergency room. The doctor was near the end of her shift and had just entered some notes into a computer when Lund approached her.

"Doctor, I don't want to get into a pissing contest with you. This is a murder investigation. Two recent college grads were slaughtered just a few miles from here–"

"I'm aware of that, Agent Lund, but–"

"Your patient was seen running from the scene within twenty-four hours of their murder. He was terrified. Just a little while ago when I show up at his grandmother's house to interview him, I spot him leaving a car looking like he was thrown from an airplane without a parachute. Are you trying to tell me all of these things occurring within, what, forty-eight hours wouldn't raise any red flags with you if you were in my position? Give me a break." Lund's voice remained calm and conversational, but his gaze was intense. The doctor was unfazed, however.

Lund was frustrated, so he tried a different angle. "Look, I am convinced the kid was not involved with the murders. The timing is all wrong. Still, my hunch tells me something happened to him out on that road. Please, how did he get his injuries?"

Doctor Pullman-Batista sighed. She appeared torn between various courses of action. Finally, she relented. She knew nothing about the Old Bay Road incident. Ryan hadn't said a word about that. She did relate Ryan's accounts of his experiences with his "twin", and how he was injured.

Lund had the impression the doctor expected him to blow off Ryan's stories as a kid's overly active imagination, but he didn't–and that encouraged the doctor a bit more in her report. For his part, Lund realized he was embarking on something horrifying, a trip down a darkened road containing nightmares and madness. Unbeknownst to any but a handful of people, Lund felt increasingly positive he had a clear image of what they all were looking for. The one thought that kept echoing in his mind was, *Oh God, not again.*

"Hey, mister, is that a real gun?"

Lund looked up from his smart phone where he searched the agency's database to find a chubby boy of about nine standing before him. Running stains of purple and red down the front of a pale yellow T-shirt suggested the boy had been eating rapidly melting Popsicles—at least two judging by the artificial colors. Hidden behind the boy was another one around six who was just barely peeking around the older kid and sporting his own running colors. Judging from his chubby face and assorted stains, Lund guessed this was the speaker's younger brother.

"What, this?" Lund lifted his arm slightly so the shoulder harness and weapon was slightly more visible. He noticed a middle aged couple scurrying towards him. These were the parents, he surmised. Body fat rippled in T-shirts stretched taut over their bodies as they moved. Lund saw combinations of environmental factors and genetics playing a role in the growth of their children.

Both boys nodded their heads vigorously.

For the benefit of the anxious parents, Lund stalled for a few seconds so they heard what was going on.

"Yep, it's real. I need it for my job." The parents were now in earshot, and Lund saw the mother ready to take action if necessary.

"Teddy," the mom said loudly, but with an attempt at sounding casual. "You can't just walk up to people and start talking." The father's eyes were riveted to the gun. They were clearly tourists, possibly coming into town to break up the monotony of being on the beach.

"Mommy, it's a real gun," Teddy announced. "He has it for his job."

Lund kind of shrugged for the parents' benefit, as if to say, "Kids. What're you going to do?"

"Are you a policeman?" Teddy asked. His sibling had now come out from behind his big brother.

"Sort of...can you read this?" Lund held out his identification and badge.

"FBI...wow. Do you see that Dad?"

Dad nodded, a little nervous as most people tended to be in his presence.

"Okay you guys," Mom announced, "it's time to go back to our tour. We can't keep bothering this man."

The kids groaned, and Lund added, "You need to listen to your mom, now."

"Ahh, darn. Hold on, are you trying to solve a case?"

"Yep, but the case is top secret so I can't talk about it." Lund's voice faded to a whisper.

"Okay," Teddy whispered in reply. He looked to his mother who jerked her head in a "let's go" manner. "It was nice to meet you." Teddy held out a sticky hand, which Lund shook. Seeing the situation was safe, the little brother did the same. Lund ended up with a booger on the heel of his hand. He waited till the family left and then wiped his hand with a tissue. Lund had two kids of his own, so he was relatively familiar with the dangers of hand to hand contact with children.

Lund prepped himself for approaching the Tryon house, and especially the boy inside who was his main concern. He would readily admit being troubled by the fact that another adolescent was the focal point of these events. Likewise, he would be the first to acknowledge his personal experiences sensitized him to this reaction.

The pattern of the attack on the young couple demonstrated some agonizingly similar characteristics to Lund's other unsolved murders. There were claw-like gouges and scratches, means of dismemberment were comparable, along with a bizarre set of physical evidence. Human hair and skin scrapings were found, but the quality was not good. That was because they were contaminated by physical evidence suggesting the involvement of an animal or animals.

Even though the cases he was interested in dated back at least five years, Lund suspected there may be pockets of others around the country. Over that time period, there was another frustrating feature that was becoming clear to him because he had the temporal context. The evidence suggested the animal was changing, or maturing. Or molting.

While these types of attacks were infrequent and occurred mostly, if not exclusively, in the summer, some geographical centers had been identified. One was South Carolina, which didn't surprise him.

Son, if anything strange happens here—and I do mean "strange"—I want you to come and talk to me.

Lund thought of calling his wife to see how the day had gone, but decided it was too early. Hannah fully understood the nature of his work. She had a home-based web design company which made his leaving at the drop of a hat a manageable event. That meant she was home when the kids returned from school, and provided the stability his work didn't permit.

Neither one was thrilled with the setup, but both saw he couldn't up and quit. He had a talent for this work, and since it sometimes involved the protection and rescue of children, they both knew he couldn't desert his position. Who could do this, if not him? There were some, but not many.

Lund met Hannah while attending the University of South Carolina. He noticed her in his economics class junior year, and then later saw her working out in the gym. When their eyes connected and she smiled in the weight machine area, he thought, *what the hell*, and talked with her. Turned out she knew his name—as she had done her own investigation of him— and they began dating the next weekend. When their relationship went to the next level involving sex and discussions of marriage, Lund was faced with a terrifying dilemma. Should he stay with vague accounts of his background and upbringing or tell her the difficult and virtually unbelievable truth? His anguish disrupted his sleep, his studying, and his interactions with Hannah. Finally, he decided it had to be done.

While taking a walk on a beautiful fall Sunday afternoon on campus, he sat her down in the shade to tell his story. Where to start the tale was difficult, and he stumbled in his initial attempts to structure his account. Almost immediately he saw Hannah was spellbound, and he hadn't even disclosed any facts. He needed a starting point, however. So, he recalled deciding on the moment his current life began which was right before he turned thirteen.

After finishing the account, he waited in trepidation for Hannah's reaction. He couldn't even look at her, fully anticipating some form of dismissal. Tears flooded his eyes, but these didn't spill...until she lifted his face to look directly at her. Her face radiated the warmth of the first spring day. "You're an incredible man."

They'd been together ever since.

Lund stood up and walked to the Tryon house. He had a strong sense of what Ryan Perry must be experiencing.

* * * *

"Okay, so...wait... I had a twin?"

They were sitting in the kitchen while his mother was replacing the wet gauze and bandages from his face. He felt like a dope for crying in his mother's arms like a little kid, but she dealt with it pretty well by not making a big deal out of it–which was cool. They also adjusted his sling to help elevate his arm.

"I don't think you could consider him your twin, Ryan," his grandmother interjected. She had joined the conversation at the table while his mother worked on the dressing. While he was showering, his grandmother had gone to the bookstore and bought him two new nonfiction books about baseball which looked interesting.

"This doesn't make sense."

He got the part about the girl in trouble, how she died giving birth (it was hard for him to get past the fact this was his biological mother) and that the twin died too. The stuff about possession and a curse and a twin who wasn't a twin, well that was creeping him out.

"How did this girl find you? Where did she come from?"

"I don't have an answer for the second question, but I do know she really found Mrs. Pullman, not me."

"She's that lady doctor's mother, huh?"

"Yes, she and I used to work closely together."

"You don't want me to talk to her." This remark was directed at Ryan's mother. The issue of talking with Mrs. Pullman was the source of the "absolutely not" commentary on his mother's part.

The doorbell rang. Ryan saw his grandmother look relieved. His mother on the other hand looked to be struggling with something.

"Ryan, I just don't know if following up with all of this will do any good. In fact, it may be rather upsetting. Some people who live in the Low country are steeped in superstition and folklore–things we don't even consider in our day-to-day life."

Ryan heard his grandmother talking to someone at the door. The timbre of the voice indicated it was a man.

"Does it scare you?" Ryan asked.

"Yes, maybe, I just don't understand it. I do think there are more real-life things that are more frightening."

Ryan nodded. He thought he understood. The superstitions were scary, but look at all the other crap that has happened to them in the past year.

"Miranda..." Ryan turned to see his grandmother walking into the kitchen, followed by some guy he had never seen before. He was wearing light blue pants, along with a shirt and a tie. He didn't have a jacket on because of the heat, and Ryan clearly saw the shoulder holster and hand gun. A badge was clipped to his shirt pocket. "This is Agent Lund from the FBI. He would like to talk to Ryan."

"Me?" Ryan actually squeaked. He felt his face flush. His mother looked at him expectantly as if he could offer an immediate explanation.

"This is my daughter, Miranda. This is Ryan."

Ryan almost blurted out, *but I didn't do anything!* The guy actually chuckled, probably in response to his shocked expression.

"Easy, Ryan, I just want to chat. You may be able to help me." He took out a small notebook from a back pocket and tossed it on the kitchen table, right in the midst of the old dressing and bandages.

"May I sit?" He extended his hand to a vacant chair at the table.

"Of course, please," Ryan's grandmother replied. "Let me remove this mess." She scooped up the debris.

"Oh, no bother."

Still, his grandmother finished cleaning the scraps. She used a plastic bag from a pharmacy that had been tossed on the counter to collect the gauze, bandages and tape. She tied the handle together and placed the bag in the trash.

"How can we help you, Agent Lund?" His mother looked unsure of herself, "We've had a difficult time of late." Her last comment made no sense to Ryan. What did that have to do with anything?

"Yes, I can see. You head must really hurt, and the arm, too. Man."

Lund leaned about a foot closer to Ryan and pointed to his own face. Ryan felt himself moving back in response, and made a concerted effort to stop.

"See this...and this?" Lund had one scar right above his eyebrow and another on his cheekbone in exactly the same area as Ryan. "My brother did this to me, pushed a door open right into my face. I was probably around your age. To this day, he claims he didn't know I was there. Don't fret though, the scars will make you look tough." Then he motioned Ryan to lean closer to him by wagging his index finger. "Chick magnet, too. Girls will love it."

Ryan smiled in spite of himself. The agent was young, but not that young–maybe in his thirties. He didn't look like cops he saw back in Wisconsin, who tended to have bellies sagging over their belts. This guy looked like he worked out, and could probably beat the shit out of anyone.

"So agent, how can we help you?" his mother asked again. Ryan thought she sounded a little peeved.

Lund turned his attention to his mother, all business again. "I wanted to talk to Ryan about his run into the woods on Old Bay Road two days ago."

How does he know about that?

His mother also looked at him with an expression that asked *what haven't you told me?*

"What about it?" Right off the bat Ryan knew he sounded defensive.

"You had quite a scare."

"Ryan what is this about?"

"Nothing...I...oh, shoot...I don't want you to get all weird on me." This last part he said directly to his mother.

"Agent Lund," his grandmother said. "Maybe if you provided us with some context..." She was not seated with the rest of them, but stood next to the sink.

"Ryan..." Lund was insistent, ignoring the two women.

"I think..." Ryan closed his eyes and shuddered. "I think there were two kids after me."

"Ryan, who?" His mother was practically out of her seat.

"What is this about, please?" his grandmother added almost at the same time.

Lund held up his hand to both his mother and grandmother to ask for silence. "Ryan, what did you see?"

Ryan told them about the kids he saw and how they ended up chasing him.

"When I turned around to protect myself, they were gone."

"Oh, Ryan, honey, why didn't you tell us?"

"What was I supposed to say," he yelled back suddenly. "There was nothing there! I thought maybe I was dehydrated. I wasn't feeling well when I finally got back home."

Ryan turned to Lund. "How did you know I was there?"

"You ran into Mister Beaumont." At the sound of his name, Ryan thought he saw his grandmother tense just a little bit.

"Oh, yeah."

"Who is Mister Beaumont?" his mother asked.

"A high school teacher," his grandmother replied.

"Biology," Ryan added.

"He said that you came running out of there like you were scared out of your mind."

"I guess I was...it was...weird."

"Can you describe the kids?"

"Nah, it happened so quickly, and I never really had a good look. Although," Ryan paused as he thought about it. "I don't think they had any clothes on."

"Did you see anything else? Any other people? Strange cars you haven't seen before?"

"They're all strange," Ryan said. "We just moved here."

"Good point."

His mother was still staring at him. Whether she was mad or afraid, he couldn't tell.

"Agent Lund, what is going on?" his grandmother asked again.

Lund slid his notebook across the table toward him. He never took any notes. Ryan guessed that was a good sign.

"A young couple disappeared from the area three days ago."

"I remember hearing something about that," his mother said. "We just arrived in town so I never really followed the story."

"Neither have I, actually," his grandmother said. "Has something happened?"

"Yes, their bodies were found, or parts of them anyway. In the area where Ryan was running the other day." His mother tensed, and Lund added, "Sorry for sounding insensitive. It happened early yesterday, when a Boy Scout troop was picking up litter. One of the kids literally stumbled upon the bodies.'

Lund looked to Ryan, and reached into his shirt pocket behind his badge. "If you think of anything, or if anything strange happens, anything at all, no matter how insignificant it may seem, please call me. Here is my card." He started to hand it to Ryan, but then pulled it back. He took out a pen and wrote something. "I've included my cell number. Feel free to call that. Understand?"

Ryan took the card and nodded.

* * * *

The day had been intense, both physically and emotionally, for Ryan. Miranda wanted to keep the dinner and the evening relatively stress free. She asked Ryan if there was anything he wanted to watch on TV, hoping he would rest. He did mention there was a baseball game on ESPN, or one of those sports networks, and that it was the Brewers. She hoped that would be the choice of the evening.

Miranda watched Ryan eat his dinner. His appetite was voracious, so it appeared at least that aspect of his functioning had not been impacted by his mishaps. He had finished his salmon, rice, and salad before she and her mother had a handful of bites.

"Can I have seconds?"

"Of course, dear. You can have as much as you like." Her mother was of the generation that food cured all ills.

"Thanks, Grandma." Ryan nearly spilled a glass of milk in his eagerness to obtain additional portions.

Miranda was amazed at his resilience. She was still shaken from the hair-raising beginning of the day, not to mention the visit from the FBI agent. Ryan, however, rebounded when he learned the details and gained information. She realized now that withholding facts from him earlier in the day was the cruelest course of action she could have taken from his perspective, which only served to increase her guilt about how she has handled the morning.

"Hey Grandma?" Ryan said around a mouthful of food. "What did you think of the FBI agent?"

"I didn't understand a thing you said, Ryan. Why don't you swallow and ask me again?"

Ryan nodded as if this was a reasonable request. *If I had said it, he'd have rolled his eyes and glared*, Miranda thought. At least the two of them had a comfortable relationship. She wondered how her mother was feeling about having another growing boy in the house. She had to feel a little cautious, after the heartache she experienced with Charlie— and was still facing, more than likely. Then again, who knows? Ryan might be a real gift for her.

Ryan finally swallowed his mouthful, and adopted a stiff posture in his effort to mimic upper class snobbery, as if table manners were the exclusive right of the upper crust. When he opened his mouth, he was trying to fake a British accent, but not too successfully.

"So, Mrs. Tryon. Your opinion on the FBI agent, if you would be so kind."

Miranda knew her mother enjoyed his antics and expected her to play it straight.

"He was a pleasant enough fellow, but I wish he could have been more forthcoming earlier in the sequence of events. I didn't like the way he kept us in the dark initially."

"Really? Huh." Ryan considered that. "Yeah, I guess he did do that, didn't he. I don't know, maybe he has to keep things secret."

"Hmmm. I do believe he was a southern gentleman, though," she responded.

"I thought I heard something in his accent, but it was very faint," Miranda said.

"Yes, it was there. I have a feeling most of his accent was probably washed out by all the riff-raff in northern Virginia."

"Riff-raff." Ryan scoffed, and then laughed. He took a few final mouthfuls, finished chewing, swallowed and then made his next point. "I don't know. I think working for the FBI might be cool."

"Oh, dear. You would need to work all those horrible crime scenes, and interact with very unpleasant people."

"Those are just the northern Virginians," Miranda inserted.

Ryan guffawed. Miranda was heartened to see him having a good time.

"Solving those crimes, though," Ryan said when his laughter subsided, "that would be exciting. Man, that would be cool. Plus, I bet you meet a lot of hot girls. You can have one hanging on each arm. That would be sweet."

"Hot girls, indeed. I don't think Agent Lund has too many."

"Grandma, how do you know he doesn't?"

"He's married."

"But, wait...how?"

"He was wearing a wedding ring," Miranda informed him. "Your grandmother is actually quite observant."

"Huh. I didn't see that." He thought for a second. "I bet he married a hot one, though."

After dinner was over and the dishes loaded into the dishwasher, they retired to the den to watch TV. Ryan was the main beneficiary, watching his former home team, the Brewers, play the Cardinals. Miranda watched with him on the couch, but also spent time considering some illustration work. Her heart wasn't in the work so she gave up and spent the evening reading magazines piled on the coffee table. Her mother was of the same mind, thumbing through most of the same magazines. Occasionally, she would recommend an article for Miranda, and leave the magazine propped open to a particular page. By the fifth inning, her mother called it a night and went to her room. Miranda stayed up to the end of the game. The Brewers won, which made Ryan happy.

"What do you say, kid, it's been a long day. Bedtime?"

"Yeah, I'm tired. I hope early mornings in the emergency room don't become a habit."

"I doubt they will. Tonight will be different. Get a good night's rest."

"Okay." He leaned over to her on the couch and placed his good arm over her shoulder. He planted a kiss on her cheek. "Goodnight Mom."

"Good night, sweetheart," she responded, but not before Ryan fled from the room and bounded up the stairs.

Miranda tossed the magazines into the recycling bin, completed her bedtime bathroom routines and retired to bed. She opened a novel she had started the previous day and began to read. After less than a paragraph she knew this was hopeless, closed the novel and turned out the light.

When she awoke sometime later, she checked her clock and saw it was sometime after four. That jolted her since she knew it was around this time Ryan had his visits with his twin the past two mornings.

Had she heard a noise? Did something wake her?

Miranda was instantly haunted with horrifying images of an injured Ryan. She was out of bed and rushing the door before she consciously made the decision. In the hallway, she scanned both directions expecting to see Ryan in a heap, but nothing was amiss. Approaching his door, she paused only for a second out of respect for his privacy, but she thought the risk of finding him engaged in something highly personal was unlikely at this hour. She entered as quietly as she could.

Ryan was sound asleep in his bed. Her mother had placed one of the hallway nightlights in his room yesterday afternoon after the previous incidents so he wouldn't feel disoriented if he woke up at night. Surprisingly, Ryan was fine with the idea.

The light was rather faint with a bluish tint, but Miranda

saw her son clearly. Ryan was on his side with his arms and legs spread out to one side. His hair was askew, and Miranda was reminded of a golden retriever puppy. Her breath caught with tenderness. She felt her eyes welling up, but blinked the tears away and chided herself for being foolish. Nonetheless, the sight his him looking peaceful and innocent was somehow overwhelming.

Gently, Miranda moved his desk chair close to his bed. She did not want to leave just yet. Sitting by the head of his bed, she cautiously reached his disheveled hair and patted it down. He reacted to her touch, mumbling something and then resuming his relaxed breathing.

Miranda was typically cold at night, whether from winter drafts or air-conditioning in the summer. Ryan was the exact opposite. He had always been a warm sleeper. When he was a preschooler, she referred to him as her "little heater". He never liked covers, so he always kicked them off, and slept in his boxers. This pattern started when he was eight, and it took years for Miranda to get used to the idea that he wasn't going to freeze to death while he slept.

Ryan turned over to his back, and shifted the broken arm rather abruptly. The weight of the cast made the movement cumbersome and off balance. Miranda was concerned he might hit the wall on the other side of the bed, but his arm collapsed by his side just shy of impact. Still, the awkwardness of repositioning roused him slightly, and he lifted his head and shoulders.

"Mom?" He was barely conscious.

"Shhh, honey." She gently touched his chest to ease him back down. "You're okay, I was just checking on you. Go back to sleep"

"Okay." He was instantly asleep again and snoring lightly.

Miranda let her hand linger on his chest for a minute more, feeling his heart beat beneath his skin. The clock read nearly five and she felt confident this night would pass safely. She stood from the chair, but not before kissing Ryan's forehead.

The curtains were parted slightly on the window at the foot of Ryan's bed. Miranda tiptoed over to close them so the sunrise would not flood the room. While drawing the curtains together, she thought she glimpsed someone standing on the sidewalk below near a streetlamp. She spread the curtains back open quickly to double check, but not a soul was present.

The entire street was deathly quiet and deserted. She tried to shrug it off as a trick of her imagination, but felt uneasy. She could have sworn a boy of around Ryan's age or younger was positioned just below on the sidewalk and staring intently up at his window.

Chapter Five

Ryan finished getting dressed and sat down on the chair by the small writing platform which held a computer keyboard and LCD monitor. The physical exam was completed and the doctor left temporarily so he could dress in privacy.

The exam was not as nerve-racking as Ryan expected. He had tons of them in the past and those were fine, but those exams were for school attendance. This particular exam was to look for or rule out something wrong with him that might be causing his hallucinations, as his mother called them, and his falling.

As he could have predicted, the morning was stressful. He was anxious and his mother was a whirling dervish of commands and criticisms. She didn't like what he was wearing, and what possible difference could that make since he had to take his clothes off anyway. She also announced she expected to come in with him for the exam.

"What? No way. You are not." They were sitting at the breakfast table when she brought up the idea. "Uh-huh. You can't be there when she gives me the exam." Ryan pushed away from the table with his good hand as a matter of emphasis.

"Ryan, don't argue. I need to be able to answer the doctor's questions, and I want to make sure you tell her everything."

"I will, okay!"

"This is serious, Ryan, I need to be there."

"Then I'm not going. I'm not going to be embarrassed by my mother being with me. I'll look like a dork."

His grandmother kept the argument from spiraling any more out of control.

"You two need to stop it and calm down." She said it calmly, almost quietly, but her voice had power—even over his mother. They both stopped talking and turned to her. "There is a simple solution here if you both bothered to look at it. Miranda, Ryan needs his private time with the doctor. You can't be there, and it would make him look like a dork if you were." She smiled at him and it eased the tension in the room.

"Ryan, your mother is very concerned. I am very concerned. You may not be the very best reporter of what's been happening. Your mother has to share her worries with the doctor.

"The easiest way to handle this is you both spend time with the doctor, without the other present. She'll probably want to do that anyway."

His grandmother got Ryan out of the kitchen ostensibly to help with a chore but more likely to keep them from bickering.

"Ryan, I need your help outside. Something got into the garbage last night, and made a huge mess."

He dragged his feet in a purposeful display of irritation. As he got to the side of the house, he noticed two garbage cans had been knocked over. The large plastic trash bags had been ripped, and crap was strewn all over the ground.

"Grandma. Yuck." He stared in disbelief. "My poor arm."

"My dear boy, you can handle it." Ryan saw the new trash bags in her hand. "Let's just put the bags back in the cans as they are. Anything that's spilled, we'll place in a new bag."

They set to work. She held a bag open and he threw the trash in. He came upon a plastic pharmacy bag that had seen a surprising degree of frenzied tearing. A Band-Aid was stuck to it, and he recognized the bag in which his grandmother had thrown his bandages when the FBI agent showed up.

"Gross. We have a vampire squirrel."

"Or raccoon. As soon as we're done, I am going to personally oversee your hand washing young man, so no arguments."

"God, you guys..." but she was true to her word. When they returned to the kitchen, she scrubbed his hand in between hers to the point where it was getting raw.

The ride to the doctor's office was calmer than the morning, but quieter than usual. Ryan guessed they were both nervous about the upcoming appointment. As it turned out, his grandmother's prediction was very accurate. Ryan was scheduled to have his exam and time with the doctor first, and afterwards she was going to meet with his mother. So their argument was for nothing.

There was a knock on the door, and Ryan didn't know if he should reply, but finally decided he ought to. "Yes? Come in."

The doctor peeked around the door. "All set?" She didn't wait for a reply and entered the exam room, sitting on a stool before the keyboard. She started tapping the keyboard and the monitor came to life. She continued tapping, and a program appeared.

"There we go. I've got your file right here." She smiled at him.

Ryan liked Doctor Barrington. She was very pretty with dark brown hair that she kept in a ponytail. Her eyes were green, and teeth were the whitest teeth he had ever seen. He couldn't take his eyes off her. During the exam, she was very talkative and knew about a lot of things. So they talked sports, school, food, interests. She examined his stitches and cast and proclaimed they were looking fine.

"So, you know the doctor in the emergency room," Ryan said.

"Doctor Pullman-Batista? Yes, I do. We went to medical school together."

"I found out she was there when I was born."

"Oh really? She told you this?"

"Yep, in the ER. My second trip."

"What did she say?"

Ryan had a suspicion she already knew the story, but he told her what he learned from the other doctor and added what he heard from his grandmother. Ryan wondered if she would add anything, and was disappointed when she offered nothing beyond exclaiming what a wild story it was. While he awaited her return after the exam was completed, he found himself nervous about what she would want to talk about.

"First, let me say you are a very healthy teenager. You clearly get a lot of exercise and you seem to eat well. You don't seem to be sitting in front of the computer or the TV all day. All of which is good.

"This doesn't help us understand the events of the past few days, and maybe we never will. Your falls could have been coincidence. The only thing I can do now is talk with you and see if there is something else that doesn't show up on a physical exam."

"Like maybe I'm imagining the whole thing or I'm going crazy?"

"No, like maybe there are some other factors I can't measure the regular way."

Ryan wasn't sure what she meant exactly, and felt very cautious.

"I now you're probably sick of talking about them, but

could you tell me about both instances when you fell?"

Ryan hesitated briefly before replying, still wondering if she was going to dismiss his experiences as figments of his imagination. He dived into his accounts, though, figuring he could make the best case for not sounding crazy by explaining what happened in a controlled kind of way. He described being awakened in the early morning hours and all of the factors surrounding the encounters with his twin. He mentioned feeling threatened in both cases, first with the way the twin looked through and tapped on the glass and second with how his bedroom door was broken in and how the twin charged him on the stairs. The vague presence of the African American lady was difficult to describe, because the sensation was so short-lived.

"Let me ask you. Before you saw the kid these two times and the old woman, have you ever seen things that may not have been real? Or heard things or voices that weren't there?"

"No. I swear to God. Really."

"I believe you. How about the incident of being chased by the kids in the woods?"

"Oh yeah." Ryan didn't remember mentioning this to the doctor. She must have heard from his mother. "Those kids were definitely real, but the way they looked and moved wasn't human...I don't know, it was strange."

"Okay." The doctor paused, and checked her notes. "What kinds of things were going on in your life around the time when you saw your "twin" as you call him?"

"I don't know. I was asleep."

Doctor Barrington smiled. "That's true. How about in the days or weeks before these things happened?"

Ryan thought and shook his head. "Nothing much. I mean, we moved and everything. That was a big thing. I didn't like it. My mom and I fought a lot it seemed. There was a lot of packing. I had to say goodbye to all of my friends." Ryan shrugged.

"When you say you didn't like it, do you mean you didn't want to move or you didn't like the act of moving?"

"Both. Like, I didn't want to leave my friends and even though Mom said I had a say in whether we left or not, I really didn't. I knew we would do what she said."

"So, you were angry with her?"

"Yeah. Some. I got over it. I think I can meet new kids."

"So, that's a plus then. Why do you think you two fought a lot?"

"Because the move was a pain in the ass. Mom can be too. She always gets on me for something."

"Do you miss your friends?"

"Sort of. I mean, I've only been gone a short while. I get sad when I think I won't ever see them again."

"What else do you miss?"

Ryan sat for a long time unsure where to go. "I miss Dad."

The doctor shook her head in understanding. "The feeling is still real strong. Is it hard for you?"

"Yeah. Well, uhm...It may not be as hard as it used to be. I've thought about him some more recently. Maybe it's because I have time on my hands." Ryan shrugged again.

"Ryan, sometimes when people are in a lot of pain, they may try and hurt themselves. Have you ever thought of doing that?"

"Hurt myself? Do you mean, like, kill myself? No way." Was she thinking he was doing this to himself? "Do you think I was trying to throw myself down the stairs. To kill myself?" He didn't know if he should be frightened or insulted at the thought.

The doctor didn't seem to mind his reaction. "No, Ryan, I really don't. But I have to explore the possibility. You had some significant trauma in your life. First your dad passed away, then you moved, you don't have your friends to hang around with, and you and your mother are arguing. Then you get here and you have two major accidents in two days. We have to see if there is a connection."

When she explained it like this, her questioning made sense. Also, although he hated to admit it, his mother's reaction kind of fitted.

"Ryan, give me your hand...your right one without the cast." Ryan extended his arm. "Do you remember me checking out your arm on both sides?"

Ryan did. "Yes."

"Some kids—when they are feeling really distressed—try to injure themselves. They aren't trying to kill themselves, but injure themselves. It actually takes some of the emotional pain away. It helps soothe them. One of the favorite ways of doing this is cutting, especially the arms. That's why I looked. Your arms are clean, no marks—other than the bruising from your falls. I also looked, by the way, for deeper injuries in case you were trying to kill yourself."

"I'm not, though. Just because I saw this kid doesn't mean I'm crazy does it?"

"No, Ryan, but as I said, we need to figure out how well you are coping."

"I'm all right, I guess."

"What about school?" she asked. "How do you feel about going to a new school?"

"I don't know. It's kind of scary, but it'll be okay. I hope people like me. I'm a little bored now, so it'll be okay to start. Not that I want to do the work."

"What are your grades like?"

"I do okay. A's and B's, mostly. I like to read, and science is okay. So's gym. I like gym."

Doctor Barrington scribbled a few notes in his file. "You haven't met any kids yet. Correct?"

Ryan shook his head no.

"Do you expect you'll meet most of your friends playing sports?"

Ryan shrugged, and then said, "Yeah, probably."

"Is there anything you are looking forward to? Anything you'd like to do differently? Here's an opportunity...being the new kid in school."

Ryan felt himself blush slightly. "I'd like to find a girlfriend."

The doctor smiled. "Now that is a pretty good goal. Have you had a girlfriend before?"

"Nah, not really. I kinda had one in eighth grade, but..." he trailed off.

"Ancient history, huh?"

He nodded.

"Have you ever had sex with a girl?"

Ryan really felt himself blush. "No..."

"With a boy?"

This one surprised him. "No."

"Has an adult ever pressured you for sex, or tried to have sex with you?"

"God, no. No way. Most adults I know are pretty cool." He remembered the man who approached Daniel and him in the mall. "There was a guy who accosted me and a friend, wanting to take our pictures last year. He sounded...wrong, so we got the fu—oops sorry, we got the heck away from him."

"That was smart. You need to trust your instincts." She scribbled a little more.

"When you are with your friends, what kinds of things do you do?"

"Just sports and stuff." Ryan could anticipate the next question so he elaborated. "You know, basketball, touch football, we hang out, play video games. That kind of thing."

"Do you use drugs or have you ever tried them?"

Ryan was prepared for this response after his emergency room visit. "I've had beer, but not much. Total amount maybe a can and a half. No drugs."

Doctor Barrington made another short note in the file. When she finished, she looked at him in silence for a long moment. "Is there anything you want to ask me, anything at all?"

Ryan asked the one question in the forefront of his mind. "So, what's wrong with me?"

"Ah. You're a bottom-line guy."

Ryan was puzzled. "What's that?"

"I'm sorry. That means you're pretty direct and want the answer right away. No messing around."

"Is that a good thing?"

"Sure, if that is how you are. You don't waste time. You will need to accept the fact that sometimes the answers aren't always immediately available. I think this is one of those times."

"What do you mean?"

"I mean I can't find anything 'wrong' with you. Which is the good news. You're healthy, and at the moment, I don't know why you have fallen the way you have. More than likely there is nothing going on other than coincidence. That, and the fact that maybe you are overtired or a little stressed out, and you've had a string of some rotten luck."

* * * *

Miranda entered Doctor Barrington's office and sat down in a chair on the other side of a large teak desk. Diplomas and certificates were assembled en masse on one wall, displaying her undergraduate and medical degrees, successful completion of her residency and a fellowship. There were pictures of a man and children which Miranda guessed were her family. Children's artwork was posted in multiple prominent locations in the room.

Doctor Barrington sat behind the desk and rocked back in the office chair. "Ryan is a very healthy fourteen-year-old.

He's in good physical shape, and that comes from his activity level. I am pleased he doesn't regularly sit around on the computer searching social networking sites."

"Well, he does do that. I hope he didn't give the impression that he doesn't."

"Of course he does it. He did admit to playing on the computer, but, it's clear he is very active." Doctor Barrington chuckled. "He must have zero body fat. I wished I could look so good. So, physically, he is fine..."

Miranda's anxiety skyrocketed. "So, emotionally, you see something?"

"Nothing I can put my finger on. He doesn't use drugs. He does not admit to any suicidal ideation or behavior. He has good social skills."

Miranda felt herself choke up. If she tried to talk, she might cry, so she only nodded.

"The visions or hallucinations are disturbing. Ryan reports no other instances of hallucinations or delusional thinking. Would you agree?"

Miranda moved to the edge of her seat. She found her voice. "Ryan has never shown any kind of odd or bizarre behavior. I have not seen anything like that before. Even now, the two instances were rather short lived. Once he calmed down, he was able to talk rationally, and he returned to his normal self."

"So, there has been no other indication of any kind of psychoses."

"Not at all."

Doctor Barrington rocked again in her chair. "Okay, that's kind of what I expected. If he was having serious psychiatric issues, it would have been more consistent, I think." She paused, and Miranda sensed she was weighing her words. "I have not ruled out self-injury, however."

Miranda was shocked. "You think Ryan might be suicidal?"

"No, not suicide. Self-injury. I'll say up front that this doesn't fit easily. Some kids have a very hard time dealing with unpleasant feelings. They have difficulty using strategies to manage their stress. The stressful feelings are triggered by loss or conflicts in relationships. Ryan certainly has had them. He lost his father, moved away from his friends. The feelings related to this might be too overwhelming."

"Oh God," Miranda whispered. She inhaled deeply before continuing. "He didn't want to move. This is my fault."

"Wait, now. Kids move all the time. I do think Ryan is angry with you about the move, though, and he may be confused by these feelings. He certainly reports that you two have been fighting more."

Miranda shook her head. "We have. We fought over the stupidest thing this morning. I didn't like what he was wearing. It looked like something he would wear to a gym."

The doctor didn't seem concerned over the fight over clothes. "Yet, and this is important for you to hear, he is looking forward to school and the opportunity to meet new kids. While he is sad, I don't think he is seeing this as a complete betrayal or loss."

"Really?"

"Yes, really. Here is another important fact. When kids self-injure, their actions usually involve cutting or carving. While unsightly, there is no lasting tissue damage and the actions are nonlethal. They are not trying to kill themselves. They are just trying to manage the emotions.

"Ryan's falls are very extreme and don't fit. These are potentially dangerous. They've been upsetting. They haven't achieved the desired result of self-soothing. Does this make sense?"

Miranda permitted herself the tiniest of nods, feeling cautiously hopeful.

"One more thing. He seems to have pretty effective coping strategies. He works out, he is active, seems capable of making friends. All of these make me hesitant to say this is self-injury."

"So what do we do?"

"I recommend you watch and wait. The visions are troubling, yes. The falls are troubling, yes. Let's see what the next few days bring. Keep a closer eye on him. Be available. Last night was peaceful. Maybe there will be nothing in the future. Then we are in the clear. Maybe things might take a different form. If they do, or if they stay the same or become worse, let's get a referral to a psychologist."

Miranda quickly felt as though she was back in turbulent waters. "I never imagined..."

"Mrs. Perry, this may blow over. He is right in the middle of puberty. Hormones are raging. He is confused. He just may need the time to sort it out. You also have been under significant stress. Cut yourself some slack. Not everything is going to go smoothly."

* * * *

Ryan was propped up in bed reading one of his baseball books. His room was in darkness except for the illumination provided by his clip-on book light. He planned on shutting off his light at midnight in order to get some sleep for the second time this evening. He went to bed around ten thirty, but was too restless to sleep. He hoped reading would help make him drowsy. The strategy was only partially successful. His clock now said midnight, and he didn't feel sleepy enough to put the book down.

By any stretch of the imagination, the day was unusual. The ride home from the doctor's office was awkward, with his mother trying to sound diplomatic about the inconclusive comments. That alone was irritating.

"I bet you're glad to hear you're a strong healthy boy," she said brightly. "Now we just need to find out what's going on with the falls."

Ryan was disgusted, and he knew he would give a snide remark even before he opened his mouth. "We didn't learn anything. It was a waste of time."

"No it wasn't. We know you aren't seriously ill."

Ryan smirked. He shifted his gaze out his side window.

"There is the question about why these two things happened. Who knows, it may be nothing. At least we know it's nothing physical."

"Yeah, but, you think it's mental. You wanted to hear that I'm crazy."

"Ryan. That's not fair and it's not true." She looked hurt, and Ryan felt guilty. He knew what he said wasn't true.

"Sorry." The silence stretched on as they traveled multiple blocks. "I saw him Mom. I wasn't lying."

She reached over and took his hand in hers and squeezed slightly. As she drew her hand away, she said barely above a whisper, "I know, sweetheart. Like everything else we'll get through it."

He closed his book and tossed it on the bed with the book light still attached. Light cascaded briefly across the room until the book settled in its final position. Was this what it was like to go crazy?

He remembered a girl in fifth grade who was very afraid to speak in class. When she was forced to, she looked at the floor and mumbled. Outside of class she was painfully shy. He felt sorry for her because she was always by herself. Some of the other kids in his class, mostly girls, made fun of her and talked about her behind her back. He thought they were being really mean, and one time at recess he let some of them know after he overheard them saying nasty stuff about her. Of course that started a round of rumors that Ryan liked her, which made life miserable for a while. Because he was liked and pretty popular, the teasing ended quickly. It was tough for the few days it went on. He couldn't imagine month after month of dealing with it. The girl was new to their school that year, and she only lasted a few months. Before she left, she came to him and said, "Thanks for sticking up for me". Ryan felt bad for her in a way he couldn't describe. Later his mother explained that she might have had something like social anxiety.

Ryan knew he didn't have those kinds of personal problems. Meeting new kids when school started would be hard, but he was pretty confident he could do it. On the other hand, seeing things that people claimed weren't there...was this what it was like to go insane? The twin looked and felt so real.

He switched off his book light and placed the book on his night table. As he started to settle down in bed, he realized he had to pee. Even though he didn't want to get up he knew he should, or else he'd probably wake up and have to go later.

The hallway was quiet for a change as he left his room and headed for the bathroom. The glare of the bathroom lights felt like razor blades in his eyes when he flicked them on. While he was taking his piss, he squinted through his lids until he adjusted to light...which took almost as long as it did to pee.

As he was shaking off the final drops, he heard the shower curtain ruffling behind him. The sound was fleeting, but there nonetheless. Ryan spun at the sound and dribbled a small amount of urine on the floor.

The shower curtain had a repeating design of green bamboo shoots on a clear but translucent background. The tile of the bathtub and shower areas was white. A figure was visible between the curtain and the white wall behind. While the features were unclear, Ryan saw it was his twin. The hair was blond and cut like his. The facial features seemed identical despite the cloudy nature of the vinyl sheet. The arms hung relaxed at its sides.

Ryan swallowed involuntarily.

He was going to call for his mother, but found himself reaching for the shower curtain with his left arm. He grasped the edge between the index and middle fingers extending from the cast. He made a fist of his right hand and was ready to defend himself.

When I pull this back, there's going to be nothing there.

He yanked the curtain back with such force the curtain rings clattered against one another in rapid succession as the entire row reached the end of the rod.

Ryan was stunned to see the twin was still visible. The entire back tile wall was visible at the same time, and it took Ryan a second to realize the twin was transparent. He was seeing right through him.

The arms rose, palms up. Ryan watched in alarm as the hands transformed. Fingers lengthened, became claws.

The twin smiled.

Ryan swung his right fist wildly, and missed because the twin vanished. There was a peal of laughter as Ryan stumbled and almost fell into the tub. Ryan felt a claw grab his left arm above the cast and scrape across his flesh. He felt another claw clutch his right shoulder. The feel of its hand on his skin was wet and bitterly cold. He convulsed aggressively out of the grasp and fell into the sink, causing the toothbrush holder to fall over. The sound echoed like gunshots. More laughter...

"Ryan?" He heard his mother running to the bathroom. He turned swiftly, and now the twin was gone.

His mother burst into the room. "What is going on?"

Ryan was speechless. He was ready to describe what happened, but stopped when he realized how it would sound. His mother put it together instantly.

"You had the hallucination again."

"It wasn't a hallucination. He was here. He was like a ghost."

His mother remained silent. She looked at his body, not at his face. Finally she said, "Ryan, I don't know what to do. I don't think I can handle this. Look at you." She motioned to his arm and shoulder. Ryan noticed the scratches. They were tiny and inconsequential, but still there.

Ryan was about to offer them as proof as they clearly

looked like they came from fingernails, *or claws*.

"You're hurting yourself, Ryan. Why?"

Ryan realized she thought they were self-inflicted.

"I didn't do this to myself," he hissed back at her, trying to keep his voice low so as not to awaken his grandmother.

She ignored his denial. "Are you looking for attention? Am I not here enough for you?"

"Mom. God..." His voice broke. "Do you actually think I am doing all this to myself for attention?" He stopped, looked downward, and then mumbled, "This is bullshit."

"I'm sorry if what I said hurts, but I have to wonder."

Ryan groaned.

She continued. "You were laughing...that makes it even more upsetting to me."

Ryan was puzzled. Laughed? He didn't laugh. Then he remembered the twin laughing. She heard the twin laugh. Not him. This meant he wasn't crazy.

"You heard the laughter," he said excitedly. "That wasn't me."

"Oh stop, Ryan. You can't keep this up."

All Ryan could do was smile. He was relieved...and actually thrilled, despite the fact that she didn't believe him.

You heard him. He felt triumphant.

Without saying another word, Ryan edged around his mother and left the bathroom.

At least I'm not crazy.

* * * *

Miranda walked unsteadily back to her bedroom. She found herself actually treading close to the walls and tracing her fingertips along the wallpaper for support. If she didn't, she might collapse.

As she sat at the edge of her bed, a burning anguish practically consumed her. The room swayed as if on rough seas, and she feared she might be sick.

"Oh, God—Phil, I am so sorry." Miranda couldn't figure out if she actually thought this or spoke aloud. She stared at the horizontal edge of the door frame above the closet door in an effort to ease her vertigo. "Did I harm him by bringing him here?" Now she realized she was talking aloud. *Oh, God— what do I do now?*

The incident tonight completely chilled her coming on the heels of the doctor's discussion of self-injury behavior in teenagers. Could Ryan be doing this as a way of coping with all of his losses? Even taking into account that he was still likely upset over Phil's death, these three incidents involving the "evil twin"—Miranda couldn't help latching on to these words—were frightening. Not because of the ghostly angle Ryan was reporting, but rather the idea that something was terribly, medically wrong.

The possibility that Ryan was developing some heritable form of schizophrenia was unmistakable. His birth mother imagined demonic possession for her and her baby. If that didn't shout psychosis, what do you have to display to qualify? Ryan was starting to see or hear similarly themed hallucinations. Earlier today the medical advice of watching and waiting made sense. Now, sitting in her own room all alone with no support, Miranda had doubts. If Ryan needed psychiatric help, they'd better start going in that direction sooner rather than later.

Miranda sensed Ryan's bedroom door being pulled open with a sudden force. Footfalls that were unmistakably Ryan's passed across the hall towards the stairs.

"Dear God—now what?" Miranda felt a surge of strength push her upright from the bed. As she raced after Ryan, Miranda was aware she may be required to endure the impossible.

Below, Ryan had reached the bottom steps and was lunging for the front door.

* * * *

If Ryan was having difficulty falling asleep before his trip to the bathroom, he knew slumber was virtually impossible after the trip. Saying he was pissed at his mother was an understatement. He was seething, but oddly gleeful at the same time. His entire body felt flushed, and his hands were clenched painfully. He willed himself to slow his breathing and relax.

Ryan had been irritated with his mother recently. He knew that, but he also knew it was not serious stuff. In fact, most of it was stupid. He tried to remember when he felt this angry with her in the past, and came up empty. Nothing compared.

Her unwillingness to consider his side of the story hurt to the core. She thought he was mentally ill or purposely trying to hurt himself. How could she think that? Why would he make this stuff up? He felt he could scream in frustration.

The lifeline Ryan held on to was that she heard the laughter.

Ryan thought he heard a muffled voice from outside. Or, maybe it was two voices. He held his breath, and stopped moving so his bed did not make any noise.

"Ryan?" Almost like a whisper...from outside...

Oh crap...who is calling me?

The air-conditioning blowers had been silent for a few minutes, making sounds more audible. "Ryan?"

There it was again.

Ryan felt goose bumps all over and debated whether to get out of bed to look. He didn't want to. He feared what he would see.

The voice whispered louder, almost a hiss, "Ryan, get your ass out of bed and look out the window!"

Ryan sat up in bed and shifted to the edge. He thought of getting his mother, but he could only take so much stress in one night.

"Hey Ryan...you pussy..."

"Dammit," he muttered to himself. He stood and walked cautiously to his window.

Ryan's window overlooked a side street. There was no porch on his side of the house, so he could look directly below into the side yard, the wrought iron fence, and the street beyond.

There were two boys standing outside the fence on the sidewalk. Their hands grasped the vertical bars and their faces were framed by bars on either side. They looked like prisoners leaning up against the bars of their cells, looking out. These guys were looking up at his window. Ryan had a strong feeling he recognized them...they had met briefly before.

A streetlamp was further behind them and to their left, which made it difficult for Ryan to discern specific features. He saw the elder of the two was probably a few years younger than him, so maybe he was twelve. The younger one was a few years younger than that, so he was around ten or nine. They both had long hair, a lot longer than Ryan's.

Ryan slowly lifted up his window so he could hear what was going on. Outside, the humidity was its own force and felt solid. Ryan sensed the moisture build rapidly in his room. He hoped the opening of his window would escape their attention as the air deadened the sound.

No such luck. "Hey, Ryan. Hey bro." The older one was talking. "Come out and play with us, or are you too mature for that?"

"Yeah, come out and play." The younger one bounced a few times in excitement.

While Ryan heard them clearly, he realized they weren't speaking very loud. Ryan was absolutely flabbergasted to see these kids were butt-naked.

How can these guys do that? Aren't they worried about being caught? What is it with these guys?

"Cool. A cat." The little one let go of the bars and turned to give pursuit, but not before he... *changed.* The upper torso leaned forward, bending at the waist, which gave the boy a predatory stance and his haunches looked inhumanly powerful. Ryan saw the hands transform into claws.

What are they?

The younger boy launched after his prey. His arms could have been forelegs the way he was bending, but instead they extended outward to snag the cat. The tropical feel of the air with its tiny water droplets, along with the listless palms, gave the scene a disconcertingly prehistoric feel.

Yep, Ryan thought. *That's exactly what it looks like. I feel like I'm watching a movie on the Syfy channel about monsters from the beginning of time roaming a village.*

The older boy watched the younger take off and shook his head in amusement before returning his attention to Ryan. With startling speed, the boy hoisted himself to the top of the wrought iron fence. He stood with ease on the top horizontal bar that was probably only an inch wide. Ryan saw three of the pointed vertical bars between his feet, meaning he left two spaces in between in order to stand comfortably. To his amazement, Ryan watched as the kid's feet turn into talons, like a bird's, and firmly clasp the bar.

"That's Maximilian, by the way. You can call him Max, though. I'm Hugo." The boy stood nonchalantly on the fence as if this was the most natural thing. Ryan was astonished when Hugo's hand moved to his crotch and started playing with himself.

"So, bro, you gotta come over to play. Our brother so wants

to see you. We'd be all together for the first time. That would be so sweet."

Max had caught the cat. Ryan heard the animal screaming and hissing. The boy returned in his bizarre posture with the screeching cat held tightly in one arm and pressed against his chest. He didn't seem to care that the cat was scratching and clawing at him. He appeared indifferent to the pain.

Max stood up tall and looked up at Ryan's room. "Want some?"

Hugo jumped backwards off the fence like a gymnast dismounting from a high bar. His landing was flawless. The two boys faced one another and transformed again. Postures leaning forward, arms and feet becoming claws...and faces contorting into something Ryan couldn't identify...sharp teeth... black eyes tinged with red...

Max released the cat by tossing it high into the air. Both boys leapt for the cat, catching it in their claws and teeth. The cat screamed shrilly for a heartbeat and then went silent as fur and skin was torn. On the ground, they continued to scratch and tear in a frenzy, barely chewing, and swallowing with gulps loud enough for Ryan to hear.

Ryan gripped the windowsill in disbelief.

He was positive he had met these kids, these monsters, before. On Old Bay Road, of course, when they chased him through the woods.

Red smears and florets of blood were on their faces and chests. Tufts of white and brown fur stuck to the wetness. The boys licked their claws.

"See you bro. We'll play some more." They took off.

Ryan shoved himself away from the window and ran from his room. He knew he was being stupid, but he wanted to see where they went. He pulled open the door to his bedroom with more force than he intended and stifled a grunt as he tried to catch it before it slammed into the wall. He didn't want his mother on his case again.

He gave up trying to be quiet as he thundered down the steps. He heard his mother's door open.

He jumped the final steps and raced to the door, his broken wrist feeling unnatural. He tried to protect it as best he could. Ryan threw open the locks and bounded out the front door and down the porch steps. His mother called after him. He ignored her.

The front gate was just ten feet ahead. Which way should he go? Turn toward the side street that ran below his window? No, those kids had already run off, headed toward the park in front of the house, and who knew where they would go after that.

Ryan ran practically headlong into the gate, and his right shoulder hit one of the bars while his hand grasped the handle. He wanted to reach the street quickly to see if there was any trace of the kids. He was vaguely aware of the pain.

I'll probably get another bruise.

He was unable to turn the handle far enough to open the gate before something collided with him from the other side of the bars. The force violently threw him to his butt on the ground. He sat partially upright leaning on his right elbow.

Hugo was plastered to the gate, the claws of his hands and the talons of his feet gripping the bars. Sharp teeth like daggers, yes, daggers, Ryan told himself, flared at him through the bars. Hugo growled. Pitch black eyes infused with a red glare actually flashed like warning beacons from the end of the earth. Behind Hugo, Max danced with excitement, barely able to contain himself.

"See, ya, bro," he snarled...

The front door opened again somewhere behind him, "Ryan!"

...and was gone.

Slippered feet were running down the steps.

Ryan shifted his right elbow from the ground and dropped gently to the bricks making up the front pathway. He felt the heat of day that remained in the bricks against his back and legs. He stared straight up. A few clouds drifted lazily across the moon. Stars struggled to shine through the haze.

Ryan was aware he was shaking, and while his reaction could be due to fear, it didn't feel that way at the moment. An adrenalin rush was more likely...exertion, maybe. He was frustrated, since he had been taunted by these jerks and he couldn't get back at them.

Without warning his mother's face appeared before him, as if looking down at him from heaven.

"Mom. You didn't see them did you?"

She was outside in her nightgown, having run after him without taking the time to grab her robe. "Ryan. I don't know. Things happened so quickly I don't know what I saw."

Ryan sat up and folded his arms around his knees. "I feel weird."

After a moment, she offered her hand. Ryan took it and stood. He didn't know what to say. His mother placed her arm around his shoulders but not before brushing the grit off his back. They walked inside without saying another word.

Chapter Six

Miranda felt so drained her skin ached to the touch. She was reminded of the discomfort that marked the onset of the flu, with aching skin, headache, fever, low energy, and the desire to crawl into a ball and hide under the covers for a week. In her mind this was always associated with winter, a Wisconsin winter with gray metallic skies and snow flurries tossed chaotically in unsettled air.

She was in South Carolina, though, in summer no less— a season typically not associated with the flu or its aching muscles and utter exhaustion. The heat index outside was over 100 degrees, and yet Miranda still shuddered and kept her hands around a hot cup of coffee. She felt as if she was outside enduring one of Ryan's soccer games on some wind-swept field in late October. The fact that her mother kept the air conditioning on a seemingly Arctic setting ("for heaven's sake, Miranda, it's not that cold. Put on a sweater if you feel chilled") provided some solace. At least she knew she wasn't going into shock.

She recounted the previous night's events for her mother, who was sitting with her in the kitchen. The room was very bright with the noontime sun. The glare could sometimes be overpowering, so years ago Carolyn had the walls painted a sea blue color which tended to cool the room. The trick was surprising effective, combined with a low setting on the thermostat which maintained a steady flow of super-cooled air. Within an hour or two the sun would be blocked by a neighboring house, which also masked the sense of oppressive heat right outside the window. Despite the glare, both Miranda and her mother enjoyed the room, jokingly referring to it as their anti-depressant. The kitchen's powers to elevate Miranda's mood on this particular day were not in evidence.

After Miranda escorted Ryan back to his room and saw him to bed, she was too wired to sleep. The typical creaks and groans of a house settling were like unexpected thunderclaps, jolting her heartbeat into a frantic rhythm. She found herself checking on Ryan frequently to make sure he wasn't wandering or running around. Each trip to his room found him deeply asleep, with little change in position from one hour to the next. Finally, with a hint of pink sky bashfully peeking around the edges of her drawn shades, she slipped into a fretful sleep where she kept imagining Ryan calling for her. She saw herself race down unfamiliar streets and darkened hallways unable to find him. Miranda couldn't recall the specifics of the dreams, but she still suffered the side effects in the form of aches and chills when she woke up late in the morning. After a quick shower, she joined her mother for coffee and made a half-hearted attempt at eating something that tasted like cardboard as the afternoon approached.

"I don't know, Mom. This self-injury stuff scares the hell out of me. Why now? Why all of a sudden? Phil's been gone for seven months." Miranda kept her voice low, but really didn't expect Ryan to listen in. That wasn't his style...barging in on the conversation was more like it. Besides, her mother had checked on him about fifteen minutes earlier and he was still dead to the world.

"You seem to have accepted this as an explanation," her mother said quietly. "Maybe there are others we haven't addressed."

"Oh, Mom." Miranda rubbed her temples. "Like what? That the house is haunted? He is haunted? That's not exactly comforting, you know."

Miranda watched her mother's expression. It remained impassive, yet it looked as though the woman struggled internally with how to express herself. Carolyn went to a cupboard and reached for a plastic tumbler surrounded by wavy lines of green and blue waves...an abstract rendition of a nautical theme. She went to the refrigerator for a glass of sweetened ice tea, and added numerous ice cubes. She sat back down across from Miranda without making a sound.

Miranda watched her mother take a sip of the tea. "When you were about three or four and your brother was a mere baby, your father and I were invited to a Christmas party in Charleston. It was one of those lavish things down near the battery. You know how we were never into the high society scene, but we loved going when we had the chance. Who wouldn't? The food was always excellent, the liquor flowed, and the conversations were often outrageous. Anyway, on our way home we took some side roads. People had Christmas lights on, it was all very festive. On one particular county road, the darkness was pretty solid. I don't recall if there was a moon, but it was clear not many people lived in this area.

"Suddenly, out of the blue, a light appeared on the road, about fifty yards ahead. Your father slowed down, and we're asking each other what it is. The light started bouncing up and down like a basketball, and then started growing in size. Soon it's like the size of an easy chair, then a car. Then it shrank again. Your father wasn't saying a word at this point, and of course I was demanding an explanation from him. Then it started rolling towards us...and it was getting bigger again. I knew at that point that if it hit the car we would be killed. I don't know how I knew it, but I did. Your father must have thought the same thing, because he threw the car into reverse and was speeding backwards down the street. This ball of light came at us even faster, and your father lost control and drove off the road and down an embankment. Lucky thing for us that he did. The light barely grazed us and continued down the road where it disappeared after going about another ten yards.

"We just looked at each other. Finally, we achieved a state of composure that allowed us to drive home. Weeks later, your father showed me a chapter in a book about South Carolina ghost stories. I bet it's still on a shelf here somewhere. It turns out these ghostly balls of light are a common phenomenon. Evidently two soldiers were even killed when they got too close to one."

Miranda stared at her mother. "I never heard that story."

"That's because we never told you. There've been others. You father once saw a girl walking through the park across the street. There was something odd about her. He said she was 'unearthly'. That was his exact word. She just disappeared when she reached the eastern end of the park. It wasn't like he lost sight of her. She was in plain view. She just vanished."

"So, you're thinking Ryan is being haunted." Miranda's grasp on the coffee tightened.

"Miranda. You forget that I saw him being born. People can dismiss that as the ravings of a woman present at a traumatic birth who wasn't prepared for the shock. However, you know I am not easily fazed. I know what I saw."

Her mother's eyes were like reinforced steel. "My dear,

Ryan could be developing a health problem, Ryan may just be going through a phase as they so often say and the whole thing will blow over. Or, maybe something else is going on, something that a month ago had been beyond our wildest dreams."

* * * *

Ryan never thought you could get a headache from thinking too much, but he had one now. He was feeling claustrophobic in the house and needed to get outside. He wasn't in the mood for running because of his headache, not to mention the fact that the broken wrist was hurting a little and the cast was awkward as hell. He opted for sitting in the shade in the park across the street. The moss hanging from the oak trees blocked his view of the house and provided him with a sense of seclusion, even with a footpath only a few feet away.

Ryan slouched all the way down so his butt was on the edge of the park bench. His legs were stretched out in front of him and crossed at the ankles. He wore a pair of sunglasses to avoid drawing the attention of tourists to his bruised face. The darkened lenses plus the shade from the trees made early afternoon look like dusk. Ryan felt anonymous, and relished the sense of isolation.

He woke up a little before one and pulled on some clothes. He found his grandmother in the kitchen. She was shuffling through some recipe cards as if she was playing poker until she found what she looked for. She crossed the kitchen to him and gave him a quick hug.

"I hear it was an adventurous evening."

"I'll say." Ryan grabbed some fruit from the refrigerator and then three granola bars from the box on the counter. "Is Mom mad?"

"Mad? No, Ryan, she's not." She paused, then added, "Frustrated, yes. She doesn't know what to do. She is also scared. It's hard not to be when you don't understand what's going on."

Ryan sat at the table and finished a banana in three quick bites. He was tearing the wrapper off one of the granola bars, chewy chocolate chip he noticed, when he decided to ask, "What do you think?"

His grandmother sighed and pursed her lips.

"No wishy-washy, beating around the bush, Grandma. I can take it."

She smiled. "You can take it? Hmmm. I suppose you could." She joined him at the table, reaching for one of his granola bars.

"You're stalling."

This time she laughed and withdrew her hand from the direction of the bar. "I'm really not. It's just that I don't know how to answer." She paused again, but only briefly. "Okay young man, here goes. I think an emotional health issue is a distinct possibility..."

Ryan slumped into his chair, feeling crestfallen.

"Now wait, let me finish. Your health is important, so we must address it. That is a very important parental responsibility. At the same time, however, you have never showed any signs of emotional problems. I might add...I have seen many strange things in my lifetime. I think there are some things beyond our rational word that can influence us. So, I am willing to be objective."

Ryan sat forward again. "Thanks, Grandma. This helps. At least you're not writing me off as a complete nut-case."

"Nobody is writing you off as a nut-case. Your mother sure isn't."

An hour after this talk with his grandmother Ryan was still unsure what his mother thought. She stopped in the kitchen briefly to refill her coffee cup. Her warm smile was genuine, and she planted a big kiss on his forehead.

"Do you feel refreshed at all?"

"Not really. I feel kind of sluggish. What are you doing?"

"Actually, I'm considering an illustration project."

Ryan brightened. If she was going back to work, that was a really huge good sign.

"Really? Are you going to take it?"

"I might. There are things to take into account. I'll let you know."

"Can I help?" Ryan often asked this question in the past. Sometimes he gave her ideas.

"If I decide to take it, definitely."

The fact that his mother didn't start peppering him with questions about the previous night was curious. She actively avoided putting him under any additional pressure, and he was grateful. Unfortunately, that made him more cautious as to what was lurking on the horizon.

Ryan unwrapped his last granola bar and took a bite. The afternoon breeze was picking up from off-shore. The sky was a hazy blue with no clouds, which was discouraging because the heat was like a warm washcloth across his face. Rain would cool things off. Ryan was increasingly bored. He really needed to find something to do or he would go nuts for sure. His injuries prevented him from going to sports camps, and probably most camps. Maybe he'd ask his mother. There had to be some kind of activity. He'd even seriously consider some art camp or theatre camp, something he never gave a moment's thought to in the past.

The oak towering above him was truly majestic. The lower branches extended an impossibly long away from the trunk. Ryan tilted his head back to scan up the tree. He could not see the top from this vantage point. The hanging moss was spooky.

An oak tree. Oaks symbolized strength. Ryan thought of his father. What would his father have done about all of this if he was still alive?

Ryan sat up straight. Okay, what would he have done?

He would have thought about the problem from many angles. What was the problem? Well, Ryan was seeing his dead twin...a twin who never had grown up. So, this was a ghost of something that didn't live very long, but was appearing as the same age as him. The twin was appearing at the age he would have been had he lived...but what did that mean?

The twin was also not human, at least according to his grandmother, and his mother...*my biological mother*...thought she was possessed or cursed or something.

Okay, what else? There was the consideration that he was mentally ill. This was a scary consideration, but he had to look at that as objectively as possible. His mother...*my real mother*...favored this explanation. This was as scary as the ghost option to him.

How could he figure this out? Being a pain in the ass for his mother wasn't effective. He knew that.

Geez, I'm only a kid. What does she expect?

Answer? *She expects more. This is your life, you got to take charge. Okay, so what? Find proof that sheds light on one explanation or the other?*

Wait. Why not? Look for evidence. Figure this out.

How?

Talk to people. Talk to those who were there.

His grandmother was walking on eggshells at the moment. She didn't want to overstep her bounds in terms of dealing with her grandson. Ryan sensed, though, that she believed him.

Okay, Grandma is in my corner, but I am not going to get too much more out of her without more proof.

The obvious source of information was staring him, and really staring them all in the face. He needed to talk to the other woman, Mrs. Pullman, who was with his grandmother when he was born. There was also that lady doctor in the emergency room. She was another source, but the best bet was Mrs. Pullman. However, his mother was forbidding that at the moment. Why would she do that? She was afraid, probably. Of what? Ryan didn't know.

So, he'd have to work on his mother. He would need to sound confident and logical, not a whining jerk.

Then there was those two kids...those two dorks chasing him in the woods and then outside his window last night. They weren't kids...he saw them change, but how were they involved? They intimated that they were all brothers, including his twin. Yet his twin wasn't human. He was like those kids...something evil...something reptilian. Running the way they did in the woods and what he saw last night, they looked...like birds, yeah, but...they also looked like...here he was worried about sounding stupid even in his own mind... like dinosaurs...those fast carnivores...sheesh.

Okay, they were on the to-do list as well, along with finding evidence to prove the ghost theory or the mentally ill theory. He was hoping for the former.

Those little creeps shredded apart a cat and gobbled it down. In the middle of a freaking street.

Ryan bolted upright. In those crime shows on TV, they always find forensic evidence of a crime. Wouldn't there be something from last night? Pieces of cat, for instance?

Before he was completely aware of what he was doing he was on the move. Ryan wove his way through the park. He dodged trees, a handful of tourists, little kids skipping on the path...until he jogged across the street to his grandmother's place. He thought of working backwards, starting with the front gate where he last saw the kids. He discarded that idea and hurried to the side street under his bedroom window.

Ryan imagined the location as a crime scene. He closed his eyes and tried to reconstruct in his mind where Max and Hugo were standing. He kept his distance so he wouldn't trample or otherwise destroy any evidence. Using the portion of the wrought iron where Hugo was standing as a focal point, Ryan searched a ten foot circular perimeter. When he found nothing, he moved about two feet closer and searched again. He kept moving closer when each search turned up nothing. If anything was left, Ryan was beginning to think it had blown away in a breeze. He had a sinking feeling this was a bust.

A tiny ball of fur was partially hidden by an iron bar of the fence.

Ryan felt his heart pound suddenly. A rush of excitement almost sent him scampering to the location. He forced himself to maintain composure so he didn't miss anything else.

He shifted his gaze slowly, making tight circles around the fur and gradually widening them with each pass.

There. A spot on the sidewalk. Dark brown...or was it dark red? Blood. It had to be. His visual search of the ground continued without taking a step. Suddenly he saw another spot, then a larger smear. It was as if his eyes were suddenly opened. How could he miss this on his first swipe of the area?

Because you were looking for fur and these spots can be anything.

The last discovery was the most exciting. A two inch stain with three smaller stains on top. Part of a foot with three toes. That's definitely what it was, at least he thought...

This was cool. More proof he wasn't losing his mind. He felt good about that, no question. He also knew this was not enough evidence to convince his mother. The ball of fur was small and it could be anything. He slowly walked to the fence and squatted. It certainly looked like part of the cat to him. It was sticking to the fence by blood or guts or something. He would need all kinds of lab tests to prove it was a chunk of cat, but that was something he didn't have. He wasn't a do-it-yourself CSI officer and there was no way he could contact the police and ask them to do it without having to explain everything.

Nope. While this further convinced him he wasn't going crazy, as evidence to convince his mother or anyone else for that matter, this was a non-starter.

The unmistakable sound of a skateboard approached him from behind. Ryan turned to see a boy of around ten riding towards him. As the kid's speed slowed, his right foot kicked off the board and gave a series vigorous pushes before returning. The kid was barefoot, with a fair amount of dirt smudged around his ankles. He had long jet black hair that flowed backwards off his face. His shirt and gym shorts were also pitch black.

When the boy's eyes met Ryan's, his expression erupted with pleasant surprise.

"Hi, Ryan!" he squealed.

Ryan was dumbstruck. The kid zoomed by him and continued toward the park. As he passed, the kid raised his hand in greeting, and for a moment Ryan thought he saw claws.

The kid rode out of sight around the corner before Ryan could jolt himself from his trance. Speak of the devil. Max just rode right by him.

The kid probably had a minute head start, but Ryan figured he could probably catch up. Ryan sprinted after him, but resisted running full tilt into the main street in front of the park. He stopped at the corner of his grandmother's property and peeked around the wrought iron fence.

The kid was gone.

Ryan found him an instant later carrying his board into the park. Ryan followed his progress and saw he was headed towards another kid sitting on a bench at the edge of the park near the sidewalk. Hugo.

Well. This was interesting. Ryan noticed Hugo's complexion was darker, almost as if he might be Latino, but his hair was a light brown color...almost bronze. Max was pale with dark hair. There was no way these two were biological brothers.

Ryan cursed his stupidity. Of course, they weren't brothers, they weren't human. Like Max, Hugo was barefoot, but his shorts and shirt were the same matching fire engine red. Weird.

Ryan didn't notice the man approaching the bench until he was practically on top of the kids. He was carrying a plastic bag, which he kept close to his chest as he sat down between the two boys. Ryan was startled because he recognized the man but couldn't immediately place him...

Max became animated and left his place on the bench and

positioned himself in the man's lap. Hugo was seemingly indifferent to the man's arrival, and the man's presence barely registered. The guy took out two cans of soda from the plastic bag and offered it to the boys. The younger one grabbed it with relish, but Hugo remained reserved. Ryan noticed he barely mumbled his thanks when he accepted the drink.

Arthur Beaumont. That's who the man was.

Holy crap. How did he know these kids? A bigger question was whether he knew these were the kids that were chasing him in the woods.

Mister Beaumont retrieved multiple bags of chips and passed them around to the boys. He placed one or two back in the bag. Ryan felt exposed hunched down by the fence. It wouldn't take much to see him. If he tried to walk home, he would certainly be spotted. Besides, Max already knew he was around, and he may have mentioned something for all Ryan knew. He decided to back away slowly and walk home by taking the long way around the block.

A rust bucket of a car drove slowly from the direction of town and came to a stop in front of the three. As the car's ignition was turned off, it knocked and rattled a few times before it went silent and motionless. Ryan stopped his retreat to watch. A large woman stepped out, wearing a brown dress that looked a lot like a sack with arm holes and a head hole cut in it. She looked tired. Actually, Ryan thought she looked trapped. She was not excited to see any of them. When she shuffled over to the kids and Beaumont, the kids essentially ignored her and dragged themselves to the car. Max tried to jockey into position to sit in front, but Hugo shoved him aside.

Beaumont appeared to be explaining something to the woman. He was doing all the talking and making numerous hand motions. Ryan saw the woman looked as if she hadn't washed herself in days. Her face was bruised, and her arms had scratch marks. Her hair was greasy and uncombed, hanging listlessly around her head. When Beaumont was finished talking, she just nodded and returned to the car. Before she slammed the door closed, Ryan guessed there was some kind of commotion in the car. He heard the woman yell "shut up", start the car, and drive away. Only a vague essence of blue exhaust hanging in the air indicated that the car and its occupants had even existed.

Beaumont gathered the garbage from the snacks and

walked to a trash can. As he tossed the debris away, he turned and looked straight at Ryan. The eyes bored into his, and Ryan was too stunned to move. Beaumont bowed ever so slightly, and turned away.

Ryan turned and dashed in the opposite direction.

* * * *

The computer screen hurtled from one web site to another. Ryan's search was rapid but focused as he was able to assimilate material and proceed to another site. His search provided him with helpful information, but only up to a point. Then the knowledge base stalled.

He started his search with the terms "dinosaurs" and "birds" combined. The number of hits was tremendous, but he was able to close in on websites that offered illustrations and descriptions. He quickly rejected anything related to herbivores, since he wanted the meat eaters. Ryan was never a dinosaur fanatic like some boys, but he knew enough about them. He was interested in finding information of fast, running dinosaurs that might be related to birds. At least that was how he conceptualized the movements of Hugo and Max.

Ryan was soon accessing information related to dromaeosaurids. They closely resembled birds and walked on hind legs. They were fast, active carnivores. Ryan found good descriptions on *Wikipedia* and noticed one type of dromaeosaurids was a *velociraptor*. Ryan was familiar with them from *Jurassic Park*–a movie that really kicked ass, but was surprised to learn the dinosaurs in the movie were portrayed too big to be *velociraptors*, and more closely resembled the *deinonychus*. Either way, though, the behaviors were very similar, and the two boys moved like them when they transformed. There were differences, however. The kids didn't have long tails like these dromaeosaurids. The boys still maintained the use of their arms, and likely used them in the running process for balance. While their muscle structure didn't change drastically, there was some kind of change Ryan couldn't put his finger on. Of course, their skin continued to look human but there were the eyes, the black eyes with sparkles of red...

So, these guys were clearly not human, and they weren't dinosaurs or birds either. Beaumont knew them–or so it appeared, and they claimed to be brothers with his twin. That meant his twin was like them. If all this was true, what did that make Ryan?

Keep investigating, don't draw conclusions yet…

On a lark, Ryan inserted Arthur Beaumont's name in the search engine. There was an artist by that name, but he died in 1978. Ryan also found a reference to his Arthur Beaumont at the local High School. He kept scrolling through the hits, and found a link to an Arthur Beaumont, author. He clicked on it.

A web site for a book titled *Art of Dangerous Living: Chronicle of a Southern Family* by Arthur Beaumont. Available as an ebook from a number of vendors for 99 cents.

"What the hell?" Ryan mumbled to himself. He was sitting in the family room using the desktop computer waiting for dinner.

He read further. A blurb said, "This book chronicles the lurid history of the Montgomery and Beaumont families from during the Twentieth Century…vividly portrays South Carolina at its Gothic best. The author is a descent of these influential families and is currently a high school teacher."

This was too much. Ryan couldn't shake the feeling he stumbled across a bag of diamonds. Could he download this to his computer? For a dollar, sure, but….He searched the specifications. There, he could download it as a PDF file. He was in business.

"Mom?" he yelled toward the kitchen. "Can I use your debit card to download a book to the computer? It's a protected site."

She appeared at the doorway, wiping her hands. "Hold on, what kind of book?"

Ryan smirked at her. "Pornography. God Mom, what do you think? Actually it's a book written by the biology teacher I met." He read her the title and the brief description.

"Ryan…"

"C'mon, Mom. What could be in it for ninety-nine cents? You can read it first." He offered because he knew she wouldn't take the time to check it out.

Ryan watched her relent, and made room for her to enter the debit card information on the checkout portion of the website.

"Thanks, Mom. I can do the rest."

"I kind of figured you could."

Ryan smiled and started tapping away. Within a few minutes he had downloaded the document, which was only 150 pages. Even the interruption of dinner and the fact that he had to do the dishes didn't deter him from finishing the book by nine. He was quick because of one essential reason, the book sucked. Lucky for Beaumont he was a biology teacher. He wouldn't have made it as an English one.

Ryan was able to skim large sections of it because those portions offered little in the way of help. Mostly these people were shitheads, swindlers, drunks, racists, scoundrels, adulterers, and perverts. Who thought a book having all of these characters in it would be boring? Yet it was...with the exception of one section...

Ryan scrolled back to a section that described the real black sheep in the family. He thought Beaumont was trying to make too fine a distinction because much of his ancestors did not have many redeeming features. Yet, he had to admit this group was creepier than most.

He found the section: A rumor that waxed and waned but otherwise had a long shelf life until about the 1960's related to a branch of the family that was purportedly devil worshipers. The first written record from around 1910 involved the youngest son of William and Margaret Montgomery, Francis, who was eighteen. He was found wandering nude in a church graveyard masturbating among the tombstones and otherwise desecrating the graves. The boy was sent away for his own good, but was seen ten years later visiting his family with his beautiful wife and young son. Neighbors learned the young man had fared well in his studies and was a successful physician. Francis spoke with sadness about his son's twin who died in childbirth. The surviving child was very unusual. He scared other children and was otherwise a holy terror, committing acts of vandalism and being suspected in the deaths of small animals, both wild and domestic. Young Mrs. Montgomery was a dark haired beauty who was cold and aloof in her interactions with most everyone. It appears that the family was not particularly accepting of her.

Within two years the youngest Montgomery returned with his family permanently. He set up his medical practice and did well. Stories began to circulate, however, that the family hosted small gatherings involving strange rituals. Whisperings of devil worship, human sacrifice and human debauchery began to circulate. All the while, Doctor Francis Montgomery's practice continued to flourish. Some suspected dark magic was the reason, trapping townsfolk into letting the doctor minister to their needs.

The great depression put a damper on these rumors, yet talk of strange occurrences kept surfacing. Infant death rates rose, an unidentified beast was slaughtering livestock, and there were even multiple attacks on humans—with some fatalities. Other odd children, similar in behavior to young Master Montgomery, were born, and the townsfolk felt the doctor was somehow involved.

Around the same time period, from the mid-1930's to the early 1940's, persistent and unverified accounts surfaced of individuals capable of breeding children who were half human and half demon. Reports of an ancient book or pamphlet with written instructions, a how-to manual if you will, were circulating, and remain alive today. Evidently, this book has been around since the 18th century, at least, with speculation that it arrived on our coast in a slave trading vessel. None of this has ever been substantiated. Nonetheless, eye witness accounts of this book can be found within current members of both the Montgomery and Beaumont clans. Two other families on the periphery of our family tree, Benton and Lund, have also supposedly gained access to the book and dabbled in the creation of demon children.

I should mention, however, that with the advent of modern times, these accounts served mostly as entertainment value around the campfire. Close scrutiny has not produced much in the way of evidence, beyond some accounts of poorly behaved children—who have never been named. That is, no children have been identified other than Francis who jump started the rumor mill on the devil-worshiping business. Still, the stories play a unique role in the family history.

I would be remiss not to tell you that, like a bad nickel, accounts of demonic births continue to raise their ugly heads even now—with the latest reports as recent as the late 1990's.

* * * *

Ryan pondered the section he just read for the second time.

Okay, okay, okay...so what do we know?

Ryan automatically fell into a discussion within his mind which sounded a lot like the way his father would solve problems out loud. He left the chair and began pacing the room.

Someone still knew how to produce demon children. Evidently, my twin was one of these kids. Have I got this right so far? What are the odds that Hugo and Max were demon kids too? Pretty high when you consider the claws and the changing eyes. Shit...they eat cats too. Pretty high nothing...it's virtually certain they are.

Ryan stopped pacing for a moment. "How did I get so involved with all of this stuff?" He realized he was talking out loud to himself so he shut up and resumed his pacing. Besides he sounded as if he was whining, and he hated doing that.

What's Beaumont got to do with all this?

Ryan felt he was racking his brain all day, and the process became torturous. He felt tired and cranky, and wanted to escape all this stuff for a little while at least. He wanted to go do some kid things for a change...play basketball, hang out with friends, go to the movies, eat ice cream, watch TV, talk to a girl...argh...this was so frustrating. Given his current situation, only watching TV and eating ice cream were possible options.

By the time he went to bed, Ryan had done both.

* * * *

"Ryan, time to get up." Knuckles rapped softly against his bedroom door.

Ryan's eyes flew open. *Time to get up?* What time was it? He noticed sunlight around the edges of the shades.

"Let's go, it's getting late. You need to dress up today. I put some nice things out for you to wear."

Ryan noticed the navy blue blazer, pale yellow shirt, striped matching tie, and stone colored khakis hanging prominently at the front of his closet. A little confused, Ryan stood up and got dressed.

"What's the big deal?" He called through his door. The hallway was quite.

Putting on the pants went okay, but the shirt proved more of a challenge. His left arm and side complained as he stretched and contorted his body to get the shirt over the cast. Doing the tie would have been impossible, but he long ago mastered the art of keeping ties tied from the previous occasion. He slipped the loop over his head and then pushed the knot towards his neck. He didn't bother with socks and just slipped bare feet into deck shoes.

The hallway was empty. *Well, what the hell?* Outside in his grandmother's garden he heard voices. As he moved down the stairs, Ryan was aware of other voices and movement on the porch in addition to the garden. Cut flowers from the garden graced the center of the dining room table, and blue balloons rose to the ceiling from their anchors on the table in groups of four or five. A sheet cake adorned one end of the table. The frosting was an ocean blue with silver lettering. Ryan walked quietly into the dining room and circled the table in order to read what was written on the cake. The silver script became clear after a few steps. *Happy Resurrection!* The entire place was festive.

Ryan slyly extended his finger to scoop a portion of the decorative frosting from the side of the cake. Checking to make sure he wasn't being observed, he inserted his finger in his mouth. The icing had a grainy consistency, and Ryan immediately gagged and spat out what was left. The flavor was extremely sweet with a rancid aftertaste.

"God. That's disgusting." He continued to shudder in revulsion as he grabbed a napkin and wiped up what he spat from his mouth. He left the crumpled napkin on the table.

Outside, the conversation was unintelligible, but the banter was pleasant and the laughter spontaneous. The ice cubes within glasses clinked with a winter clarity.

Ryan pushed open the screen door to the garden area, and the hiss of the hydraulic closer announced his arrival. Oppressive heat and humidity immediately blanketed him, and he felt perspiration forming under his shirt.

"Ahhhh! A very special guest has arrived," a voice exclaimed within the garden. Ryan found the source, a man with thinning straw colored hair and glasses.

"Hello, Mister Beaumont." Ryan reluctantly shook the hand that was extended to him. The shake was vigorous.

"Arthur, please, call me Arthur." His left arm made a sweeping gesture of the party. White chairs and tables were placed within the garden. The front yard had many more, along with a few rows of seats that faced a baby cradle under an umbrella. "Quite a day for the event, don't you think Ryan?

A resurrection! This just doesn't happen very often." Arthur was especially jubilant.

Ryan was guided down a few a steps to the garden level by Arthur, and noticed a strong odor of decay. Arthur quickly noticed his reaction.

"Oh dear, I was afraid of this," Arthur said. He let go of Ryan's hand and dragged two large plastic garbage bags away from the door Ryan just came through. One of the bags ripped under his grasp, and the tear produced a spill of body parts. One was a head of a young man which rolled into a metal table. A high-ball glass with ice cubes sitting on the top jingled on impact.

"Oops. I'm sorry," Arthur said, "collateral damage. The boys were being rambunctious, I'm afraid and they got carried away. Marking their territory, I suppose. That's why they chased you, by the way. Anyway, they should only kill what they plan to eat, don't you think? But who am I to say? I can get this cleaned up in a jiffy."

Beaumont scanned the immediate area. "Lizette?" he called. A woman appeared from behind Ryan.

"What, Arthur?" Ryan saw it was the same woman who picked up Hugo and Max from the park. She was dressed in black pants and a white shirt as if part of the staff catering the party.

"Take care of this, would you please." Arthur motioned towards the decaying body parts. Lizette scowled and grumbled something unintelligible, but leaned towards the decapitated head swelling in the sunlight.

"Wonderful celebration, Arthur." A man appeared at Arthur's side carrying a plate of food.

"Thank you, Francis," Arthur replied. "By the way, this is young Master Ryan." He bowed slightly towards Ryan. "Ryan, I'd like you to meet an old member of the family. This is Mister Francis Montgomery."

Out of the corner of his eye, Ryan noticed Lizette picked up the head by the hair using a cocktail napkin and returned it to the plastic bag. She tossed the garbage bags to the corner of the garden.

"Oh, you must be so proud." Mister Montgomery beamed at Ryan who noticed for the first time that the man was dead, which made sense given the guy was eighteen back in 1910 when he was busy jerking off in cemeteries.

Ryan shuddered with revulsion. Turning away from Mister Montgomery, he realized all the guests were dead. Their white skin pallor was like winter overcast and their eyes had receded to a lifeless black. Their lips had drawn back into a leer that exposed teeth discolored with decay. About half the guests were jubilant and appeared overjoyed to be at the party.

The other half were melancholy and apprehensive. While the joyous dead people would nod or wave when Ryan's gaze crossed theirs, this group would avoid all eye contact and their faces were filled with foreboding. Ryan also noticed their faces and bodies were terribly scarred or beat up compared to the others—if that kind of comparison could be made between groups of living corpses.

Lizette walked past him carrying a tray of hors de oeuvres. Ryan wondered if she had washed her hands after touching the oozing head. To his surprise, she paused briefly in front of him.

"Listen, kid," she whispered. "If you have the chance, get the hell out of here while you still can." Then she was gone.

From the second floor porch hung the body of Agent Lund. His hands had been tied over his head and then attached to something out of sight on the porch, allowing his body to remain suspended over the railing and above the ground. His sport shirt was ripped open, displaying where he had been gutted across his chest and abdomen. Blood dripped from his corpse, splashing the air conditioning units surrounded by the wrought iron directly below. Flies buzzed in frenzy around his body.

Squatting on the railing on either side of Lund's body were Hugo and Max. They wore matching powder blue seersucker suits with white shirts and pink ties. The only wardrobe feature out of the ordinary was their footwear. Both were barefoot, and their feet had assumed the shape of talons and were securely perched around the railing. Their positions made them look like catchers behind home plate awaiting a pitcher's delivery.

Max saw Ryan and grinned. He bounced on his haunches and waved shyly. Hugo looked bored.

"I know, it is a bit garish, but the boys thought we needed more decorations. No accounting for taste of children, is there?" Arthur shrugged. "Poor Jeremy. He always was the failure in the family, but then again the Lunds were not quite the same class of people as the Montgomerys or the Beaumonts." Arthur sighed dramatically. "Had a devil of a time getting him up there. By the way, your mother was right to warn you about the rotten railing. We couldn't afford to lose you at this stage of the game now, could we?"

Ryan was quite flustered by this point and could not reply.

"Come, let's go check on the man of the hour–or the day I suppose."

Arthur placed his hand on Ryan's upper arm and navigated him through the guests. The happy-appearing dead murmured their hellos and congratulations. Others reached out to touch him as if he was someone famous, patting his chest or back. As they walked through the garden to the front yard, Ryan saw they were making their way toward the baby cradle, which was partially surrounded by white wooden chairs placed in a semi-circle. Blue balloons decorated a few of the chairs.

"Come to the front here, Ryan. There you go."

Ryan looked into the cradle and saw the remains of a baby. The cadaver was mostly skeleton, but there were scraps of something like leather in patches attached to the bones. The crowd of guests had filled in behind Arthur and Ryan as they passed. The morose crowd filed into chairs and huddled together in the center. The joyous guests took seats on the periphery or stood at the back, watching with a barely suppressed thrill. There had to be twenty dead in attendance at least.

Ryan watched as Hugo and Max vaulted off the railing and jumped down two stories, landing gracefully on the grass and well out of range of the fenced in air-conditioners. Ryan couldn't help being impressed with this demonstration of agility. Hugo strolled over to the seating area in manner that indicated he was trying to look cool. Max possessed no restraints. He practically skipped through the crowd and came to Ryan's right side and grabbed his hand, and then looked up to Ryan and beamed.

Arthur leaned over Max and towards Ryan. "I know what you're thinking. This is vulgar and tacky. True. It's just that resurrections are so unusual. There's no record of one attempted by the family as far as I could find. Someone may have been successful elsewhere, but..." Arthur trailed off.

"I want to name him Rex. Don't you think that would be a

cool name?" Max announced when he had the chance.

Ryan was confused, so Arthur clarified, "Your twin, when he is resurrected, that is. Max here has had it in his mind that his name should be Rex. We've started calling his ghost that in jest, so we might as well use it. Shall we make it official?" This last question was directed towards Max. The little boy shook his head vigorously in agreement, his long black hair flopping with the motion.

"Okay, Rex it is!"

"Yippee! Hey Hugo, we're gonna name him Rex for sure."

Hugo had recently joined them, looking sullen. "So? Who cares?"

Arthur leaned towards Ryan and whispered, "I think Hugo's got his nose a little bit out of joint. Jealous of the attention, I think. He won't be top dog anymore. But, never fear. I know my boy. He will come around when he has a new older brother to idolize."

Ryan finally found his voice. "Who are these people who look so...miserable?" He looked at a family sitting together, a mom and dad with two kids. All four of them had sections of their heads missing. He felt awful for them, and the mom looked so sad.

Arthur placed his hand over his heart and looked solemn. "These people gave their lives for this moment. Out of respect, I needed to invite them. These are my most cherished victims...some of the fruits of my labor. As the boys got older, I let them help some. One of the most difficult tasks with these children is to teach them restraint. There must be purpose to their efforts, not just random slaughter."

"I held that little girl's hand when Arthur shot her. I told her not to be afraid," Max offered. The dead girl buried what was left of her face into her father's side when Max pointed at her.

Ryan was so appalled he was struck dumb. He couldn't help scanning the "cherished victims". Being here was torture. He saw college kids sitting together, older people, people who could be someone's mom and dad. Beaumont killed them all, seemingly with the help of these demon kids.

Right now, one is holding my hand like I'm some kind of big brother.

"Let's not dwell on the past, though," Arthur said. "Ryan, let's talk about you. You're such an important part of this family. We will be bringing my firstborn back to life. You are such a crucial part of the process. We need you, Ryan, to complete the puzzle. With you here now, Rex will experience a re-birth, and we will all be a family again. That's what it's all about, isn't it? Family?"

Arthur's comments had escalated to being nearly rapturous. His focus was interrupted by someone approaching behind Ryan. "Ahhh, Ryan, behold your brother, soon to be re-born."

Ryan did not turn his head. He figured that the ghost of his dead twin had made an appearance. The family guests exclaimed in delight, and some scattered applause was added.

Ryan felt his twin stand next to his left side, followed by its arm being draped over his shoulder. The fingernails felt sharp as the twin squeezed him in greeting. The scent of the twin was like garbage left outside in the heat for too long. Ryan could imagine the face staring at him only inches away. He could not look. If he did he would surely faint.

"The preparations are just about done, Ryan. Then we'll need you for the glorious extravaganza. The ecstasy will be overwhelming."

Ryan sensed the twin's face move closer, and he shuddered violently when it kissed him on the cheek.

"My, my, we can't let this moment go by," said Arthur, who moved directly in front of them. He lifted his cell phone. "Hello boys. How about I give you each fifty dollars if you let me take your picture." Then he winked at Ryan.

"Ryan..."

"Ryan..."

Ryan tried to turn away. *God, get me out of here.*

"Ryan, honey, wake up..."

Ryan abruptly sat up, almost banging heads with his mother who was leaning over his bed and shaking him.

"You've been groaning in your sleep. Are you in pain?"

Ryan pulled his thoughts together. It was a dream. Thank God. He dropped back down into bed, sighing in relief.

"I was just having a dream. It was so bizarre. A nightmare, really."

"Are you okay? Do you want to talk about it?"

"No," he said, and then added, "I'm forgetting it already."

After a few more reassurances for his mother, he was able to persuade her to leave his room. He checked the clock and saw it was a little after eight. He could stay in bed a little longer.

The dream was awful. Where does stuff like this come from?

He rolled over and felt a chill like an ice pack had been placed on his back. On his desk chair, his blazer, tie, shirt, and khakis had been thrown in a messy heap.

His cell phone buzzed, and he grabbed it. He opened a text with an accompanying photo.

The picture was of him and his twin, both dressed in blue blazers, yellow shirts, and matching ties. Ryan's expression was abject horror. His face was swollen, and the bruising and bandages stood out with ghastly clarity. His twin was smiling triumphantly through chiseled teeth despite the fact that he was not yet alive and still waiting to be resurrected.

Chapter Seven

There was no way Ryan could have predicted the unbelievable turn of events since he woke up from his dream just five hours before. Here he was eating homemade ham biscuits, sitting across the table from the most incredibly beautiful girl he had ever seen. She had caramel colored skin and eyes the shape and color of almonds. Her body was lean and muscular, and he guessed she must play some kind of sport. He name was Dee Batista, the granddaughter of Eugenia Pullman who was also sitting with them at the table, and the daughter of Doctor Pullman-Bastista.

"Child, explain to me your theory about Mister Beaumont, please?" Mrs. Pullman had a warm syrupy voice which Ryan loved to listen to, even if she did call him "child" a lot.

She was also a very surprising person. When Dee showed him into her house, she introduced her grandmother. Ryan forgot his manners in the most embarrassing fashion.

"It's you!" he practically yelled. Right after the words escaped his mouth, Ryan felt his face blush. If his grandmother had heard him, she had been mortified. Mrs. Pullman chuckled and waved her hand to dismiss his embarrassment.

"I am so delighted you remember me, especially since our meeting was so brief."

Dee was confused, "What are you talking about?"

Ryan described his experience with his twin outside the dining room window a few nights before and how an African American woman appeared magically to drive the vision away.

"She was her." Ryan pointed to Mrs. Pullman, "I mean, your grandmother is the woman I saw...Right?" This last word was directed towards the older woman.

"Yes, but I wasn't physically there, mind you," she said as she gazed at him warmly. "I wish I had the strength to do more." In all honesty, she didn't look as if she had the strength to do anything. Ryan could tell she had cancer. She had lost much of her hair from the side effects of chemotherapy.

Ryan felt vindicated. He was so used to not being believed or made to feel like was losing his mind. Just this morning, after he found the picture on his cell phone, he ran down the stairs to display his evidence.

"Mom, wait till you see this," he declared as he marched into the kitchen.

"Ryan, this doesn't prove a thing. This could have been digitally created."

Ryan was momentarily stunned to silence, but quickly recovered. "You think I faked this."

His grandmother also jumped to his defense. "Miranda, you must admit, this is quite unusual."

"Thanks, Grandma." Ryan was adamant that he would not give up without a fight. "Mom, it's like you're putting your head in the sand. Doesn't this strike you as freaky–at least a little bit?"

Miranda was quiet, and seemed to be deciding how to respond. Ryan took the opportunity to lay out his reasoning.

"When I first met this Mister Beaumont, he knew who I was and that I was living with Grandma…"

"Wait, how did?"

"Because he said, 'can I give you a lift to your grandmother's?' It didn't even register at the time until this dream last night. I never told him, yet he knew about me." Ryan paused to see if his mother would offer a counter-argument. When she didn't say anything, he continued, "All these strange things started happening right after that. I think he had something to do with that couple being killed…in fact, I think he is a serial killer because all of those people in the dream were dead."

"Ryan, honey, listen to yourself. You have concocted a story based on no evidence."

"Mom, geez, listen to *yourself*. One, this guy knows who I am and he is in my dreams. Two, he may have killed some people–maybe even a lot of people. Three, my natural mother was possessed or cursed or something. Four, I had a twin who was a monster. Five, I keep seeing this twin and I'm dreaming about him and he is really creepy. Six, Beaumont has two kids who are demons, or, God, I don't know what they are, but they're not human and they're practically stalking me–I watched them kill and eat a cat the other night. Seven…," Ryan paused, "there was a seventh point but I forgot it now. It doesn't matter, though. Once you accept the supernatural part, it all makes sense."

"That's just the thing, Ryan, accepting the supernatural premise. That is one huge leap, don't you see? Other than Arthur Beaumont's comment, he's not even connected to any of this except in your dreams. Does he know about the birth? Was he involved? We have no proof, honey."

"Actually, we do," his grandmother reported in a voice slightly louder than a whisper.

Ryan and his mother looked at her in silence which lasted for several seconds. Then, Ryan sat down and placed his right elbow on the table and his head in his right hand. He stared at his grandmother, and said calmly, "I thought so. Tell me."

When his grandmother described Arthur Beaumont's role in Ryan's birth, he noticed his mother was clearly shocked. She had no idea. The strange set of circumstances could not be denied as far as Ryan was concerned. When his grandmother finished, Ryan turned to his mother and said, "I want to talk to Mrs. Pullman."

* * * *

As he reached for his sixth ham biscuit, Ryan summarized his thoughts on Arthur Beaumont.

"Everything's been so confusing. I don't know what's real any more but I need to find out."

Mrs. Pullman nodded. "Dee, could you go get my Bible from my bedside?"

Dee had been quiet for most of the lunch. She kept casting glances at Ryan. He was worried about the impression he was making. This was not exactly the best way to get to meet another kid, especially a girl. He prayed he wasn't coming across as a complete loser.

Dee returned moments later, and handed the Bible to her grandmother. She clasped the book in both hands, but didn't open it.

"I didn't figure on Arthur Beaumont's role. I've known Arthur for twenty years, take or leave. He was always involved with his church, collecting food for the shelters, volunteering for home renovation projects for the poor, that kind of thing. I got to know him because our paths would cross every so often."

Ryan couldn't believe it. "He was involved with a church?"

"Oh, yes, child," the old woman answered. "What better hiding place is there?"

"I guess." Ryan was still perplexed. "Then what happened?"

"He came to me one day. This was when I lived in my house near the shore. That house is gone now. About ten years ago I sold it to developers who put up a whole bunch of fancy beach houses. I sure miss the place." She paused momentarily. "Arthur said he knew a young couple who were in a family way. She was nearly full term, but had somehow gotten it in her mind there was something wrong with her or the baby. He wondered if I could help."

"Was the couple from around here?"

"No, but I'm not sure where they came from. The young man was from somewhere in Europe. That's all I can say. While he was here, he met and fell in love with Jenny. That was the young girl's name. They got to know Arthur. Truth be told, I thought Arthur was smitten with the girl, but he always claimed the three of them were just friends."

"Were these my parents?"

"Yes, child, they were. Your momma, I'm talking about your biological momma now, was terribly upset when Arthur brought her to me. First of all, her husband–if they were even married–had disappeared. She hadn't seen him in two days. Arthur said he hadn't either. What's more, he seemed angry with the fellow for leaving Jenny at this difficult time. What was more upsetting was she kept going on about the devil having planted his baby in her womb. She said the devil's child was going to eat hers when it was born."

"Ugh," Dee said.

Eugenia paused, and pushed the Bible in Ryan's direction. "Do you read your Bible, Ryan?"

"No, ma'am. We don't go to church much." Ryan was embarrassed of admitting this to Mrs. Pullman.

"Child, I didn't ask if you went to church. I asked if you read your Bible." She leaned closer to inspect his face.

"No, ma'am, not really."

"Well, now's a good time to start as any. Here..." She flipped to the back. "This is the book of Revelation. Go to chapter 12..." Ryan found it easily, which pleased her. "Read this sentence..."

Ryan followed her finger and read, "then the dragon stood before the woman about to give birth, to devour her child as soon as it was born." Ryan finished and looked up. Dee's eyes were wide. Mrs. Pullman sat back as if preparing what to say next.

"There are some people who are just born evil, and don't need much help from hell to make them do the bad things they do. It just comes natural to them. Or, they just may need a little push."

Ryan shifted to the end of his seat to move closer to Mrs. Pullman. He noticed Dee did the same. Neither dared to say anything.

"I have heard many stories in my life, and I've seen some strange things. But nothing prepared me for what happened the night you were born."

"How?" Ryan started to ask. Mrs. Pullman lifted up her hand for him to stop. "Sorry," he murmured.

"This young girl, Jenny, came to my house with Arthur. She was half-crazed and terrified. I brought her to one of my back bedrooms. Her contractions were coming quickly and she was going to deliver soon. Ryan, your grandmother just happened to stop by for a visit and she starting helping. We wanted Arthur out of the house because he was not related to the girl and she wanted him gone. So your grandmother came up with a list of chores for him to do, like getting supplies in town. She was very clever that way."

Ryan nodded. He saw his grandmother making a huge to-do list to get Beaumont out of there.

"I don't mind telling you this girl's ramblings were very upsetting. They made me uneasy. I must say right now, I had heard about these demon children before then. I had grown up with these stories, and they came and went, like stories do. But I never believed them. None of us really did. We thought they were just ghost stories."

"Beaumont wrote about them in his book, and he said the same thing," Ryan volunteered.

"Humpf. I wonder why he would write about it like that. Well, I'm not going to waste my time trying to figure out that man. That day when she was here, I found the girl's statements very troubling. Your grandmother was nervous too." She paused for a sip of water. Her glass was empty.

"Can I get you more, Gramma?"

"Why, yes, child, thank you." Mrs. Pullman waited for Dee to fill her glass with ice cubes and water before resuming.

"When the first baby was born—and we weren't expecting two babies at the time, mind you—it had all the features of a normal child...except it did not have an umbilical cord. We looked at each other in shock, but then we didn't have time to consider it any further, for the second baby was being born. This child, you Ryan, *was* normal.

"I remember both infants being on the bed, and then the first child screamed in a way no baby ever does. He...it started sliding over to you...it moved like a serpent...no newborn can move like that...and I saw its mouth open and the jaw started to...and then its arm reached out, except the hand looked as though it had claws for just an instant, and tried to grab you, but instead one of its fingers sliced you like a knife on your side. This all happened within a few moments, but as soon as we saw your blood we started moving and pulled you away to safety."

Mrs. Pullman's eyes were moist, and her hands shook ever so slightly as a result of revisiting these images in her mind. Dee had her hands clamped over her mouth and nose in a comical parody of horror.

Ryan, for his part, felt goose bumps all over. He whispered, "It was going to eat me?"

"Yes. I don't know any other way to say it. Somehow, this girl, who we thought might have been mentally ill, knew."

"So, what happened?" Dee asked.

"Well, your mother and Mrs. Tryon..."

"Momma was there?" Dee interrupted.

"Yes, she was in the doorway watching. They took Ryan to another room, and took care of him. We figured we couldn't go to a doctor. Between the three of us, we could stitch him up and apply antibiotic ointment. You grandmother took you to her house, Ryan, and cared for you until you were well. Meanwhile she and I talked about what to do. Your mother and father wanted children in the worst way. We couldn't think of a better ending. So your grandmother talked it over with your mother, and you went to live in Wisconsin."

His mind was racing. "What happened to my mother–the one who gave birth to me?"

"She died, Ryan. When we could focus on her, she was already gone."

"What about...the other baby? My twin?"

"It was very angry. It took out its anger on your mother's body. I'm sorry."

Ryan paled. His facial bruises stood out dramatically.

"Was she already dead?"

"Yes, child. I think she was."

"And the baby?"

"We killed it, your grandmother and me."

Dee gasped at this, but Ryan only nodded in approval.

They sat quietly without moving for what seemed like a long time. The ham biscuits were no longer appealing. Dee got up and rummaged in a kitchen drawer and came back to the table with a half-gallon sized plastic baggie with a zip-lock top. She filled it with the leftover ham biscuits. When she finished, she placed them in the refrigerator and then came back to sit at the table. Only then did Ryan ask a question.

"My biological parents...were they, like, devil worshipers or something?"

"Remember, your father was gone. I never met him. My guess is he was dead by this time, but I don't know for sure. If your mother was one, she certainly was having second thoughts by the time I met her."

Ryan thought for a moment, and then asked, "Well, how did he recruit them? Beaumont, I mean?"

"Here's what I think," Mrs. Pullman said. "I think your parents were very young, poor, and confused. They were looking for a friend. They were looking for some place to belong. I think they were rather wild, rebellious types. They may have been charmed by the man who was inviting, and who offered something that was out of the ordinary—something shocking.

"Maybe Arthur promised them some kind of supernatural power. Maybe he made it sound like an adventure. Maybe it was all of these things. I don't know, but it looks as if he convinced them to play along. Somewhere along the way they became frightened, and maybe started talking about going to a doctor, or a minister. Your father could have been planning some heroic action that ended up getting him killed."

"Why did Beaumont bring her to you?"

"I think he had to do something. It would've looked strange to the young woman if he didn't. He probably thought I was safe. After all, to him I was just a black woman who probably knew about ancient folk remedies. I would not be surprised if his choice of me was based on bigotry. Who knows, maybe he even saw the need for a woman who could deliver a baby."

"So, who was the father of the two babies?" Dee asked. Ryan thought this was a good question. Who was his biological father?

"I think Ryan's father was the young man visiting from Europe," Mrs. Pullman said, and then turned to Ryan to continue, "You even look like him."

"Wait, I thought…"

"That I never saw him? That's true, but Jenny, the young woman, had this picture which we found in her belongings afterward." Mrs. Pullman flipped through the pages of her Bible until she came to an envelope stuck in the middle. Amazingly, within the envelope was a color photo that appeared dated and washed out. She handed it to Ryan, who was startled to see a guy who looked *exactly* like him, although a number of years older. Posing with him was a girl who was kind of tiny. She was a head shorter than the guy. Her hair was reddish blond, he could tell that even though the color in the photo had faded, and she had a gleeful smile as if something absolutely joyous had just happened.

Ryan felt his heartbeat then, along with a sensation that his stomach was dropping to the floor. His eyes watered, and before he realized it tears spilled gently down both cheeks. *Why the heck am I doing all this crying?*

Dee moved around from her side of the table to look at the photo. She stood slightly over his right shoulder and then leaned closer. At the same time she put her arm around him. Her face was literally right over his shoulder. Ryan felt her cheek barely touching his. If he turned his head he could kiss her.

Mrs. Pullman extended her arm in order to place her hand under his chin. She lifted his downcast face.

"I really think they fought bravely to the bitter end. You can be sure of that," Mrs. Pullman said.

Ryan appreciated the thoughtfulness and nodded to her.

"The father of the other one? Now, I have no idea about that. Remember it was not really human—no umbilical cord for one thing. Oh, it had the appearance of a baby at first glance, but if you looked closer at how it moved, how it used its hands, and other things, you would get the sense something was off. I wouldn't be surprised if it could change shape or form from the appearance of a child to—"

"A dragon?" asked Dee.

"Yes, or a serpent or something reptilian. I can say Arthur isn't one of them, that I'm pretty sure of. I think he is more like a caretaker or a foster daddy, something like that.

"I suppose the devil could have worked through Arthur, although how that would look I don't care to know," said Mrs. Pullman. "Of course, the conception could have been done by supernatural means. Just plain old evil. To me, that is the most frightening."

Ryan considered another question, "You said before that you didn't suspect Beaumont at the time. Why?"

"Oh, that's easy. He was so helpful and very concerned. He was devastated when he heard the baby and the girl died. Even when we mentioned we were thinking of arrangements for the surviving baby, he was entirely in favor of it. He behaved as though he was our ally. We never told him about where you were taken, and he never even asked. Of course, he had his own risky job to take care of."

"What was that?" Dee beat Ryan to the question.

"He volunteered to bury the girl and the baby. He never told us where he placed them, which was fine because it was better we didn't know. Now of course, I wonder what he had been up to."

"It's almost like he was waiting for me to show up. Why bother?"

"I don't think he was waiting for you the way you think. It sounds as if he has been busy enough these past fourteen years. He has two demon children. I think, I really think, he was waiting to see what would happen. If you showed up, great...if you didn't, well, he had other things to do. Then you did show up and all of a sudden you're like a piece of food stuck between his teeth. He becomes fixated, trying to do something about it. He decided he was going to try this ghastly thing."

Dee surprised him by interjecting, "You're like unfinished business. That demon baby injured you, so you and that kid are connected. Gramma, do you think he can bring him back to life?"

"Holy crap," Ryan said, not giving Mrs. Pullman a chance to reply. "That's what all this resurrection stuff is about. He needs me somehow, but, won't he need the body?"

Everyone was silent for a moment, and Ryan felt the others were a step ahead of him. Then he saw it too. "He does have the body, doesn't he?"

"Yes, child, I suspect he does. That was part of his plan, I think. He was biding his time. When you showed up here, everything was easy as sin. Look how much has happened in such a short time."

"Oh, man. What do we do?"

Mrs. Pullman considered this. "I think he's going to need you to be physically present to make this work. In the meantime, I need to do some thinking about this and some praying. I also need to talk to someone who has had...experience...with this kind of thing."

Ryan could tell Dee was going to ask who this was, and Mrs. Pullman could see it too. "You don't need to know who. This is something I need to check up on."

Mrs. Pullman reached out both of her hands, one for Dee and the other for Ryan. "I also think we need to go to the police. They're not going to believe this demon baby story, but they will understand the rest. There was an undocumented death of a woman and child, a surviving baby that was given away without any of the legal steps of adoption, and the bodies of the dead were not appropriately laid to rest. That will be enough to get Arthur off our back, I think."

"Gramma, do you think you'll get in trouble?"

"I'm sure we will, but what can they do to me or Mrs. Tryon, two old ladies? There might be a slight risk that Ryan could be removed from his home, but where would they put him? He is fourteen now, and any good lawyer, like your father, Dee, would know how to fight this."

* * * *

Ryan and Dee spent part of the afternoon sitting at her computer doing internet searches on Arthur Beaumont and unsolved murders in South Carolina and across the United States. They weren't too successful with either venture. The only information on Beaumont was his bio at the high school webpage ("*Home of the Pirates!*") and his home address.

"My, God—he lives just two blocks away. We passed it coming over here," Dee said.

The number of hits for unsolved murders was huge, and they couldn't see a pattern that might fit Beaumont. Ryan decided he was influenced from watching too many episodes of *Criminal Minds* on TV. A team of professional agents working full time over a couple of weeks couldn't figure this out, let alone two kids on a single afternoon. This gave Ryan an idea, though. He found Agent Lund's number on his cell phone. He had entered it thinking, *you never know when you'll need the private line of some FBI agent.* He gave the number to Dee, who entered it on hers, and to Mrs. Pullman, who, Ryan was astonished to find out, had her own cell phone. Ryan and Dee had already exchanged cell numbers, and Ryan added her grandmother as well.

When it came time for Ryan to leave, Dee told her grandmother she wanted to walk him home. Ryan thought it was an odd role reversal. Typically boys walked girls home, but he was pleased, especially given how their first walk went.

Earlier in the morning, when his mother relented in allowing him to visit Mrs. Pullman, Ryan's grandmother must have contacted Mrs. Pullman to make the arrangements. Within an hour, the doorbell rang, and Ryan found Dee standing at their front door.

"Hello, I'm Dee," she said. "You must be Ryan. I am supposed to escort you to our home."

Ryan was caught off guard.

"You *are* Ryan aren't you? I was told to look for a kid with his face beat up. It was my mother, by the way, who worked on you."

"Uh...yeah, I'm Ryan. So, it was your mother, the doctor?" Ryan knew he was going down in flames. This was so unexpected. She looked at him as though he was brain-damaged. "Um, I'm sorry. Please come in."

Ryan recovered enough to perform passable introductions. His grandmother exclaimed how "delightful" the whole thing was. Ryan felt humiliated, and was relieved to walk out the door with the girl.

Initially, the walk was awkward. Dee talked only to mention that she lived a few blocks away, and her grandmother thought it would be a good idea for her to pick up Ryan and walk back and show him the sights. After a few minutes, she did point out some touristy type things, like some historic houses. Ryan kept sneaking glances at her. He wasn't all that interested in local history with her by his side.

At one point, Dee glanced at him and asked, "You lived and have this scar–are you supposed to be some kind of Harry Potter?"

Ryan shrugged. "I have no idea."

Dee stopped and squarely faced him, hands on her hips.

"That was supposed to be funny."

"Oh." He noticed a hint of a smile at the corners of her mouth. He smiled back.

"So, what part of your face hurts the worst, if you don't mind my asking?" They resumed walking.

Ryan could only imagine what his face looked like to her. He gave up wearing the dressings and bandages, so now all four sets of stitches stood out in blazing glory. One side of his forehead, both eyes, and both cheeks were deep purple with some slimy green on the edges. If there was one positive side to his appearance, it masked his complexion. He had sprouted a new set of zits recently, which his mother said was probably due to stress, and the injuries drew attention away from them.

"They seem to take turns moving into the first place position of pain rankings. It depends a lot on which part of my head I hit."

Dee laughed at this, and her laughter was deep in her throat, as a much older person would laugh. It was contagious.

"No, I'm serious," Ryan said, laughing. "I have banged my head or hit myself more times in the past few days than I ever had in my entire life. It's really funny."

Dee shook her head in amusement. "You are a strange boy."

* * * *

As they walked away from Dee's house later in the day, she turned to Ryan and asked, "Are you upset?"

Ryan couldn't answer right away. He considered a number of different avenues but none was satisfactory. Finally, he said, "I don't know what I feel. I am not very good at feelings."

"Huh? What does that mean?"

Ryan wondered where this was going. His mother talked this way sometimes. "Okay, I suppose I'm angry. If I think about it too much, I want to yell or hit something. Since that doesn't help, I try to think of a way to work it out."

"This isn't something you can work out, though," Dee countered.

"Sure it is. I just haven't got it yet."

They walked a few more steps in silence, then Dee said, "You cried before, so you must feel something."

Ryan groaned. Dee grabbed his right hand and squeezed. "No, don't feel embarrassed! It's okay to cry."

"It's just that...oh God...it's so stupid." Ryan was fully aware of their hand-holding, and he clasped his hand further around hers.

"Hold on, boy, what's so stupid?"

"It's just that I've cried a couple of times recently. How can you miss people you haven't met?"

"Are you saying you've never cried before all this started happening?"

"I'm not saying that."

"When was the last time?"

"I don't know."

"C'mon. Think."

Ryan thought. "When my father died, I cried for four whole days straight it seemed."

"See, there you go."

"There you go, what?"

"You're good with feelings. That makes you human." She squeezed his hand again.

"I like holding your hand," Ryan said, bravely he thought.

"Oh-oh, maybe we should stop." She pulled her hand away.

"Why?"

"This may be the twenty-first century, but we're still in South Carolina. A multiracial girl holding hands with a white boy. That could draw some attention."

"Will you go out with me?" Ryan couldn't believe he was talking like this.

Dee practically roared with laughter. "Boy, haven't you been listening?"

"Yeah, so?"

"We just met today. It's too soon."

They walked in an amused silence to the end of the block where Dee noticed the street sign.

"This is it."

"What?"

"Beaumont. This is the street he lives on."

"Really? It's so close to where I live, and where you live too."

They craned their necks to look down the street. There were a few parked cars, but no indications a monster lived here. Ryan walked down the street, looking at house numbers.

"What are you doing," she hissed at him, "We can't just walk down looking for the guy."

"Why not? I want to check out the house."

Dee looked at him as if he was out of his mind. "Suppose he sees us? We don't have any plan."

That was a good point. Beaumont would recognize him. When you got right down to it, how would he explain his presence? Dee was right, he needed a plan.

"Yeah, okay. Let's go."

The remaining five minutes of their walk was uneventful. Ryan was deep in thought about Beaumont, and Dee rattled on about kids who would be in their class. The brief flirting episode had come to a close for now. When they turned the corner to the street Ryan lived on, Dee said, "There's my mother."

They trotted to the car which was parked halfway down the block.

"Mom, what are you doing here? Is everything all right?"

Doctor Pullman-Batista had stepped out of her car to greet them. She leaned over the driver side door that was ajar and said, "Yes, sweetheart, everything is fine." Then she turned to Ryan. "Hello to you, Ryan. How are you feeling?"

"Pretty good," Ryan replied. "It doesn't hurt too much anymore."

"Ha! That's not what he said before."

"So, I take it you two met."

"Yeah, Gramma and I had him over for lunch."

"That's what I understand. I talked with Gramma just a little earlier."

"It was very good. I enjoyed it very much," Ryan added.

"Hmm. Including the conversation? I bet that was out of the ordinary."

"Not after the past few days, it wasn't," Ryan said honestly.

"I guess that's probably true. Listen, Dee, I have to work tonight, so I thought I would come and get you for a quick dinner. Also, I would like to know you're home with Gramma when I go back to the hospital."

Dee sighed loudly to indicate the extent of her persecution at the hands of this woman. Then she turned to Ryan and said, "Bye. I'll talk to you later."

Ryan waved back. "See ya'."

Doctor Pullman-Batista remained standing outside her door, looking at Ryan. "Now, son, I want you to stay in tonight. No messing around. I know what you talked about today, and

I don't want you getting too spooked about this whole affair. Just stay home with your family. You need the rest. Are we together on this?"

"Yes, ma'am."

"Such fine southern manners."

"My grandmother's been training me."

* * * *

Eugenia Pullman walked slowly up the stairs to her bedroom. She was eternally grateful that her daughter and son-in-law invited her to live with them.

She wasn't lying when she told the boy she missed her old house near the water.

The time came however, when living alone became difficult. Multiple bouts of cancer left her exhausted, and she needed the support of her family. Living with her daughter turned out to be a joy, with the ebb and flow of family life taking the place of the ocean tides in her daily routine.

The Lord did work in unpredictable ways. She had prayed for many folks over the years, and did what she could for their healing. She always wondered whether the boy who survived the dragon would return to her life. Sure enough, the child born during moments of hellish terror was sitting right there in their kitchen. He had hair the color of late afternoon sunshine, a shy smile, and was apparently attracted to her granddaughter. He also had been seriously battered, and she knew he faced a tremendous trial in the very near future.

When she met Ryan in Carolyn's house just days earlier, she actually thought it was a dream. The act of protecting the child from that demonic entity as it leered through the dining room windows seemed symbolic as many dreams tended to be. The combined impact of her cancer and its treatments, along with the unfinished business of her past, were the likely culprits for her experience. Or so she thought at the time. To hear that the boy saw her, well, that was strangely satisfying. Somehow the Lord saw fit to allow her spirit to be transported. She still had a role to play, to be of some benefit to Ryan and his family.

Eugenia knew she had to travel to Charleston soon. She needed to talk with the only person who had the experience and the knowledge to inform her of what she could do...if anything. *Aunt Tessa...I'm praying you can help.* The inevitable conflict was approaching quickly, more so than anyone realized. This child would face the depths of hell, and if he survived, he would turn into one of their greatest fighters. Of that she was sure.

Eugenia sat at her easy chair in her room. At her side was a table on which she had her Bible and a candle. She lit the candle, and then lifted the book and opened it to the Psalms. Then her hand drifted to the cross on the chain around her neck and she clasped it. She began praying silently to the Lord for the boy's protection from the evil she suspected would befall him very soon. In her mind, the language of her prayers switched easily between English and a dialect that extended back across centuries and miles to the western shores of Africa.

* * * *

Miranda was still kicking herself over allowing Ryan to visit with Mrs. Pullman. While his flustered reaction to the presence of the woman's pretty granddaughter was almost worth the price of admission, she made up her mind that tonight there was going to be some serious talk. She must listen attentively and respectively to Ryan's report of his lunch. She was determined, however, not to allow the supernatural explanations to rule the day. Alternative interpretations must be considered. The big unknown was when to broach the subject with him. When Miranda started questioning him immediately upon sitting down for dinner, she silently berated herself for losing self-control.

"So." She tried to sound casual. "How was your day with Mrs. Pullman?"

Expecting the start of a tirade, Miranda was absolutely flabbergasted when Ryan talked for nearly five minutes straight about the girl. Not only was she delighted he felt comfortable talking about girls with her, but also that he had the opportunity to experience some typically adolescent activity. The accounts of demons and ghosts were gone, at least for a short while. As he described her looks, personality, and her laugh, he was just thrilled with himself...as if this was a major accomplishment for him. Miranda realized it truly was, taken within the context of the past week.

"Do you think it would be a problem for her and me to go out?"

Never underestimate Ryan's ability to dive into tough issues. Miranda stalled for time. "Problem?"

"Yeah. She thinks it could be a problem for a white boy to date a multiracial girl, which is how she called herself, in South Carolina."

Miranda looked to her mother. She was thinking more about putting restrictions on fourteen-year-olds dating. She hadn't considered the racial issue, which might say something positive about her open-mindedness, she supposed.

"Honey, I don't know. That's really not a problem for me, and we shouldn't care what others think." She paused momentarily then decided to share her concerns. "I will be honest. I don't know if you two are ready at your age to start dating."

"Geez, Mom. I'm not talking like that. I mean, things like hanging out together or doing stuff..."

This sounded innocuous, but Miranda recognized this dating thing was going to be a work in progress over the next few years. Good Lord...how do girls and teen sex rate on the stress scale compared to ghosts and mental illness?

Carolyn answered, "She could have had a number of reasons for saying that. She may not be ready to go out with a boy, so it was a good excuse. Or, she may have needed some time to think. Also, and it's important to realize this, the cost to her might be higher than it is to you. Do you understand?"

Ryan reflected on this statement while taking a bite, chewing and swallowing. "I think so. I hadn't considered it. It would be okay for me to talk to her and ask her to do things, wouldn't it? I mean like friends do? Not like a date or anything."

Miranda wondered how these activities would differ from dating, but didn't think discussing these finer distinctions would serve any purpose at this point. "I think that would be fine."

She considered this overall exchange with curiosity. There was no melodrama or turmoil. She hoped Phil was listening somehow.

"Of course, I think Mom wanted to know about my time with Mrs. Pullman." Ryan said, practically daring her to contradict him.

Miranda thought honesty would be best under the circumstances. She would be damned if she would allow him to maneuver her into appearing shallow. She did decide to temper it a little. "Of course, I am very curious, but I'm glad you shared the details about Dee."

Ryan smiled, barely able to conceal his satisfaction. "Okay. I learned a lot of things. I might get some stuff mixed up as I'm talking, so don't call me on any technicalities, Mom. Let me tell the story."

"I've already decided to do that. I promise not to say a word until you're done."

So he told his story. His account started with recognizing Mrs. Pullman as the woman who came to his aid in the dining room the first time the twin appeared. He summarized Beaumont's book and how it fitted in with his dream. He described Mrs. Pullman's version of events and how they read the section in the Book of Revelation. He mentioned the horror of the birth itself and how the twin died (and here there was some stalling of Ryan's part, along with his eye contact with her mother that Miranda found intriguing but nevertheless kept her mouth shut). Ryan recounted rather tenderly how he gleaned information about his biological parents.

"I looked a lot like my biological father. Did you see the picture, Grandma?"

Carolyn cleared her throat. "I did Ryan, and even though it has been a long time since I saw that picture, you're right. You are the spitting image of the young man."

Ryan finished his story by talking about the presence of two demon kids that remained in the area.

"Hugo was on the gate right as you came out the door the other night."

Miranda, who could truthfully recall only the vaguest sense of someone standing by the gate, said nothing.

"We, Dee and me, worked on the computer the rest of the afternoon, searching for Beaumont and serial killers in general. There seem to be a lot of them, by the way."

Miranda could only imagine. Two things did come to mind. The first was that Ryan presented what he learned in a very even tone. The second was that she needed to do the same.

"You're probably aware I am having a lot of trouble with the supernatural perspective."

Ryan nodded. Miranda could tell he was biting his lip to keep from bursting out.

"I don't want you to have to experience an emotional

problem, either. So I am, let's see, caught between a rock and a hard place. Is it better to have a personal problem or be haunted by ghosts and demon children? This is a no win situation as far as I can see. It's just that," and here she paused, choosing her words, "it's just that emotional problems are recognized as real, and you can do something about them. There's no reliable documentation of the things you're talking about. For you, not having an emotional problem is very important...so therefore, the need to make the ghosts real."

Ryan didn't stir. Miranda saw he was considering how to present his counter argument.

"Mom. It's not that I want these guys to be real. They are real. It really isn't a choice for one side or the other. I have evidence, even though you don't believe it." Ryan reminded her about the laughter, the photo on his phone, and the cat blood outside on the sidewalk. "You can argue them all away or think that I somehow did all these things. I didn't. They're real. Someday that will become clear, I think."

Miranda's unease picked up a few notches. He had her pegged correctly. She did think he was creating his evidence... he was smart enough to do it. Yet his sincerity was authentic. She wanted to believe and trust him, but that meant acceptance of the bizarre alternatives.

Miranda felt herself relenting. "Why don't we see how things go over the next couple of days? That's really the only thing I can think of to do. If everything blows over, then we're all the better for it. If not, then we'll have to think about taking steps to intervene."

"Intervene how?"

"Well, finding a psychologist would be the next step." Miranda knew she was on thin ice right now. She could also hear it cracking.

Ryan wasn't happy, but he assented with a nod.

She hadn't fallen into the icy water. At least not yet.

Chapter Eight

After a number of false starts, Ryan took the plunge and dialed the entire number on his cell phone.

"Jeremy Lund."

"Agent Lund?"

"Speaking."

"Um...this is Ryan Perry...you came to my house the other day?"

"Hey, Ryan, how are you?"

"You...you said I should call if I thought of anything." Ryan was on the second floor balcony in an effort to avoid being overheard. The sun had set just below the horizon, and the sky towards the east was almost a dark purple. It made him think of autumn, despite the evening heat.

"Yes, I certainly did." There was silence, which Ryan didn't fill. "Something come to mind?"

"Not the way you're thinking. Um...oh, man...I...I think the guy you're looking for is Arthur Beaumont."

More silence at the other end. Without seeing Lund's face, Ryan didn't have a clue as to what it meant.

"You know who I mean, don't you."

"I do. The biology teacher."

"Yep."

"Ryan, can you tell me what makes you think that Mister Beaumont is involved?"

"You'll think I'm crazy."

"Would you believe me if I told you I have heard and seen a lot of crazy things in my life? Things that would surprise you?"

Ryan thought a bit. "No disrespect, but no. I'm a kid, and adults always say stuff like that, but usually don't mean it."

"I understand. How about this? If you give me information, I will seriously consider it."

Ryan had nothing better to go on, and he had committed himself by making the call.

"Are you from South Carolina, Agent Lund?"

Lund was quiet, and Ryan had a sense he was confused. "No, I was born in Alabama and moved here when I was thirteen."

Ryan was disappointed. He was positive Lund was from South Carolina.

"I moved here to live with my aunt after my mother died. The family is from the area."

Ryan couldn't believe it. "I had a feeling. I think you and Beaumont are related."

"Whoa."

Ryan knew with certainty that Lund was not expecting that one.

"All right, Ryan. I'm hooked. Tell me what you know."

"It's kind of a long story."

"Give me the short version now, and we can talk later."

Ryan recounted everything just as he had for his mother and grandmother. This time, however, he began his story by rehashing the Old Bay Road incident and proceeded from that point. He left out some details that might get his grandmother or Mrs. Pullman in trouble. He also summarized Beaumont's ebook.

Agent Lund didn't say a word during the tale. Ryan heard him tapping on a keyboard, probably taking notes. When he finished, Lund asked a few clarification questions, making sure he had the narrative correct.

"So, you don't know where these kids live? You've just seen them around the park?"

"And on Old Bay Road."

"Right, there too. Nowhere else?"

"No sir, that's it. I don't know where they live."

"You say Beaumont was with them that one time, and some woman arrived and picked them up."

"Uh-huh."

"Do you remember the make of car?"

"No. It was just a beat up piece of shit. I would've been really embarrassed to drive it. The car was white though."

"Okay, a rusty, shitty white car. Plates?"

"No, didn't see them."

There was silence for a few seconds before Ryan's phone started beeping. His battery was draining.

"Agent Lund? My battery is going."

"Okay, Ryan, I think I have enough for now."

Ryan was suddenly nervous. Was he going to say, 'it's time to take you in to the station'?

"I've got a lot to mull over. We'll need to talk again. Okay?"

"Okay."

"Your story is quite out of the ordinary, I'll give you that. Still, it's not so bizarre that I will dismiss it out of hand."

"You mean, you believe me?" Ryan was cautiously hopeful.

"Remember, I told you I've seen and heard many strange things."

"What kind of things?"

"Maybe we'll talk about them sometime. For now though, keep your mom and grandmother company tonight."

"Yeah. Don't worry. I've got nothing better to do."

"Good boy. Let's keep in touch."

"Oh wait! I can't believe I didn't think of this. I have a picture sent to me by Beaumont. You know, of that party?" The phone beeped again. "Crap. I'll recharge some and then send it to you."

"I can't wait to see it."

* * * *

Ryan awoke for no particular reason other than it was morning. He felt normal. His clock read 8:30. He remembered turning the light off at ten, so he had, what, ten and a half hours of sleep. Truly awesome. His arm and injuries didn't hurt either, so that was pretty cool.

He wanted to do something...specifically, he wanted to collect evidence. While watching one of the *CSI* TV shows last night, he started getting ideas. He could investigate as well as anyone, and he just had a brainstorm about how to check things out without being noticeable.

Ryan found some workout clothes on the floor and pulled them on. They didn't smell too badly, so he figured he had another day's use out of them. He grabbed his running shoes, and scampered down the stairs.

His grandmother sat at the kitchen table sipping a cup of coffee.

"Hey." He pulled out a chair, sat down, and immediately bent over to tie his sneakers.

"Well, you're up early," she said. "What are you up to?"

"I'm gonna go run. I need to get out."

"The warden has been too tough on you?"

"Nah." he smiled. "Just something to do."

"You haven't eaten anything."

Ryan bounced from the chair and strode to the counter. One remaining box of granola bars sat next to the coffee pot. "I don't like to eat before I run." He opened the box. "Oh, man, there's only three left." Ryan took out two.

"I bought four boxes of those two days ago," she said, sounding surprised.

"Grandma, these things don't hang around forever. I'm a growing boy."

"You rascal. Come here and give me a kiss good morning and goodbye."

Ryan did, right on the cheek, and turned to move.

"Wait, what about water?"

He returned to the refrigerator and took out a small plastic bottle and slipped it in the pocket of his gym shorts. It was uncomfortable, but he would carry it when he finished the granola bars.

"I thought you didn't like to eat before you ran?" His grandmother asked a question each time he got close to the door.

"What? These?" He held up the bars. "These don't count." He burst out the door before she asked anything else.

From the moment he got up, Ryan was considering his investigative plan. He wanted to return to Old Bay Road to see it under different circumstances. He realized this was just like the course of action stupid people took in horror movies where they check out some noise all alone and end up being snuffed out by the serial killer. He felt relatively safe though. Hugo and Max had plenty of opportunities to knock him off and they hadn't done it yet.

Ryan walked to the edge of the park and sat on the bench and finished his second granola bar. A thin film of moisture already coated every inch of his body. Once again, he was glad for the water. He took a few sips and then stood, stretched, and began a leisurely jog in the same direction he took before.

After his jaunt through the woods he would run towards town and innocently glide by Beaumont's house. Just to check it out. He couldn't imagine the whole thing would take more than an hour and a half, but he would take his time. He also had his cell phone in another pocket, in case of...whatever.

After twenty minutes, the wooded tunnel of Old Bay

Road beckoned. Ryan was pleased with how good he felt. He wasn't that winded, and the tightness he did have after days of lounging around dissipated with each passing step. The thin film of moisture transformed into a running waterfall of sweat, though, and his T-shirt was drenched. He stripped off his shirt before he entered the woods and inserted it into his waistband for safekeeping.

Ryan hadn't taken two steps into the woods when he stopped short. The thought of entering the wooded area of Old Bay Road had been wearing on his mind. How would it look? In his wildest dreams he never anticipated what he found.

There had to be twenty people exercising, walking, or exploring the area. Families with kids, men, women, you name it. Relief flooded his entire body.

"Okay, piece of cake." He resumed his run.

The run was so relaxing his mind wandered. Starting school. How would that go? He imagined himself trying to engage in conversations or people asking who he was. He thought of lines of dialogue and rehearsed them. Would he find the right kinds of kids? Girls...girls...girls, what would it be like to have a girlfriend? What about senior jerks...would he have to fend them off just because he was the new kid?

Then there were the team sports. What should he try out for? Baseball for sure, but that would be spring...track...freshman basketball? He saw himself ten years from now at bat, bottom of the ninth, his team behind by three runs, two outs, bases loaded, seventh game of the World Series. The count expanding to 3-2, runners go, the pitch, fouled off...the crowd exhaling simultaneously to momentarily relieve stress...he returns to the batter's box, the pitcher sets, runners go, the pitch, swung on...*deep to left field...waaay back...going...going...gone! Grand slam!* The crowd going nuts as Ryan sprints around the bases, turns past third base and towards home...

...and Ryan found himself at the end of the tunnel. The beach was before him. God, that was great. He knew he was grinning like a dope, but he couldn't help it.

Families and groups lounged on towels and blankets. Sounds of laughter and excited yells of kids mixed with the pounding surf of the ocean. Multicolored umbrellas dotted the beach like giant thumbtacks. The presence of other people made him feel human. He thought about running along the water's edge, but knew he had to complete his tour. His problem wasn't going away, and he still had lots to learn.

He retraced his steps down the wooded tunnel, paying more attention this time. He noticed a few strips of the yellow crime scene tape so he suspected the couple had been killed nearby. Other than that, there was nothing. Absolutely nothing that he saw that would enlighten him about Beaumont or those two little demon dorks. He reached the opposite end feeling disappointed.

He decided to take a different route back home, so ran down a road parallel to the one he took earlier. The houses along this road were a mixed breed. There were nice suburban type homes with neat lawns and shrubbery, with a few small palm trees or oak trees. Others were small and ill-kept, and some looked like run-down old modular homes. Many of these had no landscaping, or if they did it was overgrown.

His mind wandered back to his twin. Ryan was beginning to realize something. The twin's appearances were becoming more...how could he describe them...personal, maybe.

There were what, three instances. Right? Four, if you counted the dream. Each time, there was more contact between them.

The first time, the twin wasn't even in the house. Ryan saw clearly the claw tapping the outside of the glass. The figure was on the porch.

The second time he was on the inside. He pounded on the door. Neither his mother nor grandmother heard all of the commotion. The twin didn't touch him, though, but instead ran right through him. Could they have touched if the twin wanted to? Ryan didn't know.

The third time they did touch. There was the scratch...on his shoulder...the laugh. His mother heard the laugh. Then the dream...and this absolutely wasn't a dream. Well, at least not completely. Ryan still had the picture on his cell phone, so he knew it really happened. Yet, and this was the disturbing thing, behind the two of them there was nothing to see. It was pitch black. No one else was there. No party. It was night. He and his twin though. They were there. Together. The twin's arm around his shoulder. The twin's kiss moments before the photo was taken. The photo courtesy of Beaumont—who was definitely there.

Did there closeness mean the twin was somehow getting stronger? Or was he just messing with his mind somehow?

Ryan's pace slowed to a near crawl as he was trying to make sense of all of this stuff. As a result, one of the neighborhood modular homes caught his attention. He might have missed it had he been running at anywhere near his normal speed.

The house was a nondescript gray with a hint of mud or rust along the bottom. The shrubs were dense, and the palmetto trees seemed haphazardly placed. A car had been backed up towards the front door. The trunk was open, and someone moved from the car into the house and back again. This pattern repeated itself as Ryan ran along the street towards the house. A woman, Ryan now saw, was packing up quickly, tossing clothes and belongings into the trunk. As he came abreast, he saw a hand reach for the top of the trunk and pull it down. It slammed with a hesitant sound as if unsure it could handle the heavy load.

The woman saw Ryan, and recognition appeared on her face. Ryan was confused. He didn't know anyone out here.

Then it hit him. He looked straight at Lizette. The packed car was the same white piece of shit he described to Lund.

"You gonna rat on me?" She recognized him...somehow.

Ryan thought she looked torn between anger and terror.

"What? No way. Why would I do that?" He realized she was fleeing. "You're trying to get away."

"What of it?"

"Nothing. It's a good idea."

She nodded at this remark, looking as though she felt safer. "I can't take this shit anymore." She turned to look at the house.

"I know." Ryan thought he did.

"Thanks, but you really don't." Lizette paused, seeming to weigh her options. Then she plunged in. "Arthur is a sadistic fucker. All these years I've been looking over my shoulder thinking he was going to do God knows what to me, but he never did. Oh, he threatened to. That's how he kept me in line." She reached up for the front door of the house and pulled it closed. "It never occurred to me he needed me to keep these little shits in line. Supposedly they lived here and I was their mother, but Arthur came for them whenever he felt like it. I can see the writing on the wall now. My usefulness is ending, and he won't let me live to tell anyone about it."

So, Hugo and Max lived right near Old Bay Road. They had easy access to the woods...

"I'm sorry," Ryan said. "I...I'm trying to learn things about him and those two kids..."

"They're not kids," she interrupted. "They're evil, manipulative monsters. They're like animals living for the moment. They eat, hurt, and kill. They only serve one thing. You should see the inside of that house. If you only knew what they are capable of...what they've done."

Ryan had a pretty good idea and started to share his experiences, but she wasn't listening.

"Stay away from them, but I think you already know that... Don't be like me. I was so stupid. Arthur could be so charming. I thought I was cool as a kid, telling folks I was into witchcraft. I dressed in all black. Then I met Arthur, the man of my dreams. I lost two of my own babies so those things would live. Can you imagine that? Can you imagine what place in hell is reserved for me for what I've done?"

"God, Lizette...maybe talk to the police or get some help somehow."

She waved him off. "No, no, no. I'm beyond that, kid. It's hopeless."

"Do you know where you're going to go?"

"No, I miss my family, but I burned that bridge a long time ago." She walked to the driver's side and eased her frame into the front seat. "You said you wanted to learn something. I can't tell you much except those two were bred somehow. Two guys were involved, but they never knew what hit them. After they played their part, Arthur got rid of them." She stared out the front windshield, not focusing on much. "I'm haunted by their faces. They were sweet guys...Jesse Munoz and Dustin Reilly, missing for twelve and nine years." She turned back to face Ryan. "Now you know something no one else knows."

She pulled the door closed and started the car. Blue smoke erupted from the tailpipe. The noise from the engine grated on his ears. Lizette drove for five feet and then stopped. The window rolled down.

She turned back to him and stared, as if trying to find the right words. After a few seconds, she gave up and just sighed. "Good luck kid."

"Good luck, Lizette." The window closed before he finished. As she pulled towards the street Ryan yanked out his cell phone and took a picture of the rear of the car. She turned down the street, and Ryan stood in silence near the front door.

He walked about ten feet down the driveway, turned and took a picture of the house, making sure he had the house number in the frame.

* * * *

The street where Beaumont lived was not a through street so vehicle activity was minimal. Lund sat in his car sipping the last dregs of an ice coffee. He'd been parked for nearly an hour two houses down from Beaumont's address, under the shade of an oak tree. Two local officers sat in the vicinity, so he wasn't really needed. Still, he was planning to watch a bit longer, hoping to make first contact with the teacher.

For the umpteenth time, Lund shook his head and laughed to himself. Damn if that Perry kid didn't find something that practically blew him out of the water. He downloaded and read Beaumont's ebook. Lund would certainly need to explore family history more closely. The parallels between his childhood and Beaumont's description were uncanny.

Beyond this information, Ryan established a connection between Beaumont and the two feral kids. Lund knew these kids, or something like them, existed for they fitted the profile he was examining. Leads had been elusive for the past five years, but now a break. For the first time, he had potential names and descriptions.

Who was Beaumont, though? Any connection among unsolved murders that hadn't been considered before in light of where Beaumont was living? A comparison of seemingly unrelated crimes not previously examined... On and on...the databases were cranking...

His cell phone vibrated.

"Lund."

"Agent...this is Simon on the north end...this Perry kid, does he have blond hair, slender, with a broken wrist?"

Lund sat up straight. "Yeah. That sounds like him."

"Well, he's headed your way. He's jogging, and checking out our house at the same time."

"You've got to be kidding. Okay, thanks. He's coming into view."

Ryan was maybe twenty feet away, trying to look ordinary and unnoticeable, but obviously sneaking glances at Beaumont's house. He couldn't be more obvious if he was carrying a large sign reading, "I'm spying on your house".

"Ryan. Get in the car."

The kid had no idea Lund was watching and his startled response almost caused him to fall flat on his face.

"Oh...hey...what are you doing here?" Ryan peered in the car window, followed by glancing up and down the street.

"What am I doing here? What are you doing here? Don't say working out." The latter was true as far as it went. His hair hung in wet clumps, streams of perspiration flowed freely down his face and chest. His shirt was soaked and flopped limply over his waistband above his backside.

"Um..."

"Ryan. In the car. Now...Please."

Ryan hung his head and made his way to the car. He removed his shirt out of the back of his shorts and put it on. He sat tentatively on the passenger seat.

"Am I in trouble?"

"Depends on whether you tell me the truth or not. What are you doing here?"

Ryan sighed. "Investigating."

"Investigating. I think that falls under my job description. Not yours."

The boy nodded, and hesitantly looked up at Lund. "I found out some more evidence for you this morning."

"Okay, tell me."

Ryan related his discovery of the house and conversation with Lizette.

"This time I got you the plates, and I have the address." He took out his cell phone tapped it a few times and gave it to Lund. He saw the two pictures, one of the rear of the car, the other of the house.

Lund was nonplussed. He was overjoyed at the stroke of good luck, but wanted to knock the kid senseless at the same time. He radioed the information to the local police, requesting a squad be sent to the house and see if anyone was home and for everyone to be on the lookout for a fifteen-year-old Honda Accord. He described the condition and gave the plate numbers.

"That was an Accord? No way."

"You're just not used to seeing them look like this. It really was an Accord." Lund returned the cell phone to Ryan.

"I feel bad for Lizette."

Lund looked at Ryan. "Why? She did nothing all these years while some major crimes were committed. People were murdered. She could have stopped it."

"I think she was scared."

"I think you're right. She was probably petrified. As hard as it sounds, that doesn't excuse her for not doing the right thing. We could have offered protection."

Lund watched the boy consider this. "Yeah, but," Ryan said, "you guys don't know what it's like. They're monsters. I've seen them. She's lived with them and she's probably seen even weirder things. You're so scared... you don't know what to do. This is not easy." The boy's volume level rose slightly as he finished.

The car was hot since it now contained a sweating teenager, and whatever breeze came off the ocean was not making it into the interior of the car. Lund was torn about what to tell the kid, but only for a fraction of a second. The kid needed someone to trust.

"I know more than you think. I want to tell you a story, but first I am going to drive you home. We'll sit in the park across the street from your house. This car is getting uncomfortable, and it's starting to smell like a locker room. I've got to get out of here."

* * * *

The kid sat beside him on the park bench. They were both positioned slightly to the side so they were facing each other. Ryan was savoring a sports drink.

When Lund pulled up at the Perry house minutes before, the kid ran inside to get his mother. Lund walked slowly up the front porch and was climbing the steps when Mrs. Perry and Ryan appeared.

"Do you want one of these?" Ryan held up the plastic bottle.

"I appreciate your asking, but no thanks."

Mrs. Perry carried what appeared to be a sketch pad containing partial drawings of children and animals. "Ryan says you want to tell him a story. I'm wondering if I should be there."

Ryan's face immediately became stricken. Lund responded before a row could develop.

"You certainly can if you insist. The story he refers to is a personal experience of mine that might help him put his current situation in perspective. I was hoping to share it just with him. He would be free to share it with you later."

Mrs. Perry looked torn.

"We'll be sitting right over there." Lund motioned towards the park across the street.

"C'mon, Mom. It's cool."

Mrs. Perry shrugged and said, "Okay."

"All right. Thanks, Mom."

"Ryan, can you find us a decent bench? In the shade."

Ryan ran down the stairs and headed for the park.

"I'm not trying to be mysterious." Lund turned to the mother. "I've had some experiences growing up that were... out of the ordinary when I was around Ryan's age. Before, he said people like me don't have a clue what he is going through. I actually do, so I thought, what the heck. If you do have any concerns, feel free to stop over."

"I do, actually, but at the moment he's intrigued, and I expect he'd be furious if I sat in."

Lund nodded his understanding, and then took his leave.

Sitting next to him on the bench, Lund noticed the boy's demeanor had become cautious. He knew kids struggle with what role to adopt when finding themselves with unfamiliar adults in situations beyond the norm. The kid's hesitancy showed common sense.

Sometimes the dramatic worked best, so Lund plunged right in.

"I'm going to tell you the scariest thing that ever happened to me. Two days before my thirteenth birthday, I escaped from hell. I ended up at the sheriff's house, and he saved my life. My relatives tried to kill me. I think they were demons."

The kid's eyes flew open like a snapped window shade.

Lund nodded his satisfaction, and continued. "The worst year of my life was when I was twelve. My mother died..."

Chapter Nine

Jeremy Lund's Story:

The worst year of my life was when I was twelve. My mother died when her car hydroplaned on I-65 somewhere between Birmingham and Montgomery in heavy rain from the remnants of a late season hurricane. She slid into a truck which lost control and tangled the two of them into a fiery crash. She died instantly. The truck driver survived with only a broken collarbone.

When it happened, I was playing basketball after school with some kids. One of the other moms ran into the gym and pulled me aside. I couldn't understand what she was saying for the longest time. Gradually, bits and pieces sank in, and when the overall scope of the news hit me, I just fell to the gym floor. I remember just lying there thinking, *What am I going to do?*

A social worker tried to locate my father, but I knew without any facts that he was dead. We hadn't heard from him in over three years, and in terms of overall importance in my life, he scored a big zero. He showed up once when I was five, and there were cards with a couple of bucks in them for two birthdays. That was all I ever saw of my old man. Turned out I was right, they discovered the shithead died in a bar fight somewhere in Texas. The social worker was concerned I would be further traumatized with this news, so she broke it to me gently. I assured her I barely knew the jerk, so it was no great loss to me. It truly wasn't.

If they wanted devastating impact, my mom's death certainly qualified. She would never light the world on fire, but she was pretty stable in my life. She kept the books for an auto dealership in town, she rode me hard when it came to homework, and she attended games when she could. Now she was gone.

I spent November and December bouncing around some different foster families, and some of those people were crazy. Not just the other foster kids either. You know what was the worst? I don't even remember Christmas or Thanksgiving that year. I do remember crying a lot, and I guess I was depressed. Right before school started after Christmas break, my social worker contacted me.

"Your aunt is willing to take you."

"My aunt?" I knew I had one in South Carolina, my father's sister, but I never met her. My mom hardly ever talked about her, but when she did she always called her "that psycho".

The social worker said my aunt was thrilled to take me, but I didn't believe her. I got the feeling she wanted to get rid of me. Still, there I was, just a few days later on a bus to South Carolina. I arrived late in the afternoon in Charleston, nervous as hell.

I walked into the bus station not knowing what was going to happen. When my aunt did appear, she certainly wasn't what I expected.

"You must be Jeremy." She was a tall woman who seemed younger than my mother. She had bleached blond hair, with about an inch of dark roots showing. You know how you get certain things in your mind that you can't shake? For me it was a faint mustache that I spotted on her upper lip. It looked as though it had been bleached like her hair.

"You must be Aunt Leanne." I was afraid we'd have this tearful meeting, but I didn't have to worry. She wasn't the tearful, hugging type. Instead she sort of scrutinized me to the point I felt uncomfortable.

"You do look a bit like Roscoe."

"Roscoe?"

"Your deadbeat father and my deadbeat bother."

"I thought his name was Louis."

"It was. We just called him Roscoe. We started calling him that after our dog with that name died."

So, I learned my father was named after a dead dog.

"Sorry about your mother, kid. Let's get your stuff and get out of here."

The ride to the house was about an hour. As she pulled up to the driveway, she said, "Cam is excited to meet you."

"Who's Cam?"

"Didn't they tell you? He's your cousin. He's older, fifteen."

Well, that was something. I started thinking maybe this wouldn't be so bad with another kid. The house was a run-down looking ranch house. Really, though, none of the houses in the neighborhood were kept up. Paint was peeling, litter, tons of cars parked all over the place. That kind of thing.

I had to lug two suitcases down to a guest room at the end of the hall. The room was kind of ratty, with a bed, chest of drawers, and a closet. I was putting clothes into the chest when I realized this teenager was standing in the doorway. I figured this had to be Cam. He was tall like his mother, but he was soft. Like the type of kid who just sits in front of a computer all day.

I made the first step, going, "hey."

Cam didn't say anything, but just continued to stare.

I felt really stupid because I didn't know what to do. "You're Cam, right? I'm Jeremy." I held out my hand to Cam. "Your cousin."

Cam didn't move, and just when I was going to drop my hand, Cam lifted his. I shook it, but it was disgusting. The hand seemed wet and cold and he had no grip. The kid didn't know how to shake hands.

Finally, Cam spoke to me. "Do you like girls?"

I wasn't sure I heard correctly. "What?"

"Do you think my mom is pretty?"

I was getting confused.

"Do you want to have sex with her?"

Okay, now I was genuinely freaked out. "What? No. God, no."

"Bastard." Cam turned and walked away. I couldn't tell if he was mad because I looked like I wanted to sleep with his mother or didn't want to sleep with her.

Dinner that first night was pretty normal. We talked about things like TV and computer games and foods we liked, so I felt a little better. When my aunt wasn't around, Cam would look at me really strange, like he was leering. It felt creepy and dirty.

When I went to bed, I don't remember if I cried or not, but at the very least I must have felt like it. My birthday was coming up, and that was bumming me out. I also couldn't imagine spending six more years with these people.

I had no way of knowing at the time I would only be with them for a few more days.

* * * *

I spent my fist day in South Carolina avoiding my aunt and cousin. I borrowed a bike from the garage and went into town. I explored every inch of the place—parks, the downtown, main street...you name it. I found a shopping mall and went to a movie.

When I returned, my aunt was rather pissed.

"Where've you been all day?"

I told her.

"Why didn't you spend time with Cam?"

How do you answer something like this, that I thought her kid was a walking freak show? I went the white lie route. "I just needed to spend time by myself."

I remember how she smirked when I said that. I knew then and there that Cam told her what he had said to me the night before. Either that or she just knew—like one of those telepathy things. The fact that she wasn't disturbed by it really creeped me out.

Right as we were finishing dinner that night, the doorbell rang. My aunt asked me to answer the door.

There was this older guy in a uniform standing on the front porch. The way he reacted, I could tell he wasn't expecting me.

The guy said, "I'm Sheriff Hagerton. Who're you, if you don't mind me asking?"

"Jeremy Lund."

"Well, Jeremy, are you visiting?"

"No, sir. I live here now. With my aunt and cousin. My mother died."

The sheriff seemed genuinely upset. It made me feel good for some reason. "I'm sorry to hear that son. When did you get in?"

"Yesterday."

I think I asked him to come inside and then he asked if my aunt was at home.

"Yes, sir, I'll get her."

"Before you do, tell me, where are you from?"

"Alabama."

"So, a southern boy all the way around."

"Yes, sir."

By this time, my aunt showed up at the door and she was really put out.

"What do you want?" Really kind of rude, and then she

turned to me. "Go to your room now, and shut the door. This is private."

I went to my room, but left the door ajar. I was trying to eavesdrop, I admit it. I heard the sheriff mention something about missing kids. My aunt got really pissed, saying Cam had nothing to do with it.

When I heard this, I thought, *holy crap.*

The sheriff asked if he could speak to Cam, but my aunt told him to go to hell.

"You're raising your nephew now."

"My brother's boy. What of it?"

"He's going to school?"

"Yeah, he's going—seventh grade. Damn social workers…"

"Good. I'd like to talk to him."

"What part of 'go to hell' don't you understand?"

"It's about basketball, Leanne. You and Cam can join us if you like."

Then she told the sheriff to fuck off, and yelled for me.

Of course, I knew the sheriff wanted to talk to me, but I had to play it as if I had no idea. So I stuck my head out the bedroom. "Yeah?"

"Get over here. The sheriff wants to talk."

I was a little nervous to talk to the guy. I wasn't a screw up at my old home, but I had gotten into a little trouble. So I didn't like talking to cops. Turns out, I didn't need to worry.

"Come here for a second, Jeremy." The sheriff opened the door and stepped to the porch. I followed in my socks.

"Do you play basketball?"

I remember thinking, *whoa*, and getting excited. "Yeah, I love basketball."

The sheriff nodded. "I coach the seventh grade boys' team."

"You coach basketball?"

He had a sense of humor. "Yes, I coach. Is that a surprise?"

I didn't know how to respond. You know how it is when adults ask you rhetorical questions.

"I coached both of my boys. They're in the army now, but I still keep coaching. Do you want to play?"

"Definitely."

"Perfect. Right after school, in the gym."

"I'll be there."

What happened next is forever sealed in my memory. The sheriff started walking to his car but then he stopped. He had taken out one of his business cards and was writing something on it. "This is my address and home phone number." He handed the card to me. "Son, if anything strange happens here—and I do mean 'strange'—I want you to come and talk to me."

Later that night the creepy stuff really started happening. I took a shower before going to bed. When I got back to my room, I was trying to decide what to wear in the morning. You know, it was the first day at a new school, and I was pretty anxious. I didn't want to wear the wrong thing. Then I remembered I needed shorts and a T-shirt for basketball.

So I was gathering up all of this stuff, and the whole thing couldn't have taken very long. Of course, for a girl it would take a lot longer, but for a boy, simple. Meanwhile, I was just starting to get dressed for bed and I realized that somebody was watching me. I just knew it. I noticed the door was cracked about two inches. To this day, I know I closed that door. No one was in the hallway when I stepped out, but I sensed Cam's door had just clicked. That piece of shit had been spying on me.

* * * *

The first day of school was not as bad as I expected. I didn't have any of the books yet, so I didn't have to do any homework.

What was really cool was that the kids were okay. I fully expected to get beaten up or harassed like they do to new kids, but they were really curious about me. It turned out the school was rather small, so everyone knew everyone's business. Of course, that meant me as well. They all knew my story, which was a little weird, but at least I didn't have to keep telling it over and over again. Everyone also knew I played basketball, so that more than anything probably made the transition easy.

I remember that first lunch period. This kid named Parker waved me over to his lunch table. Other kids joined, both boys and girls, and the table became full quickly.

"So, you live with that weird kid," Parker said.

"Yeah. Do you know him?" There was no sense denying Cam was weird.

I discovered only that morning that Cam was home-schooled when it dawned on me that I was the only one leaving for school. I met his tutor on his way into the house as I was leaving...some college guy looking for extra cash, probably. Frankly, I was relieved. That also meant that no one really "knew" him.

"He's got a reputation," one of the girls said.

I started getting really worried that I was going to get the same reputation based on association.

Somebody else said, "He peeps in kids' windows."

Now, that I had direct experience with.

Wendy, she was Parker's girlfriend, added, "There's this girl in the ninth grade. She says she woke up and saw him staring right through an open window. There was only a screen on it. She swears his eyes were red."

"He touches kids too," Parker said. "I mean... you know." He pointed to his crotch. "Boys and girls."

The other kids cracked up. "God, Parker. Just say he's a pervert."

"I heard he set fire to a trailer once."

Anyway, it went on and on. I was very relieved to hear they weren't including me in the same category as Cam.

If the first school day was good, my first practice after school was even better. I remember the sheriff greeted me with a sincere, "So, how are things going?"

He was a hard coach. He made us go through all kinds of drills, but I loved every minute. I felt normal being there, and I really liked the guy.

When I returned to the house, my aunt announced, "Good Lord, you stink," as I walked through the door. "Take your shower now before dinner."

I wanted to argue, but I couldn't figure on what grounds without saying I was worried about Cam. That creep was watching from the hall, and I remember him smirking as I passed. I had the last laugh however. I brought a fresh change of clothes into the bathroom, which had a lock. So I could change in safety.

That night, things got even worse. I woke up from a sound sleep at 1:15 in the morning. It was a really strange sensation, like someone was trying to warn me, but in a helpful way. I felt as though I was being pulled up urgently from the ocean floor. Anyway, I awoke disoriented, and I didn't know where I was. When everything started to come together, I really started to freak out.

Something was in my room.

There was this slithering along the floor. It was something big, and it was moving along the floor beside my bed.

I tried to look, but I was really scared. Suddenly, the thing stood up on hind legs.

I thought it was Cam. It seemed like it at first. Of course, the room was too dark to be sure. Then I was having my doubts. The hands were claws, and the eyes were a deep red.

The thing dropped down to all fours on the floor, and I tried to sit up higher and look over the bed.

Next thing I knew, I was face to face with it. The thing propped its hands or, God I don't know, front claws, onto the bed like a dog. Do you know what I mean?

I fell back into the bed. I saw then that, yeah, it was Cam, but man, he had transformed. He wasn't...human.

This thing throws the bed covers off me. I panicked. Then, the claws latched on to me.

Now, of course, I am absolutely terrified. I started to scream, "No, no" and I twisted to turn on a lamp by my bed. When I did that, I felt the claws scrape my skin.

The lamp turned on...

I sensed something bolt from the room, but it was so fast... I was alone in the room.

I started talking to myself out loud, "It was a dream." Still, I stood up and looked around the floor. Naturally, there was nothing there.

I remember I got back in bed and turned off the light. I was afraid I was going to lose my mind before I turned eighteen and could get out of there.

When I awoke the next morning, I felt like hell. I had no idea how much I slept, but I figured it couldn't have been good sleep. Dragging myself to a sitting position took every ounce of effort I had.

I took off my undershirt and reached for my jeans and began to pull them on. What I saw almost knocked me over. I had to close my eyes to stop my head from spinning.

There were three scratch marks on the skin right here, on my lower right abdomen.

My mind started racing. *You felt those claws scratch you when you turned away to turn on the light.*

Somehow I got the courage to pull the waist band of my boxers away from my skin, and then pull downward. The scratches extended an inch or two further towards my hip.

At this moment, the sheriff's words came back to me—"Son, if anything strange happens here–and I do mean 'strange'–I want you to come and talk to me".

I finished getting dressed, grabbed everything I needed for school, and got the hell out of the house as fast as I could. Cam's tutor was arriving again as I was leaving, but I must have looked panicked because he asked me if I was okay. I remember mumbling something like, "yeah sure", but this guy must have felt obligated to make small talk. He started telling me how much he appreciated the opportunity to work with Cam, which I thought was weird because who could ever enjoy being around that sleaze bag. I just kept walking and telling him how I was late. I didn't want to hang around for any longer than I had to for anyone.

* * * *

Somehow, I made it through that school day. Maybe it was relatively easy because I felt safe. Looking back on it, I remain impressed at how well I was able to hold it together. I don't think anyone noticed I was a wreck.

I was going to talk to the sheriff after practice. I had only been in that house for three days and I had enough of all the weird shit that was going on.

When I arrived at the gym, I was devastated. There was some other guy doing the coaching. My expression said it all, because this guy came over to me right away.

"You seem disappointed. We haven't met."

"What? Oh, no. Not really. I was just expecting to see the sheriff."

It turned out this was the assistant coach, one of the dads. He filled in whenever the sheriff couldn't make it due to some emergency. Just my luck something happened that day which kept him tied up at the office.

"Hey Dad." I turned to see Parker walking up. "This is Jeremy, the new guy."

I was really pleased to meet Parker's father. Parker ended up becoming one of my closest friends, and his dad was a great guy. He just couldn't address my immediate problem.

Parker's dad ended up bringing me home with Parker for a snack after practice. I think he must've had some kind of parent sixth sense operating and knew I really didn't want to go home right away. Anyway, this is another one of those memories that remain crystal clear. The weather was pretty warm, so we ate chocolate chip cookies outside on the porch in our gym stuff. I shared for the first time how I hated living with my aunt. I didn't go into the creepy details, but confided I was having trouble hitting it off with my cousin. I was so happy when Parker said I could come over anytime, and even sleep over whenever I wanted.

I must've stayed for about an hour at Parker's. When I got back to the house, I found it quiet.

"Hey, it's me," I called as I walked in the door and dropped my backpack. I took off my sneakers and dirty socks at the door, an old habit instilled by my mother. I wondered where Cam and my aunt were. Almost immediately, I heard a faint sound from outside in the back yard. A window was open because of the pleasant evening, that's how I think I heard it.

Only the living room and kitchen lights were on, and I worked my way towards the kitchen. If you can picture this, the garage was detached and away from the house. So, from the kitchen, I could look outside and see the entire garage. The door was shut, but I saw lights on inside through the windows.

That's when I noticed my aunt and Cam. They were beside the garage in the shadows. It was starting to get dark, but still light enough to see. To the casual observer, it would look like they were preparing a garden. I knew they weren't the gardening types, so I was curious what was going on. Internal alarm bells were going off, and I was torn between staying inside and going outside. Curiosity got the better of me, but I inched my way out the back door as quietly as I could so I could approach without being noticed.

They must have been thirty feet away, but I really couldn't judge the distance. As I got closer, I noticed a number of tools, which they had obviously removed from the garage. I first saw a garden rake and a shovel, and noticed they too were using shovels.

Three black drawstring plastic trash bags were on the ground by their work site. They were digging a hole and obviously planned to bury something. I noticed the hole was rather deep, because my aunt had difficulty climbing out. Cam, who was slacking off, had to lend her a hand. I remember thinking how strong he looked as he lifted her out, which really surprised me.

Suddenly, Cam started to get really agitated and shaking violently. Then, he starts to change, and he is growing these claws and his eyes are turning red. Jagged teeth elongated before my eyes. I knew at that point I wasn't imagining what I saw the previous night.

He ripped open the plastic bags, one after the other. My aunt just stood there like this was an everyday thing.

He reached into the first bag and pulled out this doll. The smell practically overpowered me, it was God awful. I realized this wasn't a doll, but a little kid. I remembered then what the sheriff had said on my first Sunday night. Something about missing kids. I put it all together.

Oh, God.

It got worse. He didn't seem to like this one, so he tossed the kid in the hole. He did the same with the next one. Then he got to the last, and I swear to God he smiled. His jaw seemed to keep falling open, I swear, and he tossed the kid in this wide open mouth, and swallowed it without chewing. The dead kid slid down his throat without resistance.

They heard me somehow. I think I gagged or retched or something.

Cam bent over at the waist, his arms were extended in front of him and his hands were sharp claws. I was in deep trouble.

"The serpent needs another heir. So we need him. You know that." My aunt was talking to Cam. "Get him, but keep him whole, for now." Cam growled deep in his throat.

I must have said something stupid like, "What?" or "Who?"

"The evil one. The prince of darkness...you're old enough."

I started backing away.

"Get him," my aunt roared.

Cam charged. He was fast. I backpedaled and saw there was no way I could escape. I tripped over the rake. I fell to my knees and I knew I was dead. My last coherent thought was to grab something, and I think it was the shovel.

I stood and raised it just as Cam pounced—honest it was just like that. The mouth opening seemed way out of proportion. He was flying towards me.

Somehow I got the shovel right at his gaping mouth on the downward arc of his leap. With a sickening sound, I rammed it down his throat as his forward momentum continued. His eyes rounded in shock and he made this choking sound. He knocked me down when he fell, and his arms flailed. His claws scraped my legs. I was trapped under him for a few seconds, but he rolled in agony and I must have screamed, or maybe it was my aunt. I still don't know. I scrambled to my feet and started running.

I heard my aunt wailing. "Cam! Cam!" then, "What did you do?" I knew she was yelling this after me. Porch lights were going on in the neighborhood. I kept running. I never went back into that house.

I ran to the street, not minding my bare feet. One or two people tried to help, but I just skirted them.

Somehow I found the sheriff's house. I still can't believe that. A new kid only there a few days was able to run in a blind panic and find a house and an address for which he only had a vague knowledge.

I ran up the path and stairs. I fell once, skinning my knees, but didn't care. I kept pounding on the door until someone answered.

I heard the sheriff yelling, "All right already! Jesus."

When he yanked the door open, I somehow had the breath to practically scream, "You said to contact you if I need help. Please!"

What happened next was a blur. He pulled me inside. His wife came running, and she held me. He went outside with his gun drawn, and then came back in. He asked me what happened. I don't know how much sense I made, but I told him what had been going on for the past three days. He accepted everything I said. He didn't doubt a word. Soon he was on the phone giving orders. He checked his house, made sure everything was secure, and told his wife to take care of me. I was surprised to see she had a gun nearby, and seemed quite comfortable with it. The sheriff left.

Of course I was a mess, so she got me in the shower. She found me some old clothes that belonged to one of her sons. I couldn't stop shaking, so she gave me a blanket. She fixed me something to eat, soup I think. I couldn't look at it because I felt sick. She made me take some, and she was right. Once I started eating I couldn't stop. She gave me seconds on the soup. Funny how I remember that.

I dozed off in the chair, and then the sheriff came back

around ten or eleven. He pulled a chair up and sat right across from me.

"Your aunt and cousin are dead. We found the remains of some children."

I nodded, but said nothing. I didn't ask how they died. Not then.

"Would you like to stay with us for a while and see if you like it?"

I said, "Yes", and then I know I cried.

Chapter Ten

"I ended up liking it there a lot. They officially became my foster parents, and then a couple of months after that they adopted me as their own son."

Lund decided to stop at this juncture. All the important points he wanted to share with Ryan were covered. Somewhere in the telling Ryan became completely absorbed. He kicked off his shoes, turned completely towards Lund and brought his legs up on the bench and sat cross-legged. His right arm was propped on the top of the seat back and served as a support for his head. His hand was clenching a clump of sweaty hair. The sport drink was half finished and sat forgotten on the grass.

Lund waited for the boy to make sense of things. He could be patient for him. God knows, people were patient with him when he was in Ryan's shoes.

"What...um...how?" Ryan ran his hand through his hair. He sighed and sounded exasperated. "Why...oh crap."

"You can't put it into words. I know."

"You better not be bullshitting me."

"I'm not Ryan. I swear. It happened to me exactly as I told you."

"What are these things?" Ryan brought his knees up to his chest and wrapped his arms around his legs. He seemed to be unconsciously protecting his core from further onslaught of the unthinkable. "Are they demons?"

"That's a good a term as any. Are they straight from hell? I don't know. No one has ever been able to answer that one for me."

"Mrs. Pullman thinks Beaumont is like a caretaker."

"Smart lady. Yeah, someone has to raise them, keep track of them."

Ryan pursed his lips. "I mean, geez ...what...what purpose do they serve?"

"You're asking good questions, but there are no good answers. There haven't been many of them, at least as far as I know. I know there have been others. I've been trying to track them down. They're perverse, vile creatures. Words can't describe...I think they are physical manifestations of pure evil. In that sense, I guess they are conceived in hell. They spread misery..." Lund shrugged and brought up his hands to indicate he couldn't explain it any better.

"So now, I'm haunted by the ghost of one." Ryan's eyes bored directly into him.

"Looks that way." Lund's phone rang. "Lund."

"Agent Lund, this is Officer Harrington over at the house you asked us to check out."

"Yes, what do you have?"

"You better get over here to look for yourself. This place is a nuthouse. We might have remains, and we're setting up a crime scene."

"Thanks, Officer. I'll be right there."

Ryan sat up straight and swung his feet around to the grass. "I suppose you can't tell me."

"It's Lizette's house. I don't know any details."

Ryan nodded solemnly.

Lund stood up from the bench. Ryan grabbed his shoes and did the same.

"Ryan, listen. Stay away from them. If you see them, call me. That's it. Okay?"

"Yeah. Sure."

"I think they may have left town or holed up somewhere. I don't know what makes me say that, other than no one has seen Beaumont or those kids."

They started walking across the park to the Tryon house. Ryan was absentmindedly kicking the grass with his bare feet while carrying his shoes and plastic bottle in his right hand.

"I'm glad you told me the story."

Lund felt relieved. "You've got to do things to get your mind off all of this stuff...as much as you can anyhow. Let me do my job."

"Okay, I will," Ryan said as he reached their front gate. "Thanks for talking to me."

"You're welcome. We'll probably talk again." Lund waved and left to examine the next catastrophe.

* * * *

Watching Ryan walk back to the house, Miranda considered how to play this. To her astonishment, she didn't need to worry because Ryan made a beeline for her once he was inside.

"You're not going to believe this. His mother died when he was twelve, and he had to go live with his aunt and cousin. They were into all this satanic stuff, and his cousin was kidnapping and killing little kids. Lund discovered this, and they tried to kill him. He got away after he beat up his cousin with a shovel. He ended up being adopted by a sheriff."

Miranda was aghast. How could an adult share this gruesome tale with a vulnerable child? She was getting way in over her head here.

"So, what...what do you think about this, sweetheart?"

"I'm not sure," he said, "I think he might believe me. I don't feel so...alone anymore."

The 'feeling alone' comment stung.

"Well, I guess we can count it as a positive thing, then. Do you plan to talk with him further?"

"No, not unless something comes up."

She decided to change the subject. "Grandma and I were talking before. What about the three of us driving to Charleston later? We can go out to dinner and there is a minor league baseball team there. They have a game tonight. Could you stand the embarrassment of spending a few hours being seen with two old women?"

A slight smile appeared on her son's face. "That sounds cool...well, you know, sorta cool. Yeah, okay, it sounds fun. Let's do it. No one knows me here, so I wouldn't be too embarrassed."

As he turned to leave her, she said, "Yes, it'll be fun. In the meantime, no sitting on, or otherwise coming into contact with, any furniture without talking a shower. In fact, go take one now. You're making my eyes water."

Ryan grunted and ran towards the stairs. Within minutes, she heard the shower running.

* * * *

During the shower, he kept going over Lund's story. Someone else not only believed him but had experience with the same things. He felt stupid for thinking this, but he couldn't believe his good luck. He had someone on his side.

The urge to investigate Beaumont intensified. Lund probably hadn't expected that to happen. Or, maybe he did...maybe his goal in telling the story was to secretly motivate Ryan to keep investigating and for Ryan to keep him in the loop. Well, he could do that.

Ryan didn't want to say it aloud, but he had no intention of sitting around waiting for things to happen to him. He had done pretty well sorting things out and discovering evidence even the pros couldn't find.

* * * *

Multiple police cars drew onlookers. Neighbors clustered in small groups chatting quietly and pointing at the officers and their movements. Two officers roamed the perimeter of the property, instructing the onlookers to keep their distance. Surprisingly, they were very compliant.

Lund parked along the curb of Lizette's house and walked up the driveway. Ryan gave him a good description of the place, and he noticed the tire tracks where the car had been backed up to the front porch.

Harrington was posted at the front door, and he nodded to Lund as he approached.

"Thanks for the call," said Lund.

"Welcome. Enjoy."

Lund paused at the top step. "What did you find?"

"The place looks like a zoo. I mean a real zoo. The hyena house or something. Carcasses, skeletons of small animals. Human skull artwork, a real treat all the way around. The chief's inside, waiting for you."

The door immediately opened into the living room. Claw marks and scratches were carved all over the walls and ceiling. The imprints were at positions nearly impossible for the average child, even one with an extreme case of ADHD. It looked as though these two kids had been walking on the ceiling, or running and jumping up walls. There was an undercurrent of fecal matter or something decaying.

Chief Templeton entered his field of vision. "There are cages back here which look like they held prisoners. Small children, to be exact. We found a corpse of one in the crawlspace. I've got an officer with a dog checking out the backyard."

Hattie Templeton was an African American woman in her early fifties. She had been one of the first African Americans on the force and worked her way up. Lund knew she ran a tight ship on short resources. She operated like a matriarch, and her officers wouldn't dare cross her much as they wouldn't cross their own mothers. Still, they called her "Mom" out of earshot of civilians, and she didn't seem to mind.

"No sign of the woman?"

"Not yet. We've sent out an APB."

Lund nodded.

"Follow me." Without waiting for a reply, she turned and led Lund down a short hallway. Lund was reminded of his aunt's house, not only in terms of layout, but also its hellish inhabitants. They entered a room distinctly different from the others. The walls were unmarked, the curtains on the windows had not been shredded, and the floor was clear of debris.

"Look at this." The chief pushed the door closed with a hand covered with a latex glove.

Five locks, three dead bolts and two sliding locks with steel reinforced plates graced the door. This is how Lizette kept her sanity, or at least her privacy.

There was a knock on the bedroom door. "Chief?"

"Yeah, come on in."

Harrington had made his way inside. "Ramona's hit pay dirt, it looks like. They found more skeletal remains. Looks like another child, and at least one, but more likely two, adults. The dog's still antsy, so there may be more."

"Okay, thanks Harry, I'll be out shortly." She turned to Lund. "You don't seem surprised. Tell me what's going on."

Lund considered what to say. "The kids have rooms here?'

Templeton nodded. "There's one. Looks like they shared a room."

"Can I see that before I answer your question?"

"Be my guest."

The chief was correct. Lund wasn't surprised. The bedroom was a scene of mayhem. Plasterboard walls were gouged. The sheets on the beds were streaked with green mold and rust colored stains. The sheets were also torn along with parts of the mattresses. A plastic dog crate sat in one corner. Blood stains could be seen on the outside plastic. Inside were a few clothing items, a small jumper, a pair of shorts, and a disposable diaper.

Lund's heart ached. "You had no reports of missing kids in the area?"

"No, not a one."

Lund saw what he initially thought were chicken bones on the floor, but guessed they probably weren't. More likely a squirrel, but he truly had no clue. One thing was clear to him. His aunt had a lot more control over Cam than Lizette did over these kids.

Along the far wall was the artwork. Six human skulls were lined up on the floor. Four were children, and two, adults. They had been painted with model paint. Garish neon colors shouted an agonizing death. Glitter was affixed to the two adult skulls. Lund had seen enough to be sure. He looked at the chief.

"Do you want a sanitized version that is more believable, or the true one which you won't believe?"

Without hesitating, the chief replied, "The latter."

Lund told her. Beyond a slight raise in her eyebrows when mentioned his experiences as a boy, Templeton's expression didn't change.

When finished, he asked. "What have you learned from the neighbors?"

"Nothing much. Oh, the kids were pains in the ass. Rude, mean, suspected of torturing small animals. But, nothing yet."

"It's still early."

"That it is. What about the connection to Beaumont? That's shaky."

"Yeah. The Perry kid connects them all, but so far, that's all. Unless we find neighbors who can place him here... we've got to find the woman."

The chief led him both out of the room towards the kitchen area. The sight was stomach-churning. How that woman could live under these conditions Lund couldn't begin to imagine.

"Let's track down reports of missing kids and see if we can find any correlation with other murders or with Beaumont's movements. We should examine the entire southeast," Lund suggested. "By the way, the remains of the adults in the backyard are probably connected to the skulls in the bedroom. I'm willing to bet they can be traced to the missing young men, Munoz and Reilly."

"Can you lead on the missing kids?"

"No problem." Lund turned to leave.

"Agent," the chief said, "you didn't ask me if I believed you."

"I don't think I want to know."

* * * *

The locals referred to the home of the Charleston RiverDogs as "The Joe". The minor league team was an affiliate of the Yankees, and what a RiverDog was, Ryan wasn't sure. His mother secured box seats some rows back from the home team dugout. Ryan was used to major league games at Miller Park in Milwaukee. This park was considerably smaller with a capacity for 6,000, and that meant the setting was pretty intimate.

Ryan tried very hard to get his mother and grandmother to dump the restaurant idea and eat at the ballpark, but they didn't budge. Neither of them cared much for baseball, so he relented, figuring he could handle any setting without difficulty. He also wore a polo shirt with a collar and a clean pair of plaid shorts without asking in an effort to be dressed up. There were no comments, so he interpreted that as an affirmation.

The only minor skirmish occurred when they entered the restaurant. Ryan wanted to keep on his sunglasses and baseball cap so as not to draw attention to his bruises and stitches. Both women argued he was doing the exact opposite, because displaying such slippage of southern table manners would draw more gasps from the other patrons than his injuries. Much to his surprise, nobody stared or pointed at him during dinner.

By the time they arrived at the park, Ryan found he didn't care whether his disguise was on or off. He tried to explain the intricacies of the game to his mother and grandmother, but they were both lost causes. By the fourth inning they were talking between themselves about everything other than baseball. He was under strict instruction to protect them from any foul balls that came their way. While a few did manage to drop reasonably close, Ryan was disappointed he did not have the opportunity to snag any.

The RiverDogs were having a rare laughter, leading 9-1 in the sixth inning. Ryan's mind wandered and he scanned the crowd. Of course, he didn't know a soul. Earlier, at the top of the inning, he went to a concession stand to look around, and some old, fat dipshit clapped him on the shoulder and said, "Hey, boy, I hope you gave as good as you got." His breath smelled like beer and hot dog burps, and he laughed as if this was the funniest line ever. Ryan almost called him as asshole, but ended up giving him a dirty look and walked away. Other than that, Ryan was just one person in the crowd, and he preferred it that way.

It was entirely by accident that he noticed the kid with long black hair in either the last section of the box seats or the lower reserve further down the right field line. The kid's face turned briefly in his direction but was then lost in the crowd.

Max?

Ryan stood to get a second look, and the fans in the seats immediately surrounding him stood at the same time. He was vaguely aware of some cries and squeals, but these didn't register until his mother started screaming, "Ryan! Ryan!" and tugged on his arm.

He looked at her and she looked at him with her mouth a perfect 'O' and pointed to the sky.

A foul pop-up was heading right towards her. Ryan barely had enough time to extend his right arm and leap above the other outstretched hands. He grasped the ball easily and everyone cheered. He waved his arm with the ball and more cheers erupted.

He sat down next to his mother who was grinning like a school girl.

"What?"

She slipped her arm around his and squeezed. "My hero. You saved us."

"God, Mom." She could be so embarrassing.

When he had the chance, Ryan examined the crowd where he thought he saw Max. He couldn't find him, nor did he see him for the rest of the game.

* * * *

With the developments of the past six hours, the case expanded. An official task force was recently established, with Templeton and her team the primary investigators and the feds providing support. Two agents from the Columbia field office would be arriving the next day to provide Lund with assistance.

Lund sat at a makeshift desk off in the corner at the police station. The discrete pieces of evidence were the rather limited forensics found at the murder scene of the young couple and the human remains found at Lizette's house. The discovery of that crime scene was a huge break, but unfortunately there was little evidence connecting the two. Nonetheless, finding and bringing in Lizette and her two sons was the main focus of the investigation. Their pictures were given to the media, and there was hope someone would recognize them.

Beaumont was a person of interest, but his identity was not disclosed to the press. There was nothing connecting Beaumont to anything other than the Perry kid's statements. Lund was following a hunch that the boy might have provided them with something that was a huge connection, and not a distraction. Unfortunately, this was something only Lund could confidently rely on, since it required a suspension of disbelief of which only Lund was capable.

Ryan told him Beaumont had killed multiple people. Even though this bit of information came from a dream, both he and Ryan had firsthand experience of feral children actually being demons. So, who was to say this was an outrageous idea. Lund examined unsolved murders and reports of missing children cases in the southeast over the past three years. Information from three of them proved most interesting. One little girl went missing from her home in Roanoke, Virginia, two years ago. Within a week, a teenage boy and girl were found murdered near Narrows, Virginia an hour or two away. Another baby girl was reportedly taken from her Manteo, North Carolina, home three days after a family vacationing on the Outer Banks were found executed by gunshot wounds to the head in a Nags Head beach house. This was last year. One month later, a little boy went missing in Savannah, Georgia... the day after three college girls were beaten to death in Hilton Head. This last case was one with which Lund was familiar. One of the girls had also received numerous claw or scratch marks, post mortem, and showed signs of vaginal penetration, but with what was unclear. No semen was found.

Melissa Tompkins' body showed similar patterns of assault...again post mortem. This was a new wrinkle not seen before.

A fourth child was taken last April from Columbia. No unsolved murders at the time, so Lund reached a dead end with that case. Still, three out of four was suggestive at the very least. Lund was troubled with the new piece of evidence, the sexual assaults. He searched on his laptop for any unsolved sexual assaults reported in Columbia with one week in either direction of the missing child. There was one that struck him immediately. A young woman awoke and found two assailants in her bedroom. They beat her mercilessly for about five minutes, after which one held her down while the other raped her. She described them as sadistic and like wild animals as their action was frenzied. While she never got a good look at them, she knew they were boys, and not teenagers either. They were young.

Okay, four decorated skulls in the boys' room, and four missing children...all under the age of three in the past two years from South Carolina and surrounding states. Three out of the four kidnappings occurred near the time of unsolved murders in nearby cities. If Beaumont was a killer as Ryan Perry insisted, here were some leads to follow. Was there any evidence that Beaumont was in the vicinity of those locations at the time? None so far. One additional disturbing trend was the sexual assaults...Lund guessed the boys were expanding their repertoire of terror.

One more thing...the death of the young couple mere days ago seemed to be done randomly. A thrill killing. Beaumont might be losing control of his charges.

Lund rubbed his eyes. Things were fitting together a bit more, but huge gaps remained. He matched all this new data with events drawing his attention since he was thirteen. Periodic deaths by undermined animals in the Southeast. Two or three of these occurred twenty-plus years ago. He could readily attribute them to good ole cousin Cam.

He knew way back then that Cam wasn't human, and had features that went beyond human understanding. The sheriff, whom he now considered his father, referred to them as monsters, which they were, but that term offered no explanatory information. When he was around fourteen after the adoption was final, his father took him to Charleston to visit with an older African American woman named Tessa Chambers. Lund felt secure enough to start asking questions, and when his parents' answers proved to be unsatisfactory, his father brought him to Mrs. Chambers.

After some initial pleasantries in the house, his father turned to the woman and said something like, "the boy has questions." Lund remembered her nodding, and then he was completely taken aback as his father said, "I'll see you later," and left the room.

What he heard from Mrs. Chambers chilled him so much he felt as though he was encased in a block of ice. Rituals capable of impregnating women already pregnant, and carrying to term a child of demonic origins...the human child being devoured at birth...the demonic child capable of transforming... being trained for some hellish future task by a human caretaker...the children being evil...no soul...monstrous...trained to kill when they were around seven...honing their skills...

The ultimate shocker was when the sheriff left that night right after Lund arrived in his home, the sheriff picked up Mrs. Chambers, of all people. They found Cam close to death due to injuries Lund inflicted with the shovel. They hastened his death. Then his aunt came for them, and she was taken out. How, he didn't know, and didn't want to find out.

As years went by, he visited Mrs. Chambers a few times. The last time was when he was in college on the suggestion from his father. He was dreaming, not for the first time, of these creatures. She said he was sensitive to them. Somehow he was blessed...or cursed...with this gift. She said when he had the dreams it meant a demon was being born. The more intense, the closer the creature was. He had a handful of dreams during his teen years, but the dreams in college were the worst.

That meant there were more out there than he ever imagined.

His experience prompted his career trajectory. He began monitoring strange deaths related to mauling or mutilation. An occasional one would occur in Georgia, or Tennessee, and then would not repeat. Were these connected to the dreams that felt more...distant? Did they stop due to the death of the perpetrator? Lund didn't know. New deaths started five years ago. The instances weren't frequent, that was true, but they seemed related to Lund. Call it a hunch, but Lund began combing reports, searching...

A frenzied attack on an elderly homeless man in Richmond. The death was attributed to a dog, because of the randomness...then a prostitute from Norfolk whose clientele was often the young military guys at Oceana. A witness described two kids nearby but they were never located, and this information was dismissed. The attack was like that in Richmond, but seemed more focused. A year or two went by, then a camper in the Appalachians outside Boone, North Carolina. Cuts very purposeful, made by claws...again, an animal to blame...no connection to the eastern Virginia deaths. Then the college girl in Hilton Head, then the young couple here...There were probably others in small towns or rural areas which did not cross Lund's radar.

The connections were not made among all of these deaths. No human DNA...only, what bird, or reptile? Lund knew the connection, though. Worse yet, more happened...this was going in directions he could not foresee.

Lund made a decision. Sometime tomorrow he would drive to Charleston and look up Mrs. Chambers. He needed another talk, and it had been awhile since the last one.

Chapter Eleven

When Ryan woke up late in the morning, he dug around in one of his drawers for his swim trunks and got dressed.

"A shirt, please, Ryan," his grandmother said when he plopped at the kitchen table with some cereal.

"I'm going to the beach. Why?"

"You should be dressed for the table."

"Grandma." He couldn't believe his ears. "I eat down here in my underwear."

"I've noticed. I'm just trying to make you look civilized."

He snickered. "You're such a blast, Grandma. Hey, where's Mom?"

"She's holed up in the office. Sketching."

"Cool. Do you think she'll take the job?"

She smiled at him. Ryan knew the answer. "Why don't you ask her?"

She was at one of two desks in her new home office. One desk held her laptop. The surface of the other was empty except for his mother's pads and supplies. Drawings lay scattered across the room. She was never particularly neat when working and the room looked like offices of the past when she was deeply involved in a project.

"Hey," he announced as he entered the room.

"Hi baby. Watch where you step."

"I see them all. Wow. Have you taken the job?" Ryan navigated the work and knelt beside his mother to peek at what she was doing at the moment.

Ryan felt his mother's hand pat down some errant hair on the back of his head before she caressed the nape of his neck.

"I have. It feels good to get back to something normal, doesn't it?"

"Yeah." Ryan pointed to a small character. "I like this one."

"Thanks. I'm still not there yet. I keep going back to the manuscript. I see you're ready for the beach."

"Yep. This'll be interesting."

On their way home from the ball game last night, Ryan

discovered he had a text from Dee. She invited him to go along on a baby-sitting job. She baby-sat for the family and sometimes accompanied them on family outings when the parents felt they would need the additional help. The mom promised the kids a trip to the beach, but she anticipated being on the phone most of the time so she hired Dee to come along. Dee said the kids, two boys eight and ten, were monsters and she often was at wits end trying to figure out what to do with them. Dee negotiated for additional help. Ryan would even make some money.

"When do they pick you up?"

The words had just escaped her lips when the doorbell rang.

Ryan laughed. "Right now."

"Okay. Kiss." She pointed to her cheek.

He obliged, and hopped around her work to answer the door.

She yelled after him, "Ryan? Grandma and I may be out later when you come back."

Five hours later Ryan couldn't understand what Dee's problem was. The kids, Henry and Vincent, were a lot of fun and between Ryan and the two boys they were able to come up with all kinds of things to do. For his part, Ryan was thankful for the opportunity to interact with two brothers who didn't eat cats. He noticed they had all the markings and the confidence of being privileged. Their athleticism was polished from experiences with multiple organized sports, private lessons, and camps. Artistic and creative abilities were nurtured from the top private school in the area.

Their first attempt at an ordinary sand castle quickly became an ornate sand kingdom. Nearly six feet long in length along the shore and four feet wide, the kingdom held castles and cathedrals, armories, blacksmith shops, houses and huts. A wall two feet high with turrets at the corners protected the kingdom from the onslaught of the Atlantic. As the tide began its inevitable approach, the three boys struggled in vain to maintain the wall. Melodramatic groans and cries of futility rose from the shoreline when a huge wave took it all.

Ryan noticed Dee tried to keep up with the frantic pace, but gave up, just watching and making suggestions for the design. She commented on everything, and exclaimed delightfully as the young boys displayed some original construction.

Ryan could see why the kids loved having her as a baby-sitter.

They took turns tossing a Frisbee, and then Ryan ended up standing on the shore and throwing a football to the boys in the water just out of their reach so Henry and Vincent had to attempt diving catches before crashing into the waves. Ryan relished his job, and he was able to gauge the kids' abilities and the waves after a short period of time to alter the level of difficulty. It seemed like months when it fact it was only a week or two since he was this active.

The mom was a stockbroker and spent large periods of time on the phone or checking messages. When she was busy, the baby-sitters were totally in charge. The kids were not to bother Mom. She had designated "Mom-time" when she turned off her phone and played with the boys in the water. Dee and Ryan could then take a breather. She would designate a specific length of time and it was Dee's job to keep track and let her know when the time was up. Then she left the water and the baby-sitters were back on duty.

Ryan had never seen anything like it.

"Don't you think this is kind of strange?" Ryan asked during one of their breaks. They were sitting under a green and white umbrella in beach chairs that leaned back and had footrests.

"Yes, but they pay well. She's pretty nice, I like her. She's just..."

"Weird?"

"No, uh-huh...intense."

"I'll say."

Ryan watched the waves tumble onto the beach. The water wasn't rough, but the waves were slow moving rollers that seemed big to him. Pelicans skirted the surface of the water, and the little sandpiper birds danced and skittered along the advancing waves.

"Your dad's a lawyer," Ryan said. "Does he know what's going on?"

"Nope. I have no problem telling him, but he's out of town for a few days. Some big meeting in Washington."

Ryan was quiet for a few minutes. "I had a long talk with Lund yesterday."

"Get out. Really?"

Ryan decided he needed to tell her what he learned, especially after meeting her grandmother. Somehow, he felt it was important to do, to convince her he wasn't a freak. So, he told her everything. By the time he finished, she had changed her position in the beach chair so she was sitting upright.

"Oh, my God. You know, that couldn't have been them at the game. How would they know? Your mind was playing tricks."

"Yeah, I guess so. Still, all the other stuff...don't you think it fits together somehow?"

Dee sat back. "Sure sounds like it. Are you planning something?" She sounded worried.

"I really want to check his house out. I'd love to sit and spy on it somehow. Without being seen."

"The police..."

"I know. That's what I mean. They're probably still there. Although, don't you think they'd give up if Beaumont wasn't around?"

"I don't know."

"Hey, Ryan!"

Both Ryan and Dee turned to see Harry and Vincent storming the beach.

Dee checked her watch. "She gave up early. She still had three minutes of Mom-time left."

"That is so weird." Ryan grunted. "So, what do you think about my baby-sitting?"

Dee laughed. "I think you stole my job away from me."

* * * *

Lund guessed it was at least twelve years since he last visited Tessa Chambers, but he recalled the location as if it was last week. After he rang the doorbell, an old man with white hair in sharp contrast to his dark skin answered the door.

"Hello, Mister Chambers. I don't know if you remember me, I'm..."

"Jeremy?" he interrupted. "Is that you, boy?"

"Yes sir." Lund couldn't help being surprised. "It's been awhile. I should've stopped by a lot sooner."

"Ah..." Mister Chambers dismissed the notion with a wave. "We all get caught up in life. Tessa's been expecting you."

"She has?"

"Of course. You know her. Please come in, son." Mister Chambers shuffled backwards to allow Jeremy to enter their house.

The small house was spotless, with a faint smell of lemon scented furniture polish. Lund noticed a number of potted plants decorating the living room. A TV was turned on, but the sound was muted.

Mister Chambers was a retired janitor for the school system. Over forty years of cleaning every conceivable mess generated by elementary school children produced little wear on the man other than whiter hair and more lines in his face. Mrs. Chambers told Lund many years ago her husband never minded the antics of young children. He never tired of the work, and was visibly sad when he had to retire.

Once Lund was in the room, Mister Chambers placed his hands on his shoulders and held him at arm's length.

"Now, let's take a look at you dear boy." He paused and actually looked Lund over. "Seems like you filled out some since your college days."

"Are you saying it looks like I'm getting fat?"

The old man's chuckle sounded like a rumble deep within his chest. "Fat? Heavens no, son. That's all muscle, ain't it? Isn't that what we men like to say?"

Lund never mentioned a word about his experiences to Mister Chambers, but he was sure his wife told him about them. No matter how infrequently he needed to talk with Mrs. Chambers, Mister Chambers accepted his presence without question.

"Yeah, right. All muscle."

Another rumbling chuckle came from Mister Chambers.

"We see your daddy every now and again. He keeps us informed. He says you're doing good. Real good."

"That's kind of him. I'm sure he embellishes things."

"Now, you know that ain't true. Your daddy keeps to the facts."

Lund shrugged. "I suppose..."

"Not to change the subject, but Tessa said when you showed you'd likely be in a hurry. So shootin' the breeze with an old goat like me isn't getting the job done. She's given me instructions to tell you where she's at when she's not around. Which she ain't at the moment. Anyway, I won't keep you. She's at the City Market in Charleston. Our son's wife has a sweetgrass basket stand. She's helpin' today."

"Thank you Mister Chambers. You're right—I was hoping to talk with her. I'm trying to figure something out. I do appreciate all you've done."

Mister Chambers stood rooted in front of Lund, not saying a word. He raised his hand and placed the palm on Lund's cheek and his long fingers extended to his neck.

"We keep praying for you, son," the old man whispered. "You be careful with this one."

Lund brought his own hand up, and caressed Mister Chambers' hand. "Yes sir. I appreciate the prayers."

* * * *

The Charleston City Market served as a public market going back to the early 1800's, with the current building standing since 1841. Lund had been here a few times in his youth, but it wasn't a regular destination for him. He disliked shopping, and could not understand the attraction for people who appeared to do this on a daily basis. Short of dealing with serial killers and demonic children, spending periods of time wandering a shopping mall was the closest thing to hell he could imagine. The Market hadn't changed much since his last visit. Vendors still sold artwork, clothing, souvenirs, food, vegetables, and fruit, much of it locally crafted or grown.

One mainstay in the Market was vendors, typically women, who sold sweetgrass baskets. The art of sweetgrass basketry was passed down from one generation to the next, originating with the slaves who brought the skill to the coastal areas of South Carolina from West Africa.

Lund remembered talking with Mrs. Chambers at this location once before. Many people were surprised to see a white teenage boy sitting within the crowd of African American women. He felt awkward at the time, but he recalled Mrs. Chambers not being troubled in the slightest.

Now, twenty years later, he felt like an intruder again. Lund quickly found the Chambers' spot for selling their baskets. He spotted her sitting on a lawn chair, casually working on a basket while she conversed with another woman. Lund didn't recognize her companion, but he readily noticed a scarf tied over her head to hide hair loss from chemotherapy.

Lund paced around the vendors in the near vicinity waiting for the opportunity to approach her. He was conscious of the fact it was hard to mistake him for anything other than a federal agent, or at least some kind of law enforcement. He didn't want to embarrass her, or create a sense of drama for the tourists.

His phone rang. "Lund."

"Agent Jeremy Lund?"

"Yes?"

"Hold on for a moment."

Lund was puzzled.

"Jeremy. I see you roaming around. You're making me dizzy. Get your butt over here so we can talk."

Lund smiled. He should have known. "Yes ma'am."

When he made his way across the crowd, she stood and wrapped her arms around him in a deceptively strong hug.

"Oh, my boy, my boy, here you are." She straightened out the lapels on his seersucker suit jacket and pressed down his collar. Then she fussed over his hair. "I knew you'd be coming soon."

"So I gathered." Lund smiled. "Mister Chambers told me."

Mrs. Chambers introduced Lund to her niece, Eugenia Pullman.

"Nice to meet you ma'am," he said, and then turned to Mrs. Chambers. "I would sure like to speak to you. When would be a good time? I can come back."

"Come back, nothing, we all need to talk."

Lund glanced at Mrs. Pullman and saw she was unsure where this was going, but wasn't moving at the same time. She was staying put.

"Lonnie?" Mrs. Chambers leaned around Lund to call a burly black man. "Could you bring young Jeremy that chair behind you? We'll be talking for a bit."

The man was clearly suspicious of Lund. He kept a wary eye on the weapon and badge as he passed an unused lawn chair to Lund without saying a word.

"Thanks," Lund told him, and the man nodded.

He situated the chair to be at right angles to Mrs. Chambers, and directly across from the other woman. "I'm curious. How did you get my cell number?"

"From Eugenia." She tilted her head towards Mrs. Pullman.

Lund must have looked confused because Mrs. Pullman added, "Ryan gave it to me."

Lund sighed and shook his head. "I've been one step behind that kid for days now." He quickly realized where he heard the name Pullman...from Ryan's account of his experiences. "Ryan told me about his meeting with you. He trusts you very much, by the way. I'm still trying to earn that with him."

Mrs. Pullman smiled. "Yes, sir, he has told me about you as well."

Mrs. Chambers spoke up. "Eugenia, you remember me talking about how I've met these things before? How a sheriff brought me along to a house that contained a demon, which was wounded by an orphan boy?"

"Yes, Auntie, I recall. That's what brought me to you when Ryan was born."

"Well..." Mrs. Chambers smiled wistfully. "Jeremy here is that boy. *The* orphan boy." She reached for his hand and squeezed.

Lund saw it was now Mrs. Pullman's turn to be surprised.

"In the flesh," Lund added.

"You both probably don't know it, but you're up against the same enemy. It's time y'all talked."

Lund looked at both women, and recognized that sharing case detail with them would be highly unusual. Under the circumstances, however, they were the most qualified to offer expert opinion and advice and could entertain the discussion at face value.

He summarized for them what he knew, and what he suspected.

"My. Our Mister Beaumont fooled the whole bunch of us," Mrs. Pullman said when Lund finished. "He's been riding around murdering folks all these years and is also planning to bring a demon child back to life...not to mention that he has two of them already. I gathered parts of this from Ryan. What you said sets everything in stone."

"Our mistake, Eugenia, was not destroying that baby completely. Now Mister Beaumont has unearthed a ritual to resurrect it. Or so he thinks. Do you have any reason to doubt him?" Mrs. Chambers turned to Lund.

"I don't doubt he thinks he can. Whether he can or not doesn't matter. He looks like a major threat for the boy."

Lund leaned forward to get closer to the women. He lowered his voice to avoid being overheard. "What exactly are these things? How are they born? I never asked you because I didn't want to know. Now, I need to know..." Lund shrugged, unable to express himself further.

Mrs. Chambers reached for his hand again. "You know what they are, Jeremy. You've read the book. *The dragon stood in front of the woman ready to give birth so that he may be able to devour her newborn child, but the male child was saved...*" Mrs. Chambers tilted her head back slightly, and closed her eyes. Her face was illuminated from within as she recited from memory,

"*...and there was a war in heaven and Michael and his angels fought against the dragon and the dragon fought with his angels. But the dragon was not strong enough and was defeated, and hurled out of heaven and sent to earth. When the dragon saw that he and his army were defeated, he chased the woman who gave birth to the male child. The dragon was enraged with the woman, and went to war with all of her offspring.*

"Jeremy, child..." she paused briefly to focus on Lund. Her gaze was intense. "Evil comes in all shapes and sizes. There are many beasts and dragons living among us. Some are people and some are ideas, but sometimes the dragon and the beasts are real. Some actively seek the devil, child, and these are the very slime of humanity, like the palmetto bugs we can never exterminate. They live to command, to lead an army of the devil's minions against all the holy offspring of the Lord.

"Someone found out how to call the dragon to help sire firstborn sons to breed a race of demons to conquer the earth. Michael has been fighting this battle many times...he always seems to be victorious...but the war is costly...and the dragon keeps trying."

Mrs. Chambers released his hand and sat back. "We've been called, Jeremy, to fight alongside of the angels of heaven."

Lund sat quietly. He heard a tourist behind him trying to talk down the price of a sweetgrass basket with Mrs. Chambers' daughter-in-law. He turned far enough to see a white woman dressed in some kind of resort wear and dripping gold jewelry. She displayed an air of entitlement, and Lund instinctively found her annoying. He could not discern a northeastern accent, so she didn't seem to be from New York or Boston. He was guessing Chicago.

"Where did this start, Mrs. Chambers? Somebody had to be the first one to decode the ritual. According to the Perry kid, Beaumont wrote that the written instructions may have come over in a slave ship."

Mrs. Pullman smiled while Mrs. Chambers grunted in disgust. "Child, now where would a slave carry a book on hisself from Africa? They had no possessions. If the ritual came over on a slave ship, it wasn't the slaves that brought it. It was the traders."

Lund stared at the floor. "I'm having trouble believing some southern cracker had the brains to figure this out." He looked again at the two women, but felt bashful, worried he might insult them.

"Who said it was a cracker? It could have been one of the elite white families that started this whole thing. Jeremy, keep in mind, this just wasn't happening around here. I think it's happened other places, too."

"It seems awfully cumbersome to have to keep redoing this process of finding a pregnant woman willing to be inseminated with demon seed and sacrifice her child...there's got to be easier ways to promote evil."

"Of course there are, but who can resist such power? Your own army of demons? Jeremy, I don't think you understand what happens. The person running this show, like our Mister Beaumont, needs the ritual only for the first generation."

The Chicago tourist gave up her haggling with a huff, probably because her husband grew impatient waiting. "For Chrissakes, Jen, they have these things in the Smithsonian. There's no bargains anywhere, I checked. Just pay and let's get out of here." All the while, the daughter-in-law remained polite but refused to budge off the sticker price.

"Hold on a second. What are you saying?"

"Once the demon children come of age, they can sire their own. Think of this. They can roam and rape in gangs. In packs...in armies."

Lund needed some grounding in everyday reality. This thing couldn't get any more unbelievable. He purposely tuned in to passing conversations and the activity of the customers. Many who stopped at the Chambers' stand picked up and compared multiple baskets, trying to settle on one to purchase.

"So, those boys Ryan has seen...those demon kids...once they go through puberty...hold on, do demons do that?"

Both women remained still.

"Jesus Christ." Lund reddened when he considered his audience. "I'm sorry. My apologies." He rubbed his eyes to postpone looking at them for a few more seconds. "Okay, once they mature, these kids will be able to have sex and breed their own offspring?"

"Yes."

Lund sat upright suddenly.

"Jeremy?"

"Recently, two victims had been sexually assaulted, but no semen was found. One of those kids is trying. He's around twelve, so I guess we can assume they mature roughly on par with human teenagers."

Mrs. Chambers looked sad. "That's reasonable."

He felt he was jumping from one runaway train to another.

"Would you be very insulted if I asked you how you know all this?"

"My dear boy, you're trying to understand. That's not an insult." She looked warmly at him. "To answer your question, I know because my grandmother..." and here she turned to Eugenia, "...your great grandmother...told me. She saw much of this first hand."

Her daughter-in-law asked for some help with the display of her inventory, so Mrs. Chambers excused herself for a few minutes.

"Agent Lund," Mrs. Pullman said, "I came to Charleston today to talk to my Aunt Tessa about Ryan."

Lund nodded once to indicate he was listening.

"I've been feeling responsible. You see, a friend and I killed that other twin, that demon child, when Ryan was born, but we didn't destroy it. I guess there's a difference. Now, according to her," Mrs. Pullman indicated her aunt, "Ryan's the only one who can do that now. You see, fourteen years ago we gave the body to someone, Beaumont in fact, to get rid of. He clearly didn't, if we can believe the rumors. Oh, dear God forgive me, but I feel Ryan is in grave danger."

Lund wanted to reassure her, but knew she wouldn't believe him. "Mrs. Pullman, I don't think there is anything in the South Carolina statutes about killing those things. So, I wouldn't worry about that. Don't forget, I gravely injured my cousin as a boy. I don't feel one ounce of regret. Regarding Ryan, though, I think you're right."

"All right," Mrs. Chambers announced as she returned. "I'm back."

"You two are familiar with the family story, but I'm at a loss. Could you tell me?" Lund asked her after she finished shifting in the chair.

"I could use a refresher, too," Mrs. Pullman said. "I always thought it was a ghost story to scare the daylights out of us kids. Nothing more."

"I'm happy to oblige." Mrs. Chambers rested her hands in her lap and told the story.

* * * *

"You asked me where this started. I can't say for sure, but probably goes back to the time the Book of Revelation was written. When it started for us though, goes back about a hundred years. Who started it was Francis Montgomery, from one of our supposedly finer families."

"He was the same guy who...in the cemetery."

"The same. My gramma said he was a nasty child. Always touching hisself in public and as he got older he started touching the other kids. When all of the other teenagers started to avoid him, he would make his way over to the colored section of town. Some could fight him off, others weren't strong enough. It was a blessing that none of his juices ever took.

"He was sent away after doing sacrilegious things in the cemetery. Folks said they saw him wandering with no clothes and phantoms by his side, and those haunts would rejoice as he spilled his seed among the graves. Francis was gone for ten years and when he returned he seemed a normal man, married to a stunning young woman. They had a child who was about four at the time and was named after his daddy. Young Francis looked like his mother, with dark hair and deep set eyes. The family eventually settled back in town, and the older Francis had his medical degree.

"Everything started out fine, but then talk started, first about the boy, and then the family. The boy was cruel, hitting and biting other children. Some said he could turn into a beast, and when he scratched his playmates, they'd be hurt real bad. But it was his eyes, all black with tiny red fires... people didn't see this all the time, oh no, but sometimes when he was angry, he would change...and the children were scared. Others saw him chase small animals, squirrels and rabbits and such. He was blinding fast, and could catch them and then eat them while still alive. The animal would still be squirming as it went down his throat.

"Just like his father...that's what people said, but this was worse, far worse. He could growl like a jungle beast, and gallop faster than the winds of a hurricane. His appetite changed when he was a teen. He chased girls, and the white folk quickly learned to keep their daughters safe from the boy. Once again, a Montgomery made his way to the colored section. Girls were ravished. Some died outright. They were the lucky ones. His semen was like acid, burning and scalding. Others carried his child, but it was like no other pregnancy ever seen before. The girls would deliver within a month or two...and they delivered dragons. Human bodies, yes, but with the head of a beast. After the first one, the women helping with the birth knew to destroy them at the moment of birth. The monsters fought and screamed and needed to be pounded into pieces to keep from being resurrected.

"Around this time, my daddy and granddaddy had enough. They wanted to kill young Francis, but he was in college and wasn't always home. So they waited...until summer, and then with the other men set up patrols of the town, ready to bounce if he showed his head.

"There weren't many white folk they could trust. Oh, there were some who were hoping the colored folk would make the town safe again by killing the monster, but they were not brave enough to lend a hand. One man was, though. He ran the general store, and he was always courteous to the blacks and treated them fairly. His name was Hagerton, an ancestor or relation to your daddy, Jeremy.

"He said more strange children were being born. There was maybe five or six of them. All boys. One was nearing twelve and would begin his roaming soon. The whites were petrified. On top of this the Montgomery family was holding... ceremonies. A few other families joined, Beaumonts, Lunds, I forget who else. There were rumors of rituals to make more children. The families called them demons, and everyone guessed that's what they were. People said that Francis's wife was a witch, and that she poisoned his mind. Others re-called his actions as a child and thought that like minds came together.

"Anyway, my granddaddy said something needed to be done, and Mister Hagerton agreed, but didn't know what. He wanted to talk with other men he could trust and promised to get back to Granddaddy.

"They didn't act soon enough. Mister Hagerton came to our house two nights later. The demon children went on a rampage the night before. They were led by Francis's oldest son, who was home from college. He and his younger brothers, none of them wearing a stitch of clothes, roamed and raped their way through the town. Even the youngest demon children took part. Men were killed, three or four, I think, trying to protect their wives or daughters.

"Now both my daddy and granddaddy knew our section of town was going to be visited soon. So when Mister Hagerton asked them if they were willing to help end the madness once and for all, they said yes.

"The following night after the dinner hour, Daddy and Granddaddy joined Mister Hagerton and some other white men in the town and watched the Montgomery house. Not all the white men were there. Others were too injured or too scared, but they expected something was up. My daddy told me later he was getting worried when he saw people from the other nearby houses peek around their curtains. He thought some might object to coloreds being in the crowd, but no one said anything. I guess they knew too much was at stake. Members of the Beaumont clan arrived and entered the house, but luckily never saw the men watching.

"As darkness fell, the men watching the house began to move. A few had rifles and pistols. Others held farm tools, all had weapons. My granddaddy had an old pistol. My father carried an axe. There might have been ten men in all. One carried a flaming torch and led a charge. They stormed the house.

"My daddy and granddaddy were sent around back and were told not let anyone escape. Their plan was to kill them all. Everyone...every soul in that house.

"Screams came from inside as the men entered. Shots were fired, and the cries and yells shook the earth, or so my daddy said. The oldest Montgomery child–young Francis this would be, who was probably twenty, jumped from an upper story window, and landed near Daddy. My daddy later said that yes, when he saw the boy, he knew he was a demon. The demon was injured, but my daddy froze. There were claws where hands and feet should have been, the teeth were razors and it was shaped like a dragon. It was naked, and the sight of the manly parts chilled my daddy's very soul. A woman could be torn apart if this thing entered her. The demon charged my daddy just as he raised his axe. He got one swing in, but didn't land a killing blow. My daddy felt his guts being torn out and slashed, and then there was a flash and a loud bang, and the oldest Montgomery thing fell off Daddy. My granddaddy shot the demon in the head.

"None of the men were killed who were in the raiding party. Some were injured like Daddy. They were taken to the doctor who normally only treated whites, but on this night, he took care of my daddy too. They took stock of what they had accomplished. Francis Montgomery and his wife were dead. He had his throat cut, she had been shot. Some of the Beaumonts were dead, but others may have gotten away or weren't there that night. Four demon children were accounted for, including the oldest one killed by my granddaddy. So at least one got away.

"Mister Hagerton and the other men, including my daddy and granddaddy, met a few weeks later. They agreed they would never let a situation like this get the upper hand again. They swore to each other and before God they would always stay alert for the presence or the activity of these creatures. Over time they did just that. When rumors started about demon children, they would quietly investigate and the situation was taken care of if found to be true. This promise was passed on from one generation to the next.

"The talk of these creatures faded over time, after all how many could there be? So the more recent generations never heard anything. If accounts did come up, they were often from far away...

"Georgia? Tennessee?"

"Yes, Jeremy, like that. Usually the police had a way of taking care of the problem.

"There were still members of the old families still around. Beaumonts still lived in the area, and Lunds, and other extended family. So, there were stories...

"About twenty years ago now, your daddy, Jeremy, the sheriff, came for me and said he needed my help. This was before you were in the picture, Jeremy. He called me and said he had a situation, which is what he called it. He came for a visit and told me and my husband what he knew. There was a mom and a teenage boy, who he suspected of doing...things. There were rumors. He remembered the tales and wondered what I thought. Deep in his heart, he never believed any of the stories, but all of a sudden he was faced with these reports. Then young children started missing. He started checking into the family. He kept me updated on his progress.

"Then he had the shock of his life. He called me right after it happened. He stopped over one night at the house just to let the mom know he was watching. Who answered the door was a different boy, a nephew. The sheriff told me he felt as though the world started spinning off its axis. His baby sister ran off with a Lund thirteen years before. She had been pregnant, and was quite wild. When he saw you, Jeremy, he knew he looked at his little sister's child, his own nephew."

Lund broke in, "Whoa...whoa...whoa...Are you telling me that the sheriff is actually my uncle? Why didn't he say anything?"

"We talked about that...he didn't know where you stood on all these things or what you knew, and, he didn't know what had happened to his sister and what she knew. After you escaped to his house, you were so troubled by events of that night that he didn't want to drop another bombshell on you. Once things settled down and were working out just fine, I guess he figured he didn't want to rock the boat. He adopted you though, so he made you his son...more than a nephew. I'm sorry if I overstepped my bounds here, but we often talked about what to do if you needed to know.

"You see, he couldn't be sure of anything. Once you appeared at his door in terror, he knew to take action. We took action, actually.

"You're not seeing another connection here, Jeremy. Maybe you were too young at the time for the memory to be formed. Your cousin had a tutor. Did you know that?"

Lund was too shocked to do nothing more than nod.

"Did you know he was a Beaumont? He was in college at the time. Arthur Beaumont."

Lund stood up. He felt confined suddenly, but there was no place to walk in the Market. He heard Mrs. Pullman mumble, "Oh good Lord."

Lund squeezed his eyes shut, trying to recall the young man he met very briefly all those years ago. Was that Beaumont? Just this week he talked to the man, but only for a few minutes. Sure, it could be, but he couldn't say with any certainty.

"Looking backwards, it makes sense, right? Mister Beaumont, a descendent of the original family, has somehow uncovered the rituals. He is making his own evil children. We're starting a new cycle. Now though, he is going a step further, and wants to resurrect a baby that wasn't destroyed.

That is a new one on me, but he has found a way.

"So, here we are... we are descendants of the families that drove the demons from our section of the Earth..."

Lund noticed that she didn't finish her comment. She didn't have to.

"I am trying to get my head around all of this, Mrs. Chambers. I have so many questions. I am starting to think I need to go back and help track this bastard down."

"I understand, Jeremy. You need to do this job." Mrs. Chambers turned to Mrs. Pullman. "Eugenia, you need to get some rest."

"I know, I am hurting. I catch my bus in a couple of hours."

"Mrs. Pullman," Jeremy started, but then his cell vibrated. "Excuse me."

It was Chief Templeton. "Okay, some luck. We have a credit card receipt, one of Beaumont's, from Blacksburg, Virginia at the same time as a kidnapping of a baby in Roanoke and the murder of two teenagers in Narrows." That put Beaumont in the vicinity of the crimes. Templeton continued, "Also, get this, it looks like Beaumont may have been training those boys how to be selective. The victims of the so-called animal attacks and the families whose babies were kidnapped all lived in marginal areas. They were on the fringes of society... some were involved in criminal activities...others didn't trust the police...and others didn't give a rat's ass if anyone from the family–kids included–disappeared. Real sweet people. Anyway, it's no wonder some of this didn't come to our attention."

Lund wiped moisture from his brow. He had the peculiar impression of things spiraling out of control at the same time they were falling together. The sensation was troubling.

Lund thanked Templeton and hung up. "I sure have missed you Mrs. Chambers." He stood and folded his chair. "I'm so sorry we are meeting under these circumstances."

She embraced him, and he returned the hug. When she stood back, she said, "We know what you've been up to. Your daddy tells us. He's showed us pictures of those beautiful children of yours, and of Hannah, of course. She still is a fine girl."

"Yes she is." Lund remembered what he was going to say when his phone vibrated. "Mrs. Pullman, you're taking the bus back home? Would you like a ride with me, instead?"

She smiled. "Do you have lights and a siren?"

"Yes, ma'am."

"Then, I will gladly accept."

Mrs. Pullman reached a hand to her aunt, who in turn took it in both of hers. "Eugenia, you have stronger weapons than Jeremy. Trust the Lord. Open yourself to Him."

As they walked to the car, Lund noticed thunderheads building just to the west.

Chapter Twelve

When Ryan returned home later in the afternoon, cash in hand and the prospects of salaried play dates in the future ("Can Ryan come over and play sometime?"), the previous niggling urge to examine the Beaumont house had turned into an obsession. Ryan wanted answers and he wanted to make it go away. Most of all, he needed to find the proof to convince his mother he wasn't losing his mind.

He recognized he was trying to convince himself to canvass Beaumont's house and property. Energized, he pushed open the wrought iron gate and ran to the porch and front door.

"Mom?' he called. "Grandma?" The house was quiet. Few lights were on. He recalled his mother saying they'd be out later, so that explained the emptiness. The circumstances couldn't have been any more ideal, because Ryan wouldn't have to sneak out or lie about leaving. If only they could stay away for a few more minutes.

He rushed upstairs to go to the bathroom. He changed out of his swimming trunks and stepped into his sneakers. He searched his room for his LED flashlight. He looked around to see if he had anything else that might be good to have. His baseball bat? No, how do you explain carrying that into someone else's house?

Ryan stopped moving altogether. A flashlight? A baseball bat? He had to say it out loud to himself.

"You're actually thinking of breaking into the house."

So, what of it?

"This is crazy. This is absolutely crazy."

These guys haven't let up. Mom thinks this is going to go away. It's not.

"Stupid. You'll get caught and arrested...or worse."

No, they're gone. No one's seen them. The house looks empty.

That was the clincher. If there ever was a golden opportunity, this was it. If Beaumont was gone like Lund said, he should be able to tell, right? He could just check out the house from the outside. If there was any indication someone might be home, he could just keep walking by. If it looked as though no one was home, he could approach it in stages. Walk up to the house first, then maybe look into the windows, maybe even ring the doorbell...maybe try to open a window.

God, he'd never done anything like this before. He never sneaked out of his house at night, he never shoplifted, and he never stole anything...what made him think...

What makes you think this is going to disappear? You've got to do something.

He would definitely communicate whatever he learned to Lund, no holding anything back. He looked out his window and saw dark clouds creeping across the sky. The late after-noon light faded, and the air took on a faint olive green cast. The atmosphere had a sharp electrical edge. The weather was even cooperating.

So, it was decided. He'd take it in stages. He made sure he had his cell phone. He saw it was nearing six, so decided now was the time to get lost or else he might get trapped by his mother arriving home. He ran out the door.

Ryan was surprised to see how dark it had become since he last looked outside his window just minutes before. A gust of wind slapped him as he reached the sidewalk, sending his clothes snapping. The clouds were now menacing, and Ryan considered he might be caught in the rain before he reached his destination. That could work in his favor too. He'd be harder to see.

Street lamps came on, and people turned on their lights inside the houses for dinner. At that moment, he had a brain-storm. He texted Dee saying he was going to snoop around Beaumont's house. If he didn't contact her in an hour, she should contact Lund and let him know where he went. He felt better, knowing he had backup.

Dee's reply took mere seconds.

"What! R U crazy?"

He replied, "Yep. 1 hour. From now."

* * * *

Officer Simon was on stakeout duty, sitting in an un-marked car across the street and about thirty yards down from the Beaumont house. He felt very fortunate to have this work. Most of his buddies were still in college, with uncertain futures once they graduated. He went to the academy, a dream of his for as long as he could remember, and got this police job. He recently moved out of his parents' house, finally feeling financially secure to rent his own place. He hoped this would enhance his social life. He met this girl two nights ago, and they'd been exchanging texts. They had plans to go out when he had his next night off. She was hot, and he was already having fantasies of the two of them in his bed. He already told her he was a first-class cook, which was the God-honest truth. Mrs. Simon raised her sons to be more than handy in the kitchen. He would have her over for dinner some night, and see where things went.

For now, he was stuck watching this house. He was able to wear civilian clothes, and he dressed as if he was on his way to the gym. This helped with the heat, and he kept the windows rolled down to catch a breeze. A thunderstorm approached, and the gusts traveled through the car like a wind tunnel. He'd have to roll the windows up when the rain started, which he wasn't looking forward to. He anticipated the windows would fog up. He'd have to turn on the car for the air-conditioning.

Simon started with the window on the passenger side, so was leaning over when he saw a figure in his peripheral vision dash across the street and disappear.

He bolted upright, but saw nothing.

"Shit."

He scanned the vicinity again, but still nothing. He could have sworn it was that damn Perry kid. There appeared to be a cast on an arm.

"Shit." If this kid was roaming around, people would be pissed.

Simon opened the door, keeping his eye on the area he saw the figure disappear. He rolled up the driver's side window. Rain was imminent, that was for sure. He strolled calmly towards the Beaumont house, ready to nab that damn kid and drag him back to the car. He crossed the street and had one foot on the sidewalk when he heard a snarl within the wind.

What the hell...?

A rumble of thunder...and then Simon felt searing pain as two figures, kids, grabbed him and actually dug fingernails like ice picks into his back and abdomen. With unbelievable force, they started running and pushing him forward. He was so shocked he couldn't resist. One kid jumped on his back, pushing his upper body down. His last thought before ramming face-first into a tree was *Jesus Christ, what is this?*

* * * *

Ryan stood across the street from Beaumont's house trying to slow everything down. He ran to the house after contacting Dee, mostly out of excitement to be doing something. Now, before he went any further, he wanted to catch his breath and calm down. He wanted to think clearly once he went into motion. He was drenched with perspiration because of his run. The humidity was oppressive. The wind had picked up substantially, but that did nothing to lower the temperature. Angry clouds tore across the sky.

Ryan planned to stand across the street for a few minutes and see if there were any signs of life in the Beaumont house. If it seemed no one was home, he would investigate how to approach the house, check the rooms from the outside, and maybe get access to the inside. He seriously entertained just going up to the front door and ringing the doorbell, but nixed the idea once he couldn't come up with a reasonable script to engage Beaumont if he happened to answer the door.

Hi, Mister B. I just wanted to see if you were really trying to raise a demonic child back from the dead.

No, that wouldn't work. If it came to it, breaking and entering looked like the best option to study the place. He cursed himself, though, for not thinking of wearing black clothing like they do in the movies. Fortunately, he had thrown on a dark blue T-shirt and khaki cargo shorts while he was home. So it could have been worse.

The approaching storm was turning out to be a godsend. The evening sky became much darker than usual, and lights flicked on in all the surrounding houses. Beaumont's house remained dark. Time to move.

Ryan darted across the street, trying to stay in the shadows. As he reached the sidewalk, he recognized the click of a car door closing quietly. He knelt quickly next to some hedges and spun his head around looking for the source. A lock of his hair blew into his line of sight. He brushed the hair out of his face. A sudden gust of wind blew it right back. He repeated the gesture, all the while cursing silently to himself.

A roll of distant thunder nearly masked a thumping sound he'd heard a million times before when a coach dropped a bag of sports equipment on the ground. Silence followed. He forced himself to wait for sixty seconds. When that passed, he waited a few more seconds and then rose. Nothing.

Ryan forced himself to nonchalantly walk up to the front door. In case any neighbors were watching, he wanted to make it look as if this was the most natural thing in the world. He took a moment to survey the front of the house from his vantage point at the door. The landscaping provided excellent coverage for his first felony. There were plenty of shrubs and bushes along the house, and he guessed they continued along the sides as well. He would be able to check out the interior, along with ways of entering the house, by using the bushes as a shield.

The front windows didn't reveal much as Ryan squeezed behind the greenery to peer inside. He couldn't budge any of them, but the inside was pretty dark. There was definitely no movement, so Ryan felt safe. The right side of the house produced much of the same. There were plenty of shadows for stealth activity, but all the windows felt as though they were set in stone. Ryan was beginning to wonder if he was going to have to break something in order to get in. His only source of knowledge about how to do this was movies, which Ryan realized was probably not realistic—like breaking a window with an elbow. Ryan could just see himself trying this now, and a shard of glass come down like a guillotine, badly slicing up his arm. Ending up in the emergency room for the third time this week would not be good. Plus, he would have to explain how this happened. No, he would keep checking.

As Ryan worked his way around to the back yard, there was a brief sheet of lightning followed by a rumble of thunder. He had the terrible thought that Beaumont might be racing home just this minute in order to beat the rain. Well, there was nothing he could do about that. If Beaumont did show up, he would just haul ass out of the house and run home.

When Ryan arrived at the back door, he started looking for a hidden key. He found nothing under the door mat, nothing hiding on top of the sill, nothing anywhere. A brilliant flash of forked lightning followed by a sudden boom of thunder practically made him wet his pants. The storm approached much faster than he anticipated. A gust of wind wailed its way through the neighborhood.

"Damn," Ryan swore out loud as he slapped the back door. In his frustration, he pounded the door frame twice with his fist, and then grabbed the doorknob and gave it an angry twist. To his complete and utter shock, the door swung open smoothly and silently. Ryan stood there feeling dumb.

Still in complete disbelief, Ryan stepped inside just as huge raindrops the size of nickels splattered the ground.

With the chaos of the escalating storm outside, the inside of Beaumont's house proved a momentary refuge. Ryan entered the kitchen, and decided to take a seat at a small breakfast nook in a corner opposite the cooking area.

What exactly was he searching for? He supposed it was information or evidence related to two things. One was his birth or his twin, the other was a record of any killings by Beaumont or Hugo and Max. What that record would look like he had no idea. Ryan couldn't imagine Beaumont kept bodies in the house. Wouldn't the place reek after a while? Ryan guessed it would, but then what did he know? No, this guy would want someplace private to keep these secrets. The basement seemed likely.

A series of three lightning flashes followed closely by tumultuous thunder rocked the entire house. Various objects in the house rattled with the subsequent vibrations. Ryan remembered being scared of thunderstorms as a little kid. He would bury his head in his mother's lap and plug his ears. She would hug him and sing songs to him, all the while tapping his back to the tune of the songs. He felt deeply nostalgic and wished unabashedly she was able to console him now.

The kitchen was a bust, so he strolled down the short first floor hallway. He had taken out his LED flashlight and briefly swept the circle of light across each room he passed. When he reached the end of the hall, he was by the front door. He needed to search the rooms more closely. He decided to turn to his right and enter the living room. The house wasn't as large as his grandmother's house, but it was old like hers. The floors were natural wood and covered with area rugs and runners. The living room furniture seemed haphazardly placed and didn't really fit the architecture of the house. Even Ryan, who knew zero about interior decorating, saw that. It also smelled dusty, as though it wasn't used much. As his flashlight lit up the floor, he could also see dust bunnies pushed to locations out of reach from the typical air currents. This was definitely not like his grandmother's house, which gleamed almost unnaturally bright.

The trip through the living room led him to some kind of den or study which contained a home entertainment system and books that were mostly novels and biology textbooks. There was a desk at an interior wall, on which sat piles of paper, science education journals and a desktop computer. The storm continued its onslaught outside. Ryan heard the windows shaking in their casings, caused by both the wind and claps of thunder. He sat down at the desk and touched the mouse. The monitor screen lit up, so the computer had been left on.

He had access to Beaumont's files and internet favorites.

Much of the material was pretty mundane. It appeared he had his students send him assignments electronically, which he downloaded for grading. There were research papers and lab reports from the previous school year, all of which Ryan thought were too boring to read on a summer evening. He found Beaumont's own professional writings, things like notes for his presentations at conferences for science teachers. Boring, boring. Ryan flew through these files.

When he came to "My Pictures" he hit the mother lode.

Ryan opened the file and was stunned to see file after file of various photos. All were of people and kids he did not recognize, until he came upon "Perry". Ryan felt sick to his stomach as he clicked on the file. There were photos of him, a lot of them. Pictures of him jogging on the path in the woods right before he was attacked...

"Damn," Ryan said to himself as he recalled fleeing the live oaks.

Pictures of him sitting on the porch, helping with the moving in process, pictures of him being escorted into the hospital with blood streaming down his face, and most alarming, a picture of him holding hands with Dee from the other afternoon.

What the hell?

Ryan looked more closely at photos of other people. Many appeared spontaneous, as if the subjects were not aware they were the focus of a photographer. Ryan wondered if any of these people had attended the party in his dream.

Ryan felt an adrenalin surge. He broke into Beaumont's house looking for this type of evidence, but having found it, he was terrified. This was so wrong. This was creepy, twisted and sick.

Ryan had enough. He shut everything down. He resisted the urge to run out of the house, because he wanted to find the basement. He stood and surveyed the room and located his bearings.

Two photos on the desk caught his attention as he turned to leave. How could he have missed these? Both were school pictures of two boys. Hugo and Max. What sent another jolt of anxiety up his spine was the realization that these two guys went to school. They had to torment and terrify the other kids. How did the school put up with it? For that matter, how could a school hire someone like Beaumont to be alone in a room with a group of kids?

Ryan's progress sent him from the den to the dining room, which was ordinary. Newspapers and magazines piled on the table indicated to him that Beaumont didn't use it for eating. When he left the dining room, he was back in the hallway right by the kitchen. He had made a complete circle. It was only then he noticed the recess in the hallway, which was actually the area underneath the stairs. Hidden in the shadows was a doorway. Ryan opened the door and shone his light down the stairs.

He found the basement.

Decision time. Did he check out the upstairs first before the basement, or go right for the creepy part of the house? He definitely didn't want to be blindsided by someone in the house when he was downstairs. He'd be trapped for sure. No, as much as he needed to check the basement, he knew the smart money would be on searching the upstairs first. Remove all doubts-at least as much as he could.

Lightning helped illuminate his climb up the stairs. At the top a landing contained four closed doors Ryan assumed led to bedrooms. A fifth door was ajar, and Ryan saw it was an upstairs bathroom. Ryan forced his way to the first door and pushed it open. He turned on his flashlight and stared into the bedroom.

It was bedlam. A single bed was pushed to one side. The mattress had slid partway off the box springs, with the upper left corner far enough over that it nearly touched the ground. Splatters the color of cinnamon spread majestically across two entire walls.

That's blood. He knew without any hesitation.

Bursts of lightning and thunder rocked the house, but Ryan barely noticed.

Remnants of a fitted bottom sheet were still on the bed. Claw marks had torn parallel lines in at least four different locations. The sheet was soiled with crusted shit, and other faint stains were evident. The stench of spoiled meat and urine hit him like a delayed reaction. He staggered backwards and clasped his hands over his nose and mouth. He backed into the hallway to control the reflux by breathing through his mouth.

What the hell? How can he stand it?

Ryan glanced into the room again. With new repulsion he noticed for the first time the remnants of multiple squirrels or chipmunks, with skins and bones clustered on various locations on the floor.

Ryan thought of Hugo and Max. If they lived with Lizette, then how often did they spend time here? Whose room was this?

Ryan walked unsteadily to the next room and saw another chamber of horrors. Chunks had been gouged out of the walls. Angry stains, from God knows what, splashed across the sheets.

Skeletal remains littered the floor. Bones, and shards of bones, had attached pieces of tissue, ligaments, and muscle that looked like old leather. Ryan couldn't look closely and backed away trying to maintain a sense of internal balance.

What was this place?

The third room had to be Beaumont's. When he turned on the light, he saw a four poster bed, a desk, a chest of drawers, a small TV, bookshelves along the wall...yes, Beaumont's room.

The bed was unmade, however, and Ryan noticed the stains on the sheets...and parallel tears from claws.

"Oh God. Sick." Ryan turned quickly from the room, unable to shake the image that Beaumont sometimes slept with those kids.

Ryan doubted the wisdom of his decision to break into the house. He was encountering an evil that was somehow more disturbing than seeing his dead twin. He considered... Go home? Keep searching? If he left now without checking the last room, would he regret it later? *It's right here. Check it.*

He strode to the door trying not to think...

The room was immaculate. The bed was neatly made with a cowboy themed bedspread. On closer inspection, Ryan saw it was old and threadbare in sections, but clean. He wondered if this was Beaumont's from when he was a kid. The depth of his sickness chilled Ryan.

This was going to be his twin's room. The only thing missing was a "welcome back, Rex!" sign.

Toys were neatly displayed on some shelves. *Hotwheel* cars, *Star Wars* action figures, dinosaurs...Ryan knew what they all were but he hadn't really played with toys like this for two years or more. Was Beaumont expecting a real-life boy to come back? Especially given the condition of the other two rooms...

He descended the stairs knowing he had to examine the basement.

Don't think about it. Go down, check, and get out.

The intensity of the storm gradually weakened, but Ryan was only dimly aware. His focus was on one thing...under the stairs...in the recess...the door to the basement.

Standing at the top of the stairs looking down into the gloomy basement, Ryan made out painted walls and tiled flooring with his flashlight. He found the light switch on the wall by his shoulder and weighed whether to turn it on. Figuring he could escape this place a lot sooner if he had more light, he opted to switch on the lights.

As he walked down the steps, Ryan realized shadows were the norm instead of clearly lit areas. At the bottom of the steps, he first saw a work table about six feet long on the opposite side of the room. There were all sorts of tools, both power and manual, lying about the table. Next to the table, Beaumont had hand tools hanging up on hooks attached to wooden planks attached to the basement wall. There were three rows of these hooks, along with chalk outlines illustrating where the particular tools belonged. Many were missing, and Ryan assumed they were on the table.

In the center of the basement, a thick cinder block column reached from floor to ceiling, and probably served as a support column. Rows of three cinderblocks were on each side, and the entire column appeared to be painted pink, although that was hard to tell in the gloomy light.

Other sections of the basement contained assorted

groupings of Beaumont's belongings. Luggage was stacked in a corner, an unused exercise bike and exercise equipment stood next to a wall, boxes of books were placed near the exercise area, and cleaning supplies stored on moveable shelves.

One corner of the basement was closed off by the addition of two walls jutting into the basement. These walls were perpendicular to each other, such that they met about twelve feet into the room. Beaumont had built a small room in that one corner of the basement. Ryan wondered if it was another bedroom, which seemed odd since the house had an entire second floor that already contained four. The added walls were covered with cheap paneling that was supposed to look like wood. The door to this room was faced away from the stairs.

Ryan's imagination raced into overload again as he approached the room. He saw images of his twin lunging for him as soon as he opened the door. Or maybe it would be Beaumont waiting with an axe over his shoulder. "Hello Ryan," he would say, then split Ryan's head into two pieces.

"Stop," Ryan said to himself. He took two deep breaths, traveled the few feet he needed to reach the door, and then opened it.

The room served as an office. The walls had no openings so the only light came from the overhead bulb in the basement. Ryan felt for a light switch and found it.

Two groupings of items were in the room. One was a long folding table and chair. The table contained newspaper clippings, scrapbooks, and reference books. A bulletin board on which other newspaper and magazine clippings were tacked, hung over the table. The other item in the room was a large specimen jar sitting on a display table. Inside the specimen jar filled with liquid, motionless and staring, was the corpse of a human infant.

Chapter Thirteen

Ryan couldn't move from the doorway. He kept expecting a loud, calamitous event to scare the hell out of him. Instead, it was the sight of the baby in the jar that shook him to his core. This had to be his twin. He sensed he was very vulnerable to something, but to what he couldn't tell. The baby was just...there.

He finally broke his paralysis and walked to the jar. He guessed the baby was floating in something like formaldehyde. Strips and pieces of what looked like cloth were suspended in the liquid. They appeared to be bandages or medical dressings. With sudden dread Ryan recalled the morning he helped his grandmother pick up the garbage cans knocked over by animals...and realizing that his discarded dressings were missing...presumably taken by those animals...but actually taken by Hugo or Max...and taken here and placed in this jar...

The closer Ryan looked, the more he noticed physical exceptions in its appearance that told him this wasn't a human baby. The feet and the hands were actually claws. The knuckles seemed twice the size of what they should be—almost as if they were swollen—and the fingernails seemed incisor sharp. The body looked as though it could be a doll's, and Ryan almost wondered if this whole thing was an elaborate hoax.

Two angry gashes stretched across the baby's torso, one through the neck and the other diagonally across the abdomen. This was where his grandmother and Mrs. Pullman stabbed the baby in order to kill it. He could imagine their fear...how this act went against everything they believed in...

So, this was the thing that meant to eat him at birth. This was the beast conjured from hell by Beaumont for ...what?

God, this made no sense.

Ryan turned and strode shakily to the desk with the abundance of clippings. He felt his right hand tremble as he reached randomly for one of them. He ended up with a series of three paper-clipped together. The first was an account of a teenage boy hanging over the side of a bridge by his belt near Narrows, Virginia and his girlfriend lying face down in the New River a few miles away. The second was about a family shot to death execution style in a beach house in Nags Head, North Carolina. The last described three college girls bludgeoned in the Hilton Head, South Carolina condominium. All three occurred in the past couple of years.

The descriptions of the victims were familiar to Ryan. He remembered the family with sections of their heads missing attending the party in his dream...executed in Nags Head. The teenagers, the college students, the old people...stabbed, strangled, beaten...they had been in his dream.

Ryan reached for a scrapbook lying towards the right hand corner of the desk. He didn't bother to read the articles, he just flipped through it briefly and looked at the headlines: ...tortured...slain...dismembered...slaughtered...

Sweet Jesus, how does this happen?

Animal attacks...unknown predator...

Wait...animal attacks?

As Ryan flipped through other articles, he found separate incidents: animal attacks...attacks by wildlife...a homeless guy found torn to bits somewhere in Richmond...a prostitute near Virginia Beach...a camper in the mountains of western North Carolina...evidence destroyed by other predators... He tossed the clippings back on the desk.

Clearly the handiwork of Hugo and Max. Beaumont was starting to train them.

Liquid sloshed in a tub.

The sound came from behind him.

The specimen jar.

No way.

Ryan didn't want to look, he really didn't. But there it was again—liquid sloshing...in the jar.

There was a very faint tapping.

Ryan had to turn.

The baby was staring at him, eyes open and colored a soulless black with a hint of a burning red gleam.

Both hands were placed against the glass, palms flush.

The right index finger moved, and the talon-like fingernail tapped the glass in greeting.

Then the baby smiled.

"No...no, no...no way..."

Ryan backed away, reaching behind him for the door. He couldn't find the knob, where the hell was it? He groped, and then groped again...finally he grasped it and turned...the door opened.

The baby kicked its legs in excitement, which displaced the liquid and caused the sloshing sounds.

He snapped off the light and slammed shut the door.

He turned to go up the stairs, and ran headlong into Arthur Beaumont.

"Well," Beaumont said cheerfully, "the prodigal son has returned. My dear Master Ryan, you are indeed a pest, but a predictable one at that."

Hugo stood at his right, smirking. He flipped Ryan the bird. Max was on the other side, smiling wildly with excitement.

"What did you think about the RiverDogs game?" Max winked and then threw his arms around Ryan's neck. It almost felt like an act of affection at first, but quickly turned to something different. Hugo moved swiftly to pin his arms, and then both slammed Ryan to the floor.

* * * *

Every single nerve in Ryan's head felt as though it was transporting an electric shock of one million volts.

Beaumont gruffly yanked Ryan's his arms behind his back while the boys pinned his shoulders and legs. The cast made this process difficult, and Ryan's arm screamed in protest with each tug. The unmistakable sound of tape being jerked from a roll met his ears, but Ryan was unable to resist. The tape was wrapped around his wrists.

Ryan's face was somehow wet and laying in a puddle. Somewhere in the deep recesses of his mind, he was aware his head was bleeding again.

Beaumont roughly turned him, this time on his back. His pinioned arms were trapped awkwardly underneath him. More tape was being pulled, and Ryan saw it was packing tape. Beaumont wrapped a section around his ankles, and tore off the end. Then he did the same around Ryan's shins. With his head throbbing and the boys holding him down, he remained helpless while Beaumont shackled him.

"Now, son," Beaumont said while lifting him to a near standing position, "let's get an update on the situation." Ryan was amazed at Beaumont's strength. He was essentially dead weight, and Beaumont picked him up as if he was nothing more than a feather. "You broke into my house. That is not appropriate."

Beaumont's eyes were blue fire. While his voice tone was measured and calm, he spoke through clenched teeth. His fingers dug into Ryan's arms where he was holding him. At that moment, Ryan knew he could die. Instead of fear, he felt mostly sad. He thought about his mother and how devastated she would be.

"The door..." Ryan found himself speaking–he hadn't intended to.

"Oh, because the door wasn't locked you think it was perfectly acceptable for you to mosey right in and look around?" Beaumont's voice escalated in anger with each word. Gone was the pretense of civility. "Young man, that...was...so... rude!"

Ryan felt himself being shoved. With his ankles and legs taped together he couldn't offset the thrust with any footwork. He was going down. There was the fleeting thought, *this is going to hurt,* and the sudden crash into the cinder block pillar in the center of the basement jarred his teeth. He landed on his side, but not before he sensed some tearing and popping sounds. He had hit an edge of the pillar, and his cast conveniently took the brunt of the impact. The cast cracked when he hit, and the tape pulled away from the cast. *Beaumont must have put the tape on the cast and it just broke.* All of a sudden, Ryan had a glimmer of hope. He might be able to maneuver himself out of this mess, especially if the cast was damaged.

"Yeah, you cocksucker." Hugo was upon him tugging on his left arm in an attempt to lift him up. Ryan was aware this demon kid wanted to inflict pain too, but he wasn't as strong as Beaumont. Hugo had him partway up and then shoved him to the floor. Ryan heard more tape tearing.

Beaumont entered the office area where he kept the baby and the murder clippings. The two boys moved to the office entrance. Hugo kept shifting his gaze between Beaumont and Ryan, unsure what to do next. Max was skipping in place, all eyes on what was happening in the office.

There was a popping sound somewhere beyond his line of vision, which was followed by the sounds of splashing liquid.

Beaumont made some murmuring sounds, but the words were indistinguishable. Ryan's apprehension intensified.

My God, he's talking to the baby.

Ryan's eyes flew wide open when Beaumont stepped out of the office carrying the baby.

"Ahh! There's your brother...he has been such a bad boy." Beaumont's voice had a sing-song quality.

No longer imprisoned in the specimen jar, the baby could move more freely. Its excitement grew, and just like Max its arms and legs were kicking and flailing with joy at the sight of Ryan.

"Did you notice your bandages, by the way? We needed some of your fluid to start the process. The blood was perfect, and it was there for the taking."

Beaumont took a few steps towards Ryan.

"Let's get this show on the road? What do you say?" Beaumont continued to talk to the baby. "Now give your brother a nice kiss." He lowered the baby down towards Ryan's face.

Ryan tried to squirm away from the oncoming face. A rush of pain in his hip meant Beaumont had just kicked him. "Stop moving, boy. Or I can make you feel unimaginable pain. Now let your brother kiss you."

Ryan squeezed his eyes in disgust, as Beaumont brought the baby closer. The smell was nasty, and he didn't know if that was the formaldehyde he was smelling or the fact that the corpse was fourteen years old. The sensation of the baby's face touching his lips was revolting.

"Very bad manners, Ryan, very bad, but I'll let it go. I am quite good at picking my battles, and your manners aren't important in the overall scheme of things."

When Ryan opened his eyes, he was surprised to see the baby sitting on its own on the basement floor. In the short time he wasn't watching it, the baby actually matured...actually *grew*. Beaumont was squatting next to the baby, and was talking like a teacher to a high school student.

"This is the boy who was supposed to be your sustenance. Due to some unfortunate turn of events, he survived while you were kept in limbo, if I may use such an antiquated term. Now your time has come." He gently gathered the baby's face in his hands. "Grow. Grow to the strong young adult you were meant to be. Eat well. Take everything from this young pup, take what is yours."

Beaumont stood then and patted the baby's head. He turned to Ryan. "The experts here tell me I cannot stay." He motioned to the other two boys. "The next little ceremony is meant to be private."

"Arthur, I've already told you. When it comes time to eat, he'll be starving. He could go after you," said Hugo. "Do you really want that?"

Beaumont sighed loudly, clearly frustrated with Hugo's remark. "So, Master Ryan. This is goodbye. We won't be seeing one another again. I'll tell your mother you went down fighting."

He strode purposely for the stairs, then abruptly turned and addressed the baby. "I almost forgot. After you're done with your meal, come to his house for your party. You know the way. I cannot wait to introduce you to his family." Beaumont nodded his head in Ryan's direction. He disappeared up the stairs with Hugo and Max following, closed a door behind them, and left the house.

Ryan started calculating. *Are they leaving me with the kid?* He tried rotating his left arm and heard the promising sound of tape pulling from the plaster. At the same time there was a very evident crack near the wrist which he could manipulate, although with punishing agony.

A gasp was torn from his chest when he turned to focus on the baby. His attention was diverted for what, twenty seconds? Thirty? In that time the baby had matured, maybe one year or two years. The body was bulkier, and it was on hands and knees and rocking. Ryan wondered if it was trying to stand.

Panic surged through his nervous system. Ryan probably had minutes at most until he was face to face with the real-life version of the twin he'd been seeing the past few nights. He resumed turning his left wrist one way and then the other, grateful for the tearing or ripping that the movement produced.

The twin, he couldn't think of it as a baby anymore—nor would he allow himself to consider it a boy— was now standing, although it was very unsteady. It was maybe the equivalent of five years old. When their eyes met, Ryan saw they were still black with that hint of red glow. Its lips smiled, revealing teeth like glass shards, serrated and deadly. Ryan didn't want to find out what happened when the thing reached fourteen.

The tape wasn't tearing from the cast quickly enough. He

tried to scramble backwards, but with his feet fastened to-gether progress was very difficult. His panic escalating, Ryan lost his balance with his effort and fell into the pillar. The cast crunched again.

Ryan heard the crack, and had an idea.

Oh God let this work please.

He shifted position so he could ram the cast into one of the pillar's edges. He checked on his adversary.

The twin was now about seven, and taking tentative steps. Balance was still an issue, and the figure stumbled.

Time was running out.

Ryan gave himself a few inches so he could force his joined arms away from his body to thrust them into the cinder block edges. The movement was awkward but he could do it. After a few attempts, there were no additional cracking noises and Ryan grew impatient. He gave up and tried sawing the cast against the edges. That worked somewhat better, as he sensed frayed pieces falling on his hands. Still, the process was ago-nizingly slow.

The twin was nearly ten.

This clearly wasn't working fast enough.

Ryan scooted a number of inches further away, wanting additional force in his thrusts. In position, he threw his entire body back towards the pillar. He screamed in pain when his shoulder blade made contact before the cast.

"God damn it!" Every nerve now shrieked in agony. How could he be so stupid? Of course, his upper body would con-nect first with such an uncontrolled effort from this distance.

The twin was twelve, clearly. Ryan couldn't help but pause to observe this chilling spectacle. The body looked like a twelve-year-old boy, more or less. Like Hugo. The body musculature was different—abdominal and pectoral muscles didn't line up the same. The body would shimmer and the surface of the skin *changed*, as if a camera was having diffi-culty focusing on detail. The shimmer would result in normal hands for a second, and then claws the next, as if the body had trouble deciding what form to take.

Even freakier was the back. Blond hair like Ryan's grew out of its head and tapered down the back of the neck. Instead of stopping, a line of thick individual hairs grew out of the knobs of the backbone. They appeared as spikes, like those of an iguana or a...dragon.

"No way, man."

Holy crap, get moving! Ryan forced himself to concentrate. This time he focused on ramming the cast as hard as he could into the pillar without heaving his upper body backwards. He alternated the thrusts with sawing movements and frenzied attempts to separate his arms by sheer will.

A tear.

"Yes! Come on, come on."

Deeper ripping noises... pieces of the cast being torn away...

"God, God, God...come on, damn, shit, come on..."

The thing stopped growing. Ryan recognized his double from their previous meetings. Coordinated movement had not yet developed, so the figure continued to stumble, but its attention was fixed entirely on Ryan. It smiled, and the teeth were now chiseled and jagged. He wondered if it would grow human-looking teeth after eating.

C'mon, Ryan, that's you. You're dinner.

He resumed pounding his cast, and then tried to pull his arms apart.

A tentative rip...then another...*keep pulling*...then his arms flew out to either side and he swung them around in front.

He stared in amazement. The cast was in shambles; cracks in multiple spots, layers missing. Chunks of tape hung from his other wrist. He placed a strip of the tape in his mouth and unwound the tape. It came off without any resistance. Then he did the same with another.

Ryan reached for the tape around his legs, but encountered difficulty. It held fast and he could not obtain a purchase on an edge for pulling. He examined the surroundings, looking for something with which to cut the tape.

The work table.

* * * *

Miranda was in the kitchen unpacking groceries while her mother collected recently purchased toiletries to distribute them around the house. The amount of food her mother had at home would not sustain an adolescent male for very long, so a trip to the supermarket had been long overdue. The thoroughness of the shopping session lengthened their stay far more than Miranda expected. The arrival of thunderstorm further contributed to their delay. Dinner preparation would need to begin soon, or they'd be eating rather late. In addition,

Ryan wasn't home yet, which made her slightly uneasy.

"Seems like we have a few reserve boxes of tissues here," Carolyn said.

"You can put one in Ryan's room. He uses them frequently."

Carolyn looked blankly at her daughter, and then it dawned on her. "Gosh, yes."

Miranda smiled as her mother left the kitchen, but the nagging worry over the events of the past few days erased the momentary humor.

Miranda propped open the refrigerator door and loaded fruit and vegetables into the bins. The doorbell rang, and Miranda heard her mother announce, "I'll get it, dear."

"Thanks, Mom."

The freezer items were next, and Miranda tossed in frozen pizza and two gallons of ice cream. She was amazed earlier she could struggle over the decision between buying mint chocolate chip or chocolate cookie dough ice cream while faced with the issues involving Ryan. She ended up getting both. He could inhale two gallons with little difficulty anyway.

"Miranda?"

Miranda closed the refrigerator and left the kitchen and headed down the front hallway. Her mother was standing with an odd expression. As Miranda drew near, she saw it was fear, and she was too late to react. A little boy of around nine had been positioned behind Carolyn, so he wasn't visible until she reached the door. He moved to her mother's side, and Miranda saw he gripped her mother's wrist very tightly. Another boy two or three years older entered the hall from the front porch. Both boys were shirtless and dressed in gym shorts. Their bare feet tapped silently on the hardwood floor. Long, uncombed hair fell to their shoulders. Remnants of a red liquid stained their chests.

"Do you know these boys, dear?"

"Hi," the oldest boy sneered. "We're friends of Ryan."

A man Miranda had never seen before entered the hall behind the older boy. Her mother made a barely audible sound which Miranda couldn't make out. The man smiled, but the eyes behind his glasses danced malevolently.

"Mrs. Perry. We haven't had the pleasure. My name is Arthur Beaumont."

* * * *

With his hands now free, scooting was easier. The work table was in the direction opposite from the approaching twin. Ryan purposely did not look to check on its advance. He couldn't afford the distraction of further alarm.

On reaching the table, he grasped the edge and pulled himself up. At the same time he strained to get his legs underneath him. With his head over the edge of the table he shifted his arm so his entire forearm extended across the surface of the table. Now with more leverage, he was able to push himself up and get his legs in position so he could stand on his feet and extend his knees.

He couldn't see a saw. He didn't see any box cutters. He didn't see anything he could use for cutting.

There was a crowbar. Ryan reached for it and looked for his twin.

It was about seven feet away. Walking was still a new art form, and the gait suggested the head and upper body were driven to reach Ryan beyond the ability of the lower extremities to keep up. The result was a jerky forward lean, and it was lucky not have fallen on its face with each step. Unfortunately for Ryan, the twin obviously was getting the hang of bipedal locomotion, and walking would be perfected at a pace that matched that of growing from infancy to fourteen years.

As the twin continued its advance, Ryan noticed it shuddering, as though having a fit or trying to shake something loose that was caught in its airway. It stopped, but teetered on the verge of falling over. It began forcibly opening and closing its jaw. Ryan was reminded how some people did this when flying to relieve pressure in their ears.

There was a snap, and the jaw remained open. The thing paused in this position for a few moments, and then started to open its jaw further.

"Oh, Jesus." Ryan watched in disbelief as the jaw unhinged. Its mouth became cavernous–impossibly huge beyond reason. Saliva was illuminated in the dim light as it threaded the jagged teeth rimming the opening.

It was going to eat him.

It was going to devour him whole, or as close to whole as possible.

Absurdly, Ryan imagined a British narrator on some nature channel saying, "The jaws of the demon-child unhinge allowing the creature to eat prey twice its size."

Ryan kicked himself into gear, and decided he would try to remove the tape by chopping at it with the crowbar. Grabbing it by the straight end, he aimed to hit one segment of tape at an angle using the curved end. In his haste, he missed, and ended up hitting his shin.

"You idiot," he screamed and watched as, unbelievably, blood started dripping from a fresh cut. He switched ends of the crowbar, and holding the curved end as a handle, he tore at the tape on his ankles with the flattened point. It went quickly once he made a puncture. Then he did the same with the tape around his shins.

He looked at the twin. He was walking more proficiently. His arms were outstretched, and a mere four feet from Ryan.

"Go, go, go." He reached down and found an end to one of the strips of tape and pulled, removing it from one leg and then continuing with the other. Then he did the same with the second strip of tape. Under normal circumstances, yanking off packing tape and simultaneously ripping the hairs from his legs would have been pure torture. Yet, compared to the events of the past hour, this barely registered.

The twin swiped at Ryan just as he skipped backwards, no longer hindered by the tape. Ryan felt the claw miss him by only tenths of an inch.

The rapid maneuvers caught Ryan off guard, and he found himself unable to maintain his balance and landed hard on his backside. He sprawled uncontrollably and the crowbar skidded jarringly across the basement floor a few feet away. He raised his left arm while his right propped him off the floor. The twin was upon him with stunning speed. The momentum of its attack sent them rolling one over the other. Ryan tried to dislodge himself from the twin, and couldn't.

With sudden revulsion, Ryan realized his arm was in the twin's mouth, extending down its throat.

His feet scrambling for purchase, Ryan recoiled in disgust, still not believing what was happening. He continued to thrash, desperately trying to dislodge his arm. The twin rotated away from Ryan on his hands and knees until both were a straight line and looking face to face. The twin swallowed again, and Ryan felt what seemed like hundreds of tiny suckers grab him and pull. The speed and force of the motion was beyond comprehension.

Ryan was dragged further into the twin's mouth. His left

shoulder was now below the throat, and with accelerating panic he realized his head was fully inserted in its mouth. Ryan was being swallowed alive.

He tried to scream, but instead inhaled saliva and mucus. Whatever sounds he made were muffled. He was nearly incapable of inhaling. The interior walls felt alive, and when they collapsed around his head and arm, the pressure was intense. The covering was viscous and fetid like decomposing flesh.

Another downward thrust occurred, and Ryan felt his head move further towards the throat.

Oh, God!

Again Ryan tried to kick and roll. He felt stabs of fire, and was aware the jagged teeth were tearing at his back and upper chest.

Oh, God—not this, please!

Their bodies continued the writhe and thrash, mostly because of Ryan's frantic kicking. He was able to roll slightly to his right a few inches—and his hand hit the crowbar. With a second attempt he seized it and swung wildly, in the direction he hoped the twin was located. There was a muffled thump, and Ryan felt the twin convulse.

He tried again, and actually felt a thump on the twin's body.

The twin's actions now seemed defensive. Ryan felt as though he was sliding out of the mouth, but still couldn't see. He felt the twin's hand brush his arm. He instinctively jerked his arm back and instantly swung again. He must have hit the twin near the throat or neck because Ryan *felt* the impact.

Ryan sensed being expelled. The interior squeezed further and he was ejected from the twin's throat in a caustic choke. Landmarks of the basement tumbled by as Ryan sprawled again on the floor. He retched, and wiped his face frantically.

"You dirty fuck!" he screamed.

The twin snarled in rage and leapt at Ryan.

No hesitation...Ryan swung the crowbar and connected with the joint in front of its left ear with such force the twin spun out of control across the basement floor. Ryan swore he also heard something shatter. The twin finally fell into the exercise equipment area.

Ryan was now fueled by personal rage. In a few strides he was towering over the twin as it looked up to him, seemingly pleading for mercy.

"You've got to be kidding."

A hand was held up in supplication. Ryan swatted it with the crowbar. The jaw was broken and well out of line. Ryan made sure it would never be used again. He swung downward, and the crowbar hit the upper teeth and then smashed into the jaw. Ryan kept swinging, making sure the crowbar hit the face or head with unforgiving force. Then he moved to the rest of the body.

Ryan finally stopped. The twin was a mass of crumbled bones and fibers. There was no blood. *Of course, he hadn't eaten me yet.*

The mangled face looked surprised, and then exhaled in such a way that it sounded like air escaping from a punctured tire. Fissures coursed their way through what was left of the body, quickly lengthening, deepening, and finally reaching a point where physical integrity could not be maintained. The body collapsed into pieces, which further disintegrated into dust-like substance.

The figure was gone.

Ryan reached for his cell phone and saw it had been crushed in the melee. Damn, he'd have to run like hell to get home.

His brain shifted into frenzy mode, and he was frantic to get moving and return home. Ryan bolted up the stairs, grasping the handrail and practically thrusting himself up each step. He collided with the door which swung open with a rush, and he fell onto the landing.

* * * *

"Gramma?"

Eugenia's cell phone rang as she and Lund were nearly home. She sensed the agent was more anxious to get back than she was. Much of the boy's safety was in his hands. The sense of responsibility must be overwhelming. She promised herself she would do what she could, including listen closely to her granddaughter's comments regarding Ryan. Sometimes, kids knew things but were afraid to say something for fear of getting in trouble. It has been awhile since she parented teenagers, but being around Dee was bringing back the skill. It was kind of like riding a bike. You never forgot how even though you still took big spills.

She and Lund had passed the time talking about their experiences with Ryan, but shifted into talking about families and kids.

"Yes, Dee, is everything okay?" Eugenia sensed it wasn't.

"Um, Gramma, I don't know what to do." Dee sounded terribly worried.

"Go on, dear."

"Ryan went to Mister Beaumont's house tonight. He was going to sneak in if he wasn't home."

Dear God, what was the boy thinking?

"He told me to call the FBI agent if I didn't hear from him after an hour." Dee paused. "Gramma, it's been an hour. I'm a little scared."

"Oh sweet Jesus. I wish the boy hadn't done this. Have you tried to call him?"

"Yes, he doesn't answer. I think he has his phone off."

Eugenia glanced at Lund and saw his jaw set, looking determined. "I am getting a ride back with that FBI man right now, child. We're almost home, too. I'll let him know. Meantime, you stay home and wait for Ryan. Understand? Call me if something happens."

"Yes, ma'am."

Eugenia closed her phone.

"What's he done?"

Eugenia sighed. "Dee said he wanted to go investigating Mister Beaumont's house. He told her to call you if he wasn't back in an hour. An hour's up, and she hasn't heard from him."

Lund's fingers began tapping the steering wheel in time with the windshield wipers. This was the only indication of agitation. "I'm going to kill that kid."

"I feel the same."

"Will your granddaughter stay put?"

"Hummf. I doubt it."

"Well, you wanted lights and sirens."

* * * *

"There we go." Beaumont had just finished securing Miranda's legs to the dining room chair with silver duct tape. He stood up from his kneeling position by her side and groaned softly with the effort. "That'll do, don't you think?" he asked pleasantly. "Lord have mercy, lots of taping for me tonight."

Miranda shuddered and feared becoming violently ill. She had to struggle to maintain some composure. Her mouth was taped shut, and becoming sick would be disastrous. Her mother seated to her left and at right angles to her appeared dazed, with a deathly pallor. Miranda's mind swirled, hopelessly convinced she was on the verge of losing everyone in her family.

Where was Ryan? *Oh God, please keep him away.*

Beaumont sat down and flashed a chillingly pleasant smile.

"Let me rest a bit before I set up for the evening's extravaganza." He reached over and patted Miranda's hand. Since she was securely taped to the arm of the chair, she couldn't remove her hand from his repulsive touch.

"Mrs. T." Beaumont shifted his gaze to look at Carolyn. "I want to say up front there are no hard feelings for your role in murdering my son. I understand how the sequence of events led to the course of action you and the witch took. I really do, although at the time I was furious, but powerless to do anything. Besides, good things come to those who wait, as the saying goes."

Beaumont leaned back in the chair, stretched out his legs and practically slouched his way to the edge of the seat. He clasped his hands behind his head, and began talking as though reminiscing.

"I had my son's body, you see. That was your mistake, giving him to me. My oh my. You should have changed him to a form that would be impossible to resurrect. When you didn't, I was frantic to find a way to resurrect him. Not many get that opportunity, of course. I restructured my thinking and considered the prospect a challenge...something to look forward to. Once I figured I could track down your little bastard at my convenience, the sense of urgency left me."

At that moment, both boys entered the room. The younger sat behind Beaumont and leaned over his shoulder. The elder stood next to him. Beaumont ruffled his hair.

"I was able to help sire two more sons in this town alone. Beautiful boys...and they can do such wonderful things with their mouths...and you don't need to worry about any of that psychological fallout since they aren't human." Beaumont sat up straight and eased the older boy into his lap. The boy resisted initially, but then gave in, looking disgusted.

"Anyway, I digress. Between the other boys and my summer

hobby I had my hands full. Then, lo and behold, I found him! Talk about stupid on my part. I never dreamed, Mrs. T.," and again Beaumont looked at Carolyn, "that you would farm the little brat to your own daughter. I should have considered it, but honestly, I didn't. The fact that she was long gone from your house was probably the reason. Then your hubby bit the dust." This comment was addressed to Miranda. She felt his eyes bore hatred into hers. "Anyway, you can draw your own conclusions whether there was a little unworldly help or not. We were banking on it.

"I knew you'd be back, either for a visit, or as a permanent move. I also realized you probably visited many times in the past, but only during summers or holidays, when I was likely gone. Talk about bad luck for me. If I happened to be around and saw you, maybe all of this could have taken place years ago." Beaumont shifted the boy on his lap slightly and leaned forward toward Miranda. She wanted to push back, but was immobile.

"The thing is..." Beaumont's voice tone now became intense. "I had developed my own hobby. I developed a taste for carnage. I have been honing my skills at terminating the useless lives of others in such a way that nobody makes a connection. It has been a blast. Have the authorities even suspected me in fourteen years? The answer is no." Beaumont shook his head in feigned disgust and chuckled.

"Mrs. Perry, here is the long and short of it. At their birth, your son was meant to be fodder for the growth of my son. Part was symbolic, but part transformative, if you will. Sort of like Communion. The fact is, it can still happen. Your boy will serve his true destiny. The process is supposed to be breathtaking, but I've been informed by the authorities..." and here Beaumont caressed the elder boy who pulled away in irritation, "that I can't watch because of a certain amount of risk."

The boy squirmed out of Beaumont's hold. "Let me go, Arthur. Shit." Miranda watched him walk sullenly towards the living room, where he was out of her view. She heard him flop in a chair.

Beaumont shrugged and resumed his monologue.

"This might have gone considerably smoother fourteen years ago if that Norwegian...or maybe he was Finnish...anyway, if that Scandinavian stud didn't turn chivalrous at the end. He convinced the earthen vessel something was wrong and that they needed help. Of course, I dispatched him, and let me tell you, that little shit died painfully. I made sure of that. I wasn't going to be undone by a couple of twenty-year-olds. All's well that ends well, though. Here we are ready to try again tonight. When everything is said and done, Rex will make his way on over. Rex is his name, by the way. Max named him. That's Max." Beaumont motioned with his thumb to the younger boy sitting behind him.

Miranda was beside herself when the little one flashed a brilliant smile and waved bashfully at her.

Miranda closed her eyes against the ache which coursed through her. Her life was being plundered again. If Ryan was going to die, she wanted to go with him. She couldn't survive this night without emotional destruction.

"Sorry, Mrs. Perry. This was meant to be."

Miranda kept her eyes closed. She couldn't look at this monster.

"You know," Beaumont continued after a short pause, "would you like to help raise him? There is a job opening here. Shall we have a recruitment interview of sorts? The benefits are...as they say...out of this world."

Miranda sobbed behind the tape. The cruelty of this man.

"He'll look a lot like your son, Mrs. Perry, but with some obvious personality differences, let alone some genetic ones. Your son, poor fellow, was being visited by him. He really was seeing a ghost of sorts. I bet you didn't believe him."

Miranda could have died. The pain of being reminded of her failure by this man was intolerable.

"Ah...I see that was the case. Well, no matter after tonight. Raising these boys though, now that is quite an adventure. We are shaping the first generation of the dragon's army. The first fruits, soon to be a legion. The downfall of all the woman's offspring. As boys, though, they can be disruptive. People are slaughtered. Young children are a delicacy and often go missing when the boys roam. My boys were a little too overzealous with those college kids a few days ago. They've brought some unwanted attention, and we need to teach them how to go after those who will rarely be missed. The trouble with all of these attempts over the past one hundred years is when the boys overstep their bounds. When they hit their teens, look out. Hugo there..." Beaumont motioned towards the boy in the living room, "...can't keep his pants on. Hence the parenting. Interested?"

"Drop dead, Arthur," Miranda heard from behind her.

Miranda would love the opportunity to apologize to Ryan for not believing him. *Please God*, she prayed, *please give me that chance.*

"Hugo. What's taking so long? This should be over by now. Take your brother and look outside for Rex."

"Maybe he's not coming," Hugo taunted.

Beaumont's face hardened to granite. He stood very slowly, and Miranda noted a barely controlled rage. A flush started at his forehead and shifted downward. The sight was startling.

"What do you mean, Hugo?"

"Who knows? Maybe the Ryan kid beat him. We never stayed to watch."

Miranda shuddered. She feared Beaumont's reaction.

"You said I couldn't stay."

"Shit. I made that up."

Beaumont charged the living room. Miranda could not see what was happening, but she turned her attention to her mother. Carolyn's expression was absolute shock. She stared, flinching as sounds of hitting and slapping began.

The little boy started bellowing at the sight, and then he ducked as both Beaumont and Hugo wrestled their way back to the dining room. The struggle ended in a draw, which appeared more disconcerting to Beaumont. Miranda noticed Hugo had transformed slightly. His eyes were all black and his hands were claws. He snarled at Beaumont.

"Don't ever do that again, Arthur. I held back just now. Next time, I won't."

Beaumont continued to glare, but he looked considerably uncertain. He tried to recover. "Go outside and start searching for him and bring him back."

"C'mon, Max." Hugo left the room.

Max followed at a safe distance.

Chapter Fourteen

Dee stepped onto the sidewalk and walked as rapidly as possible towards the Beaumont residence. She was fully aware of deliberating disobeying her grandmother, something she never did before. Chances are she would get to the house at the same time they would anyway. At the very least she could flag down someone to help or run to a neighbor's house if something needed to be done right away. She was parading into real danger, however, and she was aware of this.

The thunderstorm had ended for now, but Dee saw lightning flashes all around her. She suspected another round of storms was imminent, and she hoped this entire episode would be over before the torrential rains returned. Dee noted the first round increased the mugginess, if that was possible. Water droplets fell lazily from the drenched trees over her head, adding to her discomfort. After only one block she was perspiring freely.

As she turned down Beaumont's street, Dee gasped in alarm and yelled, "Ryan!"

The boy had been running in and out of the illumination of streetlights. He would have slammed into her if she hadn't yelled and he if hadn't made a last second maneuver to skirt her.

"Dee!" he shouted. His voice was strained from panting and his eyes darted around her in panic. "What're you doing?"

"You're hurt!"

He was. Dee was startled to see his appearance. Even in the dim light provided by streetlights he was nearly unrecognizable. Sweat and blood ran like a fountain from his hair. Dirt and blood smeared across his face. Blood was everywhere on his exposed skin and clothes. His hair was matted in grime. His bruises were even uglier than before.

"Bit me...tried to eat me." His labored breathing continued. He kept frantically looking around her in jerky movements, and with no warning started running again.

Dee lunged for his hand and grabbed it just before he was

out of reach. It was his left hand and he swung around grunting in pain. His cast was gone except for a few pieces.

"Ryan wait!"

"I can't. He has my family."

This time, hands clasped, she ran with him.

* * * *

Eugenia gripped the passenger door handle tightly. She didn't know if watching out the windshield or closing her eyes would make her feel less anxious. Signs, buildings, and houses swept past with startling speed. She never had been in a car going this fast. Sidelong glances at Lund didn't ease her terror, as he steered with one hand and held onto his cell with the other.

"I'm there in a minute or two," he practically yelled then discontinued his call.

"There was an officer keeping the house under surveillance. He doesn't respond to radio. That could mean a problem. Squads are headed there now."

Tires squealed as he turned a corner. Eugenia had a terrible sense of vertigo along with a feeling they might tip over.

"They got Lizette on a bus to Atlanta. Her car was found at the bus station in Charleston. A ticket agent recognized her photo and recalled where she was headed. She confirmed Beaumont orchestrated this whole thing. He'd be gone for weeks in summer. The last two or three summers he took those boys. They would bring souvenirs back, or that's what he called them. She never looked at what was in the plastic bags. She swore up and down she didn't know they were kidnapped children. By the way, they were all alive when they were brought back. Hard to miss the cries of a little kid."

* * * *

"Ryan, look!"

Dee pulled him up short with less than half of a block left before they turned down the street separating his house from the park. Ryan stood directly below his bedroom window, in almost the exact spot Hugo and Max were the other night. He saw the end of the porches from this location, and his attention was drawn to the second level porch at Dee's urging.

Hugo stood on the railing, slowly scanning the front yard. Max came into view seconds later, looking questionably up at his brother. Ryan could not take another step forward without being seen. They crept backwards.

"Shit. What am I going to do?" he whispered.

"Ryan, wait for the police."

"I can't. My mom's in there. Besides, they're all going to Beaumont's house."

The wraparound porch only extended the front of the house and the area above the garden. This side of the house where Ryan's bedroom was located and the back had no porch.

Ryan had an idea. "Over here." He slipped further down the block, but still adjacent to his house. Here he was able to speak a little louder. "They're looking for me...or the other guy, more likely. You got to help me over the fence."

"What are you talking about?" Dee staggered slightly at the idea.

"They're not watching the side. I can sneak around the back and enter the house by the garden. It's the only way."

"No. You can wait."

"For what? I can be inside in a couple of minutes. Who knows where the help is. You can call them—tell them what's going on—as soon as I'm over."

Dee didn't reply, but then Ryan never gave her a chance. He swiveled around and placed his hands on two vertical posts of the fence about shoulder width apart. The top of the fence was shorter than he was, so maybe it was five feet. If his arm wasn't hurting, he thought he could probably hoist himself up and lift a foot to the top horizontal rail and finish by somehow vaulting himself over. Tonight he needed help. He turned back to look at Dee.

"I'm sorry. I can't lose my mom, too."

Dee's expression softened and she moved to his side. "Okay, how do we do this?"

"I'm not sure. I think I'll try and lift myself up high enough to get my left foot on the bar. After that, I don't know. Just be ready to give me a boost under my right foot."

He rubbed his hands on his shirt and grasped the tops of two posts. "Here goes." He squatted for a second before using his legs to push upward while simultaneously hoisting himself. Immediately he found his waist at the level of the fence top. His left wrist began screaming in pain, and he actually felt his forearm twitching. Knowing he couldn't hold this position much longer, Ryan tried to swing his left leg high enough so his foot would land securely on the rail. His sneaker crashed uselessly against the top of the post and his leg fell back.

"Damn!"

He swung his leg again, but the initial effort had weakened him, and he realized he was operating on a dwindling supply of energy. Suddenly, he felt Dee's hands square on his butt and pushing up. There was enough momentum for him to raise his foot to the top bar and wedge his sneaker on the rail. Dee also stepped over and pushed his foot more securely between the two posts.

"Great! Now, boost me."

Ryan felt her hands under his right sneaker and as he tried to bring up his leg, she lifted. His knee banged into a bar, but he didn't stop until he had his knee resting on a railing.

His position was precarious, as he swayed at the top of the fence. He needed to get his knee up and somehow push with his left foot and jump to the ground. The swaying increased, and he noticed the tapered points of the spikes of the fence. He could see himself getting impaled if he slipped.

"Ryan, look up."

"What?"

"Above you. Look up."

He did. A limb from an oak tree extended about two feet above his head. He grabbed the limb, and the roughness of the bark was a welcomed feeling. His swaying stopped, and he was able to rest for a second.

"Thanks." Breathing heavily, he brought his painful left arm up and caught the branch. Now even steadier, he slowly stood by bringing up his right foot. After a couple of breaths, and trying not to think about it, he jumped. His landing was silent and he maintained his balance. He looked back at Dee.

"Going down was easier."

"I'm calling now."

"Okay." He ran towards the back of the house.

This part abutted the property next door, and only a narrow path separated the house from the fence. The path was comprised of blue slate pavers and some kind of ground cover Ryan couldn't identify. The area was not as well kept as the remainder of the property, and Ryan envisioned snakes and spiders the size of his fist crawling along in the darkness. He forced himself to take deliberate steps.

Darkness ruled the path, such that Ryan saw vague shapes with only the tiniest hint of color. Lights from a neighboring house or a lightning flash would display varying shades of green from the vegetation. Water dripped freely from trees and gutters to maintain the tropical feel. Wind gusts still buffeted the surroundings, and unrelenting lightning-thunder combinations foretold additional storms.

Ryan never saw the metal pail before he kicked it, and the accompanying rattle sounded louder than a jackhammer. He froze, and waited for cries of alarm or running footsteps advancing on his location. There was nothing, and he allowed himself to exhale slowly in relief. Kneeling down, Ryan felt for the obstacles in his path and found small gardening tools to go along with the pail. His grandmother must leave them here when she finished her daily pottering in the garden.

He reached the corner of the house. The edge of the garden lay directly before him, and extended to his right down the side of the house. He stole a glance around the corner. The garden stood empty. Faint light from the surrounding houses and streetlamps cast shadows, but no movement was evident. A bolt of lightning illuminated the dark recesses of the yard that Ryan's vision couldn't penetrate.

The door to the kitchen was just about ten feet away.

* * * *

Dee crept along the wrought iron fence staying as low as she could to the ground. She moved slowly enough that she was counting on the shadows and the weather to make her less obvious. Like Ryan about an hour before, she wished she had on dark clothing, but at least she wasn't wearing anything white.

Despite the inherent dangers, she was fascinated by the movements of the younger boy. He had clearly transformed into...something. Yes, a dragon could describe it, so could a dinosaur or even a bird. His gait had a hop to it, while his legs and arms extended unusually long with claws capable of ripping a person in two sprouting at the end of his arms and legs. He could pounce across the length of the second floor porch in four steps. When he had done this three times, he jumped onto the railing, landing on his feet which were actually talons. He stood firmly and comfortably watching what was going on in the front yard. After a few second, he would gracefully launch himself off the second floor and land easily on the lawn...after which he would jump and scamper up to the second floor porch. He would then repeat the pattern.

Dee took out her cell phone while still crouching close to the front gate, and called her grandmother. She watched between the bars. She could not find the older boy.

"Gramma." She kept her voice low. "Ryan was captured at Mister Beaumont's house. He escaped." Her grandmother started asking questions, but there was no time to explain. "Long story, I'll tell you later. Beaumont and those two creepy kids are at his house. Ryan thinks they have his family inside. Gramma, he did it again. He sneaked into his own house this time. Bring that FBI man here." She hung up without waiting for a reply.

Dee returned her attention to the front of the house. The little boy was gone. She swore to herself and looked through the fence at the lawn and peered towards the garden. She didn't see him. Dee was rising from her crouch when she heard a low growl. At first, she thought it might be thunder, but the sound was too close. She looked up.

The older boy was in a squatting position on the top of the fence right above her. He glared down at her, eyes indistinguishable from the night except for faint red specks of fire. The claws at the ends of his arms suggested searing agony, while his talon-like feet clutched the horizontal bar of the fence. He was balanced perfectly. The boy licked his lips to catch his drool. His teeth were shards of glass.

Something flopped right next to her, making a slapping sound as feet hit pavement. The little boy appeared from no discernible direction. He smiled at her, displaying teeth like daggers.

"Hi. I'm Max."

From above, Dee heard the older one pounce.

* * * *

Lund raced down Beaumont's street towards multiple squad cars with lights flashing chaotically. To his right, Mrs. Pullman finished her call.

"They're not here." Panic escalated dramatically.

"What?"

"Dee said Ryan escaped, but she wasn't clear from what. Beaumont and his demons are at the Tryon house. Ryan's family is in danger. Ryan just entered the house to get them. Dee is with him."

Lund braked the car sharply in front of Beaumont's house. "Are you sure? Could it be a diversion?"

Mrs. Pullman's hands fluttered to her face. "Dear Lord. I don't know. Dee sounded like herself..."

Lund threw the door open. "Wait here. I'll be right back." Lund ran around the car and saw Templeton leaning over medics who were working on someone. "What's the status?"

Templeton didn't look up. "Officer down, multiple injuries. No one inside. If you thought the other house was a chamber of horrors, wait till you see this one."

Lund started back to his car while yelling, "Get people to the Tryon house. The Batista girl said the kid, his family, Beaumont, and God knows who else are there."

He was back in the car within seconds and speeding away, light and sirens raging. He noticed Mrs. Pullman had moved her satchel to the seat between them. She had been digging through it to find her Bible.

* * * *

Ryan remained as close to the side of the house as possible and moved furtively towards the door of the kitchen. There was nothing he could do about the noise produced from opening the metal framed screen door except to open it extremely slowly. The kitchen door was ajar, and Ryan gave it a slight push with his foot as he held the outside door open. It moved soundlessly, giving him enough room to slide through the opening. Then, he closed the outside door.

He was inside his house. The tension was close to unmanageable. His breath quivered as he inhaled, but his exhale felt more like an earthquake. Breaking into two houses in one night...

The interior was eerily silent. After taking a few calming breaths, he noticed a rustling sound coming from the dining room area. Ryan tried to swallow, and realized his mouth was dry. He wanted to inspect the other surrounding rooms before entering the dining room.

He slipped into what his grandmother referred to as the

"parlor", but first checked around the inside wall by the doorway to make sure Beaumont wasn't waiting to grab him. He concentrated on softly placing each step on the floor. The living room was in darkness, and Ryan peered around the corner before entering.

Behind him and across the hall, Ryan heard footfalls descending slowly down the uncarpeted hardwood stairs. The sound was hollow and lifeless. The hallway light on the second floor evidently cast enough illumination for the person to see adequately. Ryan assumed it was Beaumont because he would recognize the footfalls of his mother or grandmother and the two boys were outside. The tap of the shoes was unsettling. Ryan stepped into the darkness of the living room.

"Son?" Beaumont softly called.

Ryan remained perfectly still. He sensed Beaumont reached the end of the stairs, but no further movement occurred. After what seemed like hours, Ryan heard Beaumont sigh and return upstairs. Ryan couldn't imagine what he was doing up there, other than watching for his precious son.

He let his eyes adjust to the dark of the room. The furnishings he associated with family and warmth now were sinister. Somehow they cast an air of betrayal making him feel even more vulnerable.

At the other end of the living room was an entry to the dining room, but it was blocked by pocket doors. Even with the doors nearly closed, a faint noise was perceptible from the other side. The chandelier was lit as evidenced by the light under the doors, but the dimmer switch must have pushed all the way down. This was terrific lighting for a romantic dinner, but now it hinted at sheer terror.

The rustling resumed as Ryan drew near. The tension was killing him, but he forced himself to maintain the slow pace. He wished he had the crowbar.

When Ryan reached the pocket doors, he slid them gently apart until he reached a vantage point to examine the dining room. He almost lost all of his composure and had to call upon every instinct he had not to cry out.

His mother and grandmother sat upright in the dining rooms chairs at the table. Their positions seemed exaggerated, and Ryan saw why. They had been taped to the seats using silver duct tape. Their mouths were also taped shut, but their eyes were very aware and opened wide in panic.

"Mom!" Ryan whispered fiercely as he slid open the pocket doors as quietly as he could. Once in the dining room, he closed the doors as silently as possible.

For the second time in an hour, Ryan found himself looking for a cutting instrument. His mother jerked her head, trying to communicate, and she made guttural vocalizations under the tape. He found a knife and cut the tape at his mother's wrists. He kept checking the two doorways into the dining room, in anticipation of Beaumont. With her arms free, his mother tore at the tape over her mouth. He worked on the tape around her waist that attached her to the seat.

"Ryan, stop!" she whispered, and forcibly grabbed his shirt and threw him off balance. "Get out of here now. Call the police, don't waste time."

Ryan ignored her and bent to free her feet.

"Mom, are you okay? Did he hurt you?"

"I'm okay honey. I'll be all right." She clasped her hands around his face. "My poor baby. Please leave and get help."

"Dee's gonna call. I can't leave you in this house with that bastard running loose inside." He gave her the knife. "Here Mom. You can finish."

"Ryan..." she pleaded.

"I love you both." He slipped into the kitchen. His mother whispered after him again, but he didn't answer. Instead he searched for something to use as a weapon. A frying pan and rolling pin were too bulky. He saw the wooden block with the cutlery, and found a carving knife that fitted his hand nicely.

The front door flung open and slammed into the wall. Cries and swearing erupted from the entrance. Even though Ryan could not see what was going on from his vantage point in the kitchen, he knew what happened.

"Arthur! Look who I found!" Hugo yelled from the front hallway. "I want her, man. She's mine."

Hugo found Dee outside.

* * * *

"Mom, almost done." Miranda gently pulled the tape from Carolyn's mouth. When she pulled the last portion, she asked, "Are you okay?"

Carolyn looked disheveled. Her hair was mussed, and her pallor had a green cast as if she was ill. Her eyes were clear and focused, however. "I'm fine dear. Shaking like a leaf of course. Where's Ryan off to?"

At that moment, a siren pierced the pandemonium in the front hallway.

"Oh, thank God." Miranda cut the tape from her mother's wrists.

* * * *

Ryan remained hidden in the kitchen clutching his knife and wondering what to do. His confidence was evaporating rapidly now that Dee was captive. All three of them clumped together with Dee in their midst suddenly made the situation seem impossible to handle without Dee or him getting hurt.

Beaumont descended the stairs with more urgency than he had when Ryan entered the house. "Where did you find her?"

"Out by the main gate. She's mine, remember. I want her." Hugo's voice was raised with excitement.

The knife handle was moist under Ryan's hand. Hugo wanting her could mean so many things.

"Stop it, Hugo. There's no time for playing."

"For afterwards, then." Hugo's voice sounded desperate.

A siren was approaching. Ryan felt relief...Dee got through.

"Did you see your brother?" Beaumont raised his voice.

"Nope," Max said timidly.

"Aww, who the hell cares? We don't need him. We were fine without him," Hugo whined.

"We don't need him?" Beaumont bellowed. "Is that what you just said?" It sounded as if he was walking towards Hugo, because additional shuffling noises followed Beaumont's movement. Hugo was backing up, dragging Dee with him. "We don't need him?" Beaumont repeated. "You little shit! It's because of your little stunt that we have bit of a crisis on our hands. We wouldn't be in this situation if you hadn't lied to me." Beaumont's voice was raging out of control. "To succeed in our plan, we need more personnel. We'll always need more! Dammit, Hugo. Here you are, only thinking about yourself.

"I'm asking you one more time, Hugo. Did you see your brother?"

"He's not coming." A small, timid whisper came from Dee.

"What did you say, dear?" Beaumont was trying to sound reasonable.

"He won't be making it," Dee's voice was louder than before. "He's dead. Beaten to a pulp. You didn't count of Ryan getting away." Now her tone was defiant.

A pause in the shouting allowed the siren to be heard by everyone.

"Is the Perry brat here?" Beaumont yelled in disbelief.

Dee didn't answer him.

"This is just...not fair! That kid is probably outside somewhere...or in here. Damn!"

By the front gate, the siren quit screeching, indicating the emergency vehicle had stopped.

"Hugo, get outside and handle whoever that is. Redeem yourself. Leave her with me."

"Arthur, I..." Hugo was pleading.

"Go, now! You have been such a bad boy." Ryan heard the front door open. "Max, go with him." Max must have left without saying a word, for the door shut with no further interactions.

Now with the two guys gone, the odds were better. Ryan made his move.

* * * *

Lund aggressively shifted the car into park. "Please stay in the car," he said to Mrs. Pullman. She didn't respond, but he didn't like the look of determination on her face. She clutched her Bible to her chest.

As he swung the door open, lightning flashed the area, making it appear like midday for a brief second. Thunder boomed immediately. *That was close*, Lund thought. A few raindrops fell.

The house stood indifferent to the ongoing mayhem. Lund was immediately reminded of his final day at his aunt's house of walking into the dark, quiet house, then through the house, and out the back door into...hell.

Lund slid past the gate and began closing it behind him. The rain suddenly came down in torrents. Distracted, he missed seeing the front door open and close, so was surprised to see two figures on the front porch.

Demons masquerading as boys.

Both crouched momentarily and then with an unearthly cry sprang off the porch and charged him.

Lund unholstered his weapon, took what aim he could and fired twice. He thought he heard a yelp come from the younger one, but then they were on him. Their lunge pushed him back into the gate, and it clanged shut.

His gun fell to the brick path, and he was reduced to fending off the attack with his hands. He swung wildly. Teeth snapped with breakneck speed, attempting to catch whatever came within reach. Claws flashed in a blur. He was never positive what he hit.

The smaller one leapt to his chest and clung to him with nails like chisels. The mouth chomped on his left forearm and squeezed. Molten pain flowed unobstructed to his chest. The older boy reared back and flung his arms around Lund's torso. As he frantically tried to remove the smaller creature, he was not prepared to ward off the older boy who widened his mouth cavity and bit down on his side under the armpit and over his ribcage.

Lund screamed in agony, which pierced the rhythm of the downpour.

* * * *

Ryan rushed from the kitchen hoping to grab Dee and push her out of the way. At the front hallway, he stopped abruptly because Beaumont stood right there looking at him as if he had expected him to appear. He also held a knife, and it was poised at Dee's neck. Beaumont's other arm held her close to him.

Where'd he get the knife?

As if reading his mind, Beaumont said, "I always carry one for protection. You never know when you might need it."

A clap of thunder shook the house. Ryan resumed walking ever so slowly.

"Let her go."

"Like I'm going to do what you say just because you say so." Beaumont laughed.

"I killed your kid. It was easy." He continued walking.

"Doesn't look like it, given how you look. Still, I am disappointed. No matter. Just a minor upset." Ryan knew Beaumont was trying to make it look as though it was only a trivial setback. It was not convincing.

Two explosions rang outside, and Ryan thought they sounded like gunshots.

Beaumont seemed sure however. He backpedaled quickly to the base of the stairs. "Get upstairs, girl. I need to check. Don't do something stupid." They started walking up the stairs together.

Ryan slowly followed.

* * * *

Eugenia recognized she was needed. She noticed the horrible demons before Lund did. She fumbled with the door to warn him, but the creatures were so fast the agent was shooting his gun as she scrambled out of the car.

Every muscle group in her body revolted against her efforts to approach the young man. He was pumping his arms to fend off the creatures, but they weaved and dodged with unbelievable agility.

Continuing to clutch her Bible, she searched frantically for ideas.

You have a stronger weapon...

She was quickly drenched, and her wet clothes contributed to her agonizingly slow progress. Eugenia prayed with each step.

A shrill cry erupted from the tangle of figures at the gate. Eugenia noticed it was the little demon, which had seen her approach. His black eyes widened in panic.

My God, he's afraid.

"Good, you should fear..." Eugenia raised her Bible in her arms. Rain coursed down, but the book appeared undamaged. Lightning flashed. The younger demon squealed again. Eugenia saw Jeremy's left arm was now free and saw the young man slap the demon off his chest. Blood spurted where the creature's claws had dug in, and then was washed away in the rain. The young demon tried to run away, but Jeremy was able to kick it before it had any traction. All the while the teeth of the older demon boy remained attached.

Eugenia knew how to disable them. Her spirits soared as she picked up speed walking to the gate. Transferring the Bible to her left hand, she held out her right hand before her, cupping it to catch some water...although she suspected this wasn't necessary given the rain was soaking everything. As she reached the gate, she thrust her hand through the posts and over Jeremy's arm. She grasped the back of the head of the older demon, and began rubbing all of the water into his scalp.

She began the rite, "I baptize you, in the name of the father, and..."

The older demon released his mouth from Jeremy's chest, screamed, and then flung itself out of her reach. Lightning exploded around them, and the thunder was deafening.

"...and of the son, and of the Holy Spirit..." but the creature was now ten feet away, rubbing its hair frantically, as if trying to shampoo the blessing away.

"Jeremy, son, you need to move away from the gate." Eugenia was trying to push the gate open, but the injured agent had fallen to the ground and was braced against it.

Somehow, the young man heard her and shifted to his knees, and crawled a few feet. Eugenia pushed open the gate far enough for her to slide through sideways. She walked calmly to the agent, all the while watching the demons who were about ten feet away. The younger was still whimpering, and the other was flailing at his head, but the movements were becoming less pronounced. She didn't have much time before they came around.

Eugenia leaned over Jeremy, and placed her hand on his head. She briefly prayed for his healing and strength. "Jeremy. The children are still in the house."

He nodded, clearing his head. "I'll get them." He staggered to his feet, and checked his injuries. He looked at her, puzzled. "I'm feeling okay."

"Yes. Now go."

Lund searched the ground until her found his weapon by the fence, and limped toward the house.

The two demons looked more like little boys again. They were scared and uncertain. Eugenia crossed the property towards them. The boys shrank back with gasps of fear. With her Bible clasped in her hands, Eugenia lifted it above her head again so they would see it.

"In the name of the Lord Jesus Christ, I command you to leave this house!"

Wails of misery erupted from both.

Again, she cried in a loud voice, "In the name of the Lord Jesus Christ, I command you to leave this house!"

More woe from the boys–they retreated from Eugenia, increasing the distance between them and her.

"The power of Christ demands that you leave. In his name I command you!"

A violent gust of wind raced around Eugenia, tearing at the boys. As the air continued to rotate, a visible vortex formed and the boys clawed their way along the ground away from Eugenia to keep from being torn helplessly from their place. Their screams increased in a crescendo with the raging wind as they managed to escape the immediate updraft, but blind panic remained as they sprinted from the property, hurdling over brick walls and fences.

As quickly as it started, the rotating wind dissipated.

Silence returned.

Eugenia walked forward, and raised her eyes to the nightmare unfolding on the upstairs porch.

* * * *

Ryan knew Beaumont might become very dangerous if he realized he was corned upstairs. At the same time, he knew he had to keep Dee in his sight. He wouldn't let that bastard take her away.

It would be impossible to run up the stairway without announcing his presence, although he guessed it would be no surprise to Beaumont if he appeared. He willed himself to slow down and take each step as softly as possible.

"Ryan?" his mother called tentatively from down below, probably still in the dining room.

God dammit, Mom, shut up.

As he neared the top landing, Ryan heard Mrs. Pullman yelling something outside.

With a burst of anger, Beaumont yelled, "What in hell is going on out there?" The suddenness of the outburst so startled Ryan that he dropped the knife. It hit the first step and then clunked its way end over end to the bottom of the stairs.

Shit!

Frantic footfalls rushed from his grandmother's bedroom to the second floor porch. Beaumont had been hiding in that bedroom and forced his way through a door that allowed him to enter the second floor porch. He had to be dragging Dee with him, and he showed no indication that he heard the knife tumble down the stairs.

More sirens blared in the distance.

Ryan scrambled to the top step on the second floor landing and pursued Beaumont. No longer concerned about whether Beaumont heard him, Ryan sprang onto the porch.

Sirens were louder now...seconds away.

Beaumont held Dee around the neck with one arm. The knife was poised beneath her neck in his other hand. She struggled to stay on her feet, but her eyes were focused and alert. She gazed intently at Ryan, and his heart ached.

Beaumont turned to Ryan. "You cannot take my son from me." Beaumont was unbalanced, his expression melodramatically evil.

"I already did. You still have two. What's the big deal?"

"He was my firstborn..." His remaining words became a frenzied mumble.

"Arthur?"

The call was calm but authoritative, coming from the ground below. Ryan knew it was Mrs. Pullman. Dee jumped involuntarily, which caused Beaumont to stiffen. Ryan's heart was in his throat.

Beaumont was confused. His head swung back and forth looking for the source of the voice.

"Arthur," Mrs. Pullman called again.

"What?" Beaumont back-peddled, dragging Dee, all the way to the railing overlooking the garden. He leaned against the railing and glanced below, searching for the voice. The knife shifted randomly as Beaumont's attention wavered away from Dee. He finally saw Mrs. Pullman. Her presence unraveled him.

"Your other boys have left, Arthur. I've sent them home. They won't be back. They're too afraid." Her voice tone was reasonable. "You can let the girl go."

"She's right, Mister Beaumont," Ryan added. "You might as well let her go. Those two boys need you."

"Don't patronize me, you little shit. You're too young."

Below, a door was yanked open and heavy footfalls sounded.

"Agent Lund." Ryan heard his mother gasp.

A second voice, Lund's, was much lower but still audible. "How do I reach them?"

His grandmother answered with surprising calm. "Upstairs, to the left, through my bedroom."

Ryan looked at Beaumont. He was frantic. He eyes shifted rapidly in all directions. He stepped back and kicked the railing. With dawning horror, Ryan realized he was leaning against the railing with the rotted wood.

With no warning, Mrs. Pullman was by Ryan's side. Though he couldn't see her, the impression was startlingly clear. There was a faint caress of his face, and the sensation reminded him of the first night his twin appeared outside the window and Mrs. Pullman appeared to chase it away. This time, instead of fear, he felt peace.

Her hand shifted from his face to the top of his head. She was whispering something to him at the same time she was trying to talk with Beaumont. He could only capture portions of it, but was enough to realize that she was praying for him.

"...defend us in battle...be our protection against the wickedness...of the devil...Oh Prince...by the power of God, thrust into hell Satan and all the evil spirits who prowl about the world seeking the ruin of souls."

Then she was gone, but the warmth of her presence remained.

Beaumont spun back to Ryan. "Your concern over Hugo and Max is touching. Don't worry, though, I can still make it, I've perfected the art of self-preservation."

As the police cars sped closer, Beaumont again scanned the view over the porch. As he did so, Ryan saw the knife lowered away from Dee's neck. Amazingly, Dee saw it too. They looked at one another.

Dee, did you see? When it happens again, run...please understand.

"You watch. I can walk out of here. They won't touch me. You and I will meet again."

Police cars and emergency vehicles appeared from all directions. Rainwater splashed. Doors swung open, and police officers with guns drawn raced through the gate. Ryan heard Agent Lund behind him somewhere in the house, trying to make it to the porch. He gave instructions about securing the area and setting up sharpshooters.

Beaumont twisted to watch the excitement below. He glanced over Ryan's shoulder expecting Lund to appear any moment and then back to the activity below.

"Arthur," Mrs. Pullman called again. The rain pounded the porch roof and the runoff over the gutters was nearly solid. Yet her voice carried. She called again, "Arthur?"

Beaumont's arm around Dee's neck loosened, and the knife swung away from her neck.

Dee saw the opportunity.

Ryan yelled, "Now!"

She bolted and was nearly clear of Beaumont's grasp when he recovered and lunged, grabbing her hair. Dee screamed.

Ryan screamed, "No!" and charged Beaumont. He rammed him as hard as he could in the chest with his shoulder. Ryan flung his arms around Beaumont and continued to push him backwards. Beaumont needed to release Dee in self-defense. Ryan felt white hot pain as the knife in Beaumont's left hand was pushed into his side. Ryan screamed again but kept pushing in an attempt to escape the blade ripping into him.

They crashed into the railing and Ryan's forward motion pushed both of them precariously over the barricade. Ryan tried to reverse his course and gain purchase on the porch. He briefly let go of Beaumont as his arms flailed. Then he heard a series of sickening cracks. The railing moved.

Ryan lost his balance and fell forward into Beaumont who screamed in his face, "You can't!"

The railing shattered and Ryan was flying over the side with Beaumont below him still in his arms. Ryan was dimly aware of screams and chaos, and he barely had enough time to recognize the decorative wrought iron railings surrounding the air conditioning units waiting to greet them when they landed.

Chapter Fifteen

"...need an ambulance..."

"...Ryan..."

Mom?

"Oh, my God..."

Movement...faces...pouring water...

"...adolescent male...multiple injuries..."

Talking about me?

"...oh my baby..."

Hands caressing him...faces...more water...shivering

Bright lights...flashes...

White sleeves...green masks and caps...

Those are doctors...

He opened his eyes and moved his head.

His mother sitting in a chair, asleep. Mom?

Did he call her out loud or only in his head? He closed his eyes...slept some more.

Fingers gently stroked his face. He opened his eyes again. His mother looked down at him, her eyes red with dark circles underneath.

"Hello, sweetheart." She smiled

"Mom." It came out as a croak.

"It's okay, you keep resting."

"Thirsty."

She moved out of his vision. "Here, have some ice chips." A plastic spoon appeared, he opened his mouth. The ice chips tasted delicious. He slept.

* * * *

His mother and grandmother sat off to the side, reading magazines. They had been whispering to each other, which woke him up, but then returned to their reading.

"Hey."

They both practically jumped to his side.

His mother rubbed his head. It felt funny. "You're in the hospital. Did you know that?"

"Yeah. I gathered."

"Are you in pain?"

"Um...I don't know. I've been sleeping."

"It's okay, you can rest."

"I'm tired of resting."

Ryan shifted to place his arms behind him in order to sit up. He was surprised to see both arms in a cast. A jolt of pain stunned him. "Oh, man."

His mother reached across his chest and pressed a button. "This is pain medication."

"Thanks." Ryan eased himself back down. "Is there a way to sit up?"

This time his grandmother pushed a button on a bedrail. The head of the bed rose.

"That's good." The bed stopped rising.

"I fell." A statement.

"Yes, you did, but you'll be okay." Then his mother added, "Do you remember what happened?"

"Pretty much." Ryan looked at her. "Beaumont?"

She paused, and pursed her lips. "He's dead."

Ryan nodded with satisfaction. "Good." He glanced out the window and saw that it was raining. Again or still, he didn't know. "Hugo and Max?"

"Those horrid boys?" his grandmother asked.

"They aren't boys," he said flatly.

"I know." This came from his mother. She added, "They're missing. Mrs. Pullman scared them away."

Somehow, that didn't surprise him. He smiled slightly. "Can you tell me everything, please?"

Ryan listened to the synopsis of events beyond what he saw and experienced. Agent Lund being attacked, Mrs. Pullman saving him and chasing the demon kids away, Lund trying in vain to reach the porch despite being hurt...he actually dived to try and catch him...the tips of his fingertips briefly brushing his sneakers as he went over the edge...

"Is Mrs. Pullman okay?"

"She developed a fever and they kept her in the hospital overnight to watch her, but she was fine the next morning. Both she and Dee really want to see you. Right now you aren't allowed any visitors."

"Was Dee hurt at all?"

"No, just badly shaken up."

He let it all sink in and then asked a question he'd been dreading. "What's wrong with me?"

"You have a lot of broken bones." She started counting off on her fingers. "Both wrists, a couple of ribs, cheekbone, elbow, ankle. I think there is a dislocated shoulder in there somewhere. You may have set a hospital record."

Ryan smiled, but then grimaced as his cheeks hurt.

His mother continued, "you also have hundreds of stitches...some are second attempts at closing your previous wounds, some on your head and arms, and you were cut very badly on your side and back." She rubbed his head again and said, "They had to shave your head."

"So, that's why it feels strange."

Later, Doctor Pullman-Batista came in and went over his injuries in detail.

"You're lucky to be alive, you know."

Ryan nodded to her.

"When people fall from the height you did, they either get disabling injuries or die altogether. Neither happened to you. Mister Beaumont took the brunt of the iron spikes, and you managed to hit some branches which helped cushion the fall." Her expression was unreadable, but she was trying to remain professional. "All your breaks are relatively simple fractures. Oh, they'll hurt while you're healing, and you will have some scarring from the stitches, but you'll be more or less good as new in a couple of months."

"Can I still play baseball?"

"Once you heal, yes. I will prescribe physical and occupational therapy to get you up and going. Even though you won't feel like it, we'll need to get you up and out of bed–starting today."

Ryan paused and considered his next question. "Are you mad at me?" When she didn't answer right away, Ryan experienced a sinking feeling.

"Initially, yes. I was very mad. You put yourself unnecessarily at risk and you put my own daughter at risk. Ryan, there are adults who are professionals...they are trained and paid to handle these situations. I know your heart was in the right place, and you were very brave. Having your heart in the right place and being brave are not the same things as being smart. In fact, in your case, it meant the exact opposite."

Ryan dropped his gaze to his casts. His face burned. She was right...sort of. He was going to counter argue that he tried to rely on adults, but they didn't believe him. She was one of those who didn't. Instead, he said, "Yes, ma'am. I'm sorry. I never meant to harm Dee or anyone else." That was the truth.

She reached for his fingers of his right hand that stuck out of the end of the cast. "I know that. I said initially I was angry, but I've mellowed some."

Ryan looked up and saw her smiling. He did the same in return.

"I am happy and relieved things worked out. I know of one silly fourteen year old girl who thinks you were so heroic and courageous."

His smile broadened despite the pain.

* * * *

The rest of the day contained a lot of activity. Nurses came and went. Technicians checked his machines and intravenous lines. The catheter was removed so he had to pee in a jug. An OT therapist came in and taught him and his mother about getting dressed with injuries. A PT therapist helped him sit up and then transfer from bed to a chair and then a wheelchair. When all of this was done, Ryan was exhausted and in intense pain.

He was able to use his pain medication pump once he returned to bed. His mother watched him anxiously.

"What?"

"Nothing...I can't believe how brave you are."

Ryan dozed for about an hour before dinner. When it arrived, his mother fed him like a baby, but he didn't care. She left after dinner for the first time in two nights. Ryan tried to watch TV, but had difficulty focusing. He fumbled with the remote and learned how to turn it off. Just then, Agent Lund walked in to the room.

"Knock, knock," he said. "May I come in?" He didn't wait for a reply. "I'll only be a few moments."

Ryan smiled weakly, not knowing how to react. Lund was walking cautiously and his arm was in a sling. Ryan realized he hadn't heard about his injuries, so he asked.

"Nothing serious. Those guys have sharp claws, so I have a

few stitches. This..." he indicated the arm in the sling, "...came when I tried to catch you. Almost did too..." He shrugged.

"Sorry."

"Don't worry about it. It's not your fault."

Ryan wasn't so sure.

"I wanted to let you know that the official word is that Mister Beaumont was a serial killer and he captured you and your family as his intended next victims. You were able to escape, there was a fight, and you both went over the edge. All of that is actually true, well, more or less. We have enough evidence from his home to close a number of unsolved murders. Turns out Beaumont and those two kids broke into a house across the street and down a ways from Beaumont's own house. An older man, kind of a recluse, lived there. They killed him and took up residence for a few days and kept watch on the house...hoping you'd turn up, I gather."

"Hugo and Max got away though."

"So they did. Who knows how well those two can survive on their own. We'll find them. Your room is being guarded, by the way." Lund lifted his leg and placed his foot on an empty chair. He rested his arm on his elevated knee. Ryan noticed something in his hand for the first time.

"Really? You think they'd try to get me in here?"

"No. You're not exactly important to the overall plan. You were just a pet project as far as Beaumont was concerned. Wouldn't make sense for them to be that risky. By the way, we've kept their existence a secret."

Ryan found he wasn't sleepy at the moment, and something occurred to him.

"What happened to you after your cousin and aunt were killed?"

Lund nodded and said, "I'm glad you asked. Can I sit for a second?"

Ryan said, "Yeah, please." He shifted slightly to face the agent.

Lund didn't say anything for what seemed the longest time. Ryan guessed he was trying to organize his thoughts. When he did start talking, he was obviously relating things rather carefully.

"I enjoyed living with the sheriff and his wife. As I said the other day, they became foster parents at first so they could keep me. Soon after, they adopted me. It was easy to start calling the sheriff 'Dad', but I had trouble with calling his wife 'Mom'. She recognized this, and said it was perfectly fine to call her whatever I was comfortable with. It took a while, but eventually 'Mom' flowed off my tongue with no problem. What made it final was a dream that I had where my real mom said I should use 'Mom', and that she—my real mom that is—was honored to share the title. I also gained two older brothers which was really cool. They were twenty-one and nineteen at the time, and they enjoyed having a new kid bother to play with when they visited home."

"That would be cool."

"It really was. They were jocks in high school, so I had someone to play basketball with." Here he paused and looked at Ryan, which Ryan found curious. Finally, he resumed, "I think my aunt and Cam considered my arrival an amazing stroke of good luck. I think they initiated their plans right away, beginning with the 'serpent needing an heir' craziness. I'm positive that's what Cam was doing with his leering and his efforts to check out my body. He was seeing if I was ready or 'old enough' as my aunt said. What the plan involved I have no clue, I am just fortunate things ended before I had to find out. That's where my experience differed from yours."

Ryan felt awful for him. "God."

"I learned more about my aunt and Cam. The sheriff, that is my dad, helped me. Some of it was hard to believe, but he let me accept it at my own pace. I'll never forget the first thing he showed me. It was the Book of Revelation from the Bible. It mentions the dragon and the beast. He said this was the reference for understanding what I was facing."

"Mrs. Pullman showed me the same thing."

"Now that is an amazing woman. Talk about a superhero with amazing powers. Anyway, the rest is history. Went to college, got married, and got a job, so on and so forth. So here I am."

"I'm glad you were."

Lund bowed theatrically at the comment. "Suffice it to say, we've been tracking down people like him for a long time. You handled yourself pretty well, even if it was a bit too risky for my taste." Lund smiled at him. "You look tired. I'll let you go." He stood and started to leave.

"Oh, my main reason for coming was to give you this and I almost left without doing it." The object in his hand turned out to be a rolled up T-shirt, which was dark green with small white lettering on the front. "Welcome to the club." He placed the shirt unfolded on Ryan so that he could examine the words more closely.

Ryan squinted and then looked up at Lund. "What does it mean?"

"I tell you what...Why don't you figure it out, and when you do, give me a call. We can talk then." He saluted Ryan, and left the room.

Ryan returned to the shirt front. The lettering was three words in a single line:

Twelve: Seven-Eight.

* * * *

Agent Lund left the hospital and walked to his car. He felt lighter than he had in a week. The immediate threat had passed, and the kid looked as if he would recover. Ryan was strong and determined, more so than he was at that age. Lund was curious to find out if he was up for a new challenge. He had a hunch Ryan would be, but he had wait patiently. It might take a while.

Lund planned on spending the night at his parents' place instead of the hotel. They still lived in the same house as when he was a teenager, despite now growing very frail. He and his brothers have been bringing up the topic about selling the place for a few years now. Finally, it seemed they were willing to listen, but Lund had his doubts about them making a move unless they are forced to because of health. He hoped it never came to that.

His father was the person who started the gimmick with the T-shirt. Lund was the first recipient, and the first T-shirt being an old white undershirt with the numbers written on with a black laundry pen. His brothers now wore the shirts, more as honorary members instead of official members. Lund picked up on the idea and updated the design.

Lund had only a handful of opportunities to distribute the shirts, but he continued to use his father's strategy for introducing the topic. You couldn't force people, and many of them were adolescents and young adults, to recognize they have been "drafted", like it or not, because of their experiences. They had to dwell on it for quite a while and warm up to it. Some eventually grabbed for the ring, others didn't.

Epilogue

Nearly seven weeks after leaving the hospital Ryan felt normal again. He was outside after dinner taking a walk in the park across the street from his house. The wind was harassing the trees, making them sway back and forth. A hurricane was a few hundred miles off shore, but was forecast to turn northward and hit the Outer Banks instead of the South Carolina coast. Ryan took every opportunity to exercise in one capacity or another before school started. That, sadly enough, was about ten days away.

His time home from the hospital was not easy. The recovery period was painful. He and his mother fought often, although there were a number of times when she was happy and planned cool outings. It was a strange mix.

The physical therapy was torturous, and he had to suffer the indignity of having his mother give him sponge baths every few days. They were both relieved when all the casts were removed so he could shower on his own.

Nightmares were pretty frequent, so he didn't sleep well. There were occasional flashbacks like mini-clips from a movie playing right before his eyes. He started counseling with a shrink, someone who knew Lund. He dreaded the first appointment, wondering if he would be thrown into a psychiatric hospital for months on end. The shrink, Doctor Marshall her name was, turned out to be nice. She was funny and compassionate, and accepted everything he said without being judgmental. A lot of the time was spent making sense of things, and planning ahead for the future.

Dee came over often to visit. He was finally able to kiss her ("Now I am able to see what your face actually looks like"). They went out on a date of sorts. The other night they walked for ice cream and back. Ryan wasn't sure how this whole "going out" thing worked, and he missed his father. A guy couldn't really talk to his mother about this kind of thing.

Dee introduced him to kids who would be their classmates in high school. Ryan found he had gained a certain kind of notoriety. He was the new kid who already killed a teacher. Some kids came just out of curiosity, he was sure, but a few returned multiple times and he started developing friendships. Much revolved around mutual interests in sports, especially baseball. One guy named Connor was a competitive swimmer with the local USA swimming club. He took Ryan with him to the pool the previous week, because a single lane was reserved for people in physical therapy. Ryan joined adults recuperating from things like knee replacements and back surgery. So he paddled, walked, and floated with some old people. Within two days, he surpassed them in terms of recovery, and swam with the swim team. He couldn't keep up with any of the star swimmers like Connor, but he pushed his personal limits and found he could manage pretty well. The swim coach was impressed enough to suggest he join the team.

"At the very least, you can prepare for the boys' high school swimming season, which will also get you in shape for the baseball season in the spring."

Ryan accepted, so he was off to swimming practice every day with Connor. His scars were a sight to behold. Ryan just shrugged off the attention he received from being stabbed by Beaumont. This new scar traveled the exact same trajectory from his shoulder blade to his hip given to him by his twin when he was born.

As Ryan finished his walk through the park, he started heading home. Tourists still frequented the park, but their numbers had dwindled slightly over the past week or so. He noticed a blond haired woman walking with two kids. He didn't pay much attention to them until they had gotten closer. The woman was pretty, and seemed rather young to have kids the ages of the two at her side. Her expression looked strained and her glances at him were furtive as if she was apprehensive.

Then he saw why. The two kids had changed since he saw them last time. Their hair was cut short and their clothes were clean. They both wore button down collar shirts and pressed khaki shorts. They looked preppy.

Hugo had grown an inch or two while Max was a little more subdued than he used to be. Still, he smiled at Ryan, and gave a quick wave.

Ryan stopped on the path and waited. The woman pulled back and turned around, not wanting to watch. The boys strolled up nonchalantly to greet him. They stared at one another in silence.

"New caretaker," Ryan finally said.

"She'll do...for now," Hugo answered.

Earlier in the summer, Ryan might have been alarmed or even frightened. Now, he was just disgusted.

"This ain't over, you know," Hugo said.

Ryan snorted. "Give me a break. You two haven't got the balls."

Hugo smiled, genuinely amused. "That's pretty funny."

Max was rocking back and forth on his feet, becoming a little more excited. "Hugo's gonna be a daddy. I'm gonna be an uncle." He skipped a step. "You too, I guess. Cool, huh?"

Ryan turned to look at the young woman again. She was a mere ten feet away, in profile. He noticed for the first time the slight swelling of her belly. He groaned inwardly.

Ah shit. What does this mean now?

Hugo seemed to read his mind. "Y'all are in for quite a surprise. You've got no idea what's coming. It'll be awesome, real kick-ass." He folded his arms, looking smug.

The woman turned back to the three of them. One hand was in front of her mouth. Ryan saw she was chewing on her thumb nail. Her eyes were vacant and soulless. Whatever made her human fled her a long time ago. She was Hugo's now. God help her.

Ryan walked across the street and through his gate. He turned around to close it. Hugo and Max were gone. So was the woman.

Lund had instructed Ryan to contact him immediately if he saw the two boys. Ryan took out his new cell phone, courtesy of his grandmother again, and texted Lund all of the information, including details about the woman.

Lund replied moments later, "Thanks."

It was at that exact moment that Ryan thought he understood the meaning of the T-shirt Lund gave him. To make sure, he entered the house and went to the bookcase. Searching, he found what he looked for and opened the book to confirm his hunch.

* * * *

Ryan sprawled on the couch and dialed Lund's number to

talk instead of text. He answered on the third ring.

"Hello, Ryan."

"Agent Lund," Ryan replied. When Lund didn't say anything more, Ryan continued. "I figured out the words on the T-shirt."

"Very good. Are you with us?"

"Yeah, I'll do it."

About the Author:

Anthony Hains is a university professor in counseling psychology, with a specialization in pediatric psychology—his research involves working with youth who have a chronic illness. He is married with a daughter in college. *Birth Offering* his is first novel.

Visit him online at:
http://www.anthonyhains.com/

Also from Damnation Books:

Within This Mortal Coil
by Anthony T. Pate

eBook ISBN: 9781615724987
Print ISBN: 9781615724994

Thriller Horror
Novella of 24,402 words

There are some things you can't un-do. You face the result of your actions and move on, but what if you were forced relive those moments over and over again, experiencing the horror of your past mistakes as if they had just unfolded?

For Corey Aston, this nightmare became reality after waking up in his bathtub with his wrists slit. A mysterious stranger to say his wife left him and taken everything. Then he is being hunted by two men in ski masks.

When things worsen and the sweet embrace of death takes a hold of him, he isn't lifted up to the heavens, but dragged back down to his bathtub to repeat the events that just transpired. As reality blurs and his sanity dissipates, Corey must unravel the tangled web his life has turned into or be forced to repeat his mistakes and brew in his own personal hell.

With so many knots, where does one start to untangle the mess? And, without the person you love by your side, is it even worth trying?

Also from Damnation Books:

Severed Ties
by Angie Skelhorn

eBook ISBN: 9781615728206
Print ISBN: 9781615728213

Paranormal
Novella of 28,819 words

By the use of divination and magic, some ties can never be severed.

In the beginning, by the light of the Full Moon, Frankie connects with Candice's energy through dream time and witnesses her involvement in a terrifying act of violence. After receiving information from Sandra that their childhood friend is missing, they pack their bags and head to the inner city to find her.

Frankie, afraid for her own safety, has a chance encounter with a local named Calvin who is plugged into what's happening. Using his workable ideas—as well as Frankie and Sandra consulting tarot, ordinary playing cards, astrology, and spell-casting—they set forth to free Candice from the dangerous situation she is in.

Visit Damnation Books online at:

Our Blog—
http://www.damnationbooks.com/blog/

DB Reader's Yahoogroup—
http://groups.yahoo.com/group/DamnationBooks/

Twitter—
http://twitter.com/DamnationBooks

Google+—
https://plus.google.com/u/0/115524941844122973800

Facebook—
https://www.facebook.com/pages/
Damnation-Books/80339241586

Goodreads—
http://www.goodreads.com/DamnationBooks

Shelfari—
http://www.shelfari.com/damnationbooks

Library Thing—
http://www.librarything.com/DamnationBooks

HorrorWorld Forums—
http://horrorworld.org/phpBB3/viewforum.php?f=134

CPSIA information can be obtained at www.ICGtesting.com
Printed in the USA
BVOW07s1711231013

334449BV00001B/12/P